heartwood

Also by Amity Gaige

Sea Wife
Schroder
The Folded World
O My Darling

heartwood
AMITY GAIGE

FLEET

FLEET

First published in the United States in 2025 by Simon & Schuster
First published in Great Britain in 2025 by Fleet

1 3 5 7 9 10 8 6 4 2

Copyright © 2025 by Amity Gaige

The moral right of the author has been asserted.

*All characters and events in this publication, other than those
clearly in the public domain, are fictitious and any resemblance
to real persons, living or dead, is purely coincidental.*

All rights reserved.
No part of this publication may be reproduced, stored in a
retrieval system, or transmitted, in any form, or by any means, without
the prior permission in writing of the publisher, nor be otherwise circulated
in any form of binding or cover other than that in which it is published
and without a similar condition including this condition being
imposed on the subsequent purchaser.

Excerpt from "October" from POEMS 1962–2012 by Louise Glück.
Copyright © 2012 by Louise Glück. Reprinted by permission
of Farrar, Straus and Giroux. All rights reserved.

Excerpt from "The More Loving One" by W. H. Auden.
Copyright © 1957 by The Estate of W. H. Auden. Reprinted by permission
of Curtis Brown, Ltd. All rights reserved.

A CIP catalogue record for this book
is available from the British Library.

Hardback ISBN 978-0-349-12755-2
Trade paperback ISBN 978-0-349-12756-9

Interior design by Paul Dippolito
Printed and bound in Great Britain by Clays Ltd, Elcograf S.p.A

Papers used by Fleet are from well-managed forests
and other responsible sources.

Fleet
An imprint of
Little, Brown Book Group
Carmelite House
50 Victoria Embankment
London EC4Y 0DZ

The authorised representative
in the EEA is
Hachette Ireland
8 Castlecourt Centre
Dublin 15, D15 XTP3, Ireland
(email: info@hbgi.ie)

An Hachette UK Company
www.hachette.co.uk

www.littlebrown.co.uk

To Keith and Mira

and to Tim

*A wind has come and gone, taking apart the mind;
it has left in its wake a strange lucidity.*

*How privileged you are, to be passionately
clinging to what you love;
the forfeit of hope has not destroyed you.*

—Louise Glück, "October"

Dear Mother,

You used to call me Sparrow.

Why Sparrow? Well, because the woods are full of sparrows, and you loved everything outdoors. Songbirds, wildflowers, wind. You could read the weather like a poem.

But why did I remind you of a sparrow and not another songbird? I never thought to ask. With their white cheeks and dingy underparts, plain brown sparrows are everywhere. They beg at outdoor tables and hop under city benches. They nest in chimneys and rafters and even tailpipes. Sparrows are not much to look at, but they're smart. Canny. Tiny, feathered battle-axes.

Sparrows are survivors.

I like to think that's what you meant.

Back then, I followed you as if you were a fixed star. Fumbling against your leg, mouthing a bit of your skirt, I kept you close, better to go wherever you went. I'd straggle after you to the garden and right back inside. Up the stairs and back down. Sometimes, in your lap, I would press my hand against your chest so that I could feel the center of you—your heartwood, your innermost substance, like the core of a tree that keeps it standing. When I couldn't see you, I listened for you. Your puttering was the music of my life. An equivocal sigh, the crack of a knuckle, a stifled *Shit!*, an avalanche of baking sheets.

When I grew taller, I stood beside you in the kitchen, the apron strings tied three times around my middle. You were magical. You had machines for every task. A tool that peeled apples.

An apparatus for scraping the fragrant part of the lemon peel but not the bitter pith. A wand of turned wood used for withdrawing honey from a jar.

I was four or five when I began to sense the truth of my position, which was that we couldn't go on like this forever. That, in fact, we were never meant to. I'd have to leave our country of two. I couldn't bear this news. I didn't want to grow up.

Naturally, I had no choice. I grew up anyway.

Kindergarten, grade school, high school.

I survived the ordeal. I liked the hustle of adult life, in fact. The changing faces. The possibilities, the open road, and even the solitude.

Spitting in the eye of my numerous anxieties, I became a nurse.

Eventually, I understood that motherhood, as the child imagines it, is unperformable.

No woman is a star. No woman is a god or a tree or a magician.

But for a while, in your arms, the universe was the right size, and I knew where I was.

Lt. Bev

Any woodsman who says he's never been lost in the woods is a liar. It's inevitable. Up here in the North Woods, everybody goes woods queer now and again. That's because we spend so much time outdoors. Ice fishing, hunting. Kids grow up following their parents into the backcountry, where they learn the basics of outdoor survival. How to build a camp. How to dead reckon by the sun. Up here, we tend to think of being lost as something you can be good at.

I've been in the business of finding lost people in the woods for thirty years. I know how hard it is to keep a clear head when lost. The disorientation can be shattering. A lost person is like the believer who is told "There is no God." After that, everything seems like a lie. But loss of mental control is more dangerous than the lack of food or water. Panic crowds out common sense. It makes the lost person crave a quick, easy solution.

Imagine you're her. Valerie Gillis. You have been hiking for a long time. Three months. You're no young lass, though you're tougher than you thought you were. Like a lot of people, you'd always wanted to hike the legendary Appalachian Trail. Since taking the plunge, you have hiked through mud, water, pain, and heat. Maine is even harder than you heard it would be. One difference is the density of the woods. Walls of vegetation hem you in on both sides. In the past, when the trail got hilly and punishing, you stared at your boots, willing yourself forward one step at a time.

But now, you raise your head. You pause. Somehow, for some reason, you step off the path. Maybe you've seen something—a rare bird or flower. Or maybe you just need to pee and want some privacy. Hikers are supposed to chug two hundred paces away from the trail before they urinate, and you're a polite person. Or you're spooked by a sound in the woods, voices approaching. You step off the path and fight your way through the head-high saplings and sticky bushes. You look up at the sky, which is barely visible through the dense, netted canopy.

Time passes.

Rested, relieved, you look for the path. Ten steps, twenty. Nothing. But the path was *right there*. You don't backtrack. Lost people seldom do. Rather, you push on farther, because you are dead certain this is the direction you came from. Every direction you turn, the view is identical, a claustrophobic wall of foliage and shrubbery. You wade forward into the mass of vegetation.

You begin to run. Branches beat your head. Buckthorn snares your feet. Brambles tear your skin. You're desperate to get a view, to reorient, to understand.

We frequently find lost people looking very beat-up. They've been lanced by thorns and snags. Their clothes are filthy and ripped or even torn off from falling down or crawling or stepping into dangers they would have otherwise seen.

That's what the terror of being lost makes people do.

By the time they get up here, northbound Appalachian Trail hikers have trod 1,900 miles. The class of hikers that starts as a mob down in Georgia really thins out by the end of the season. The beleaguered few who make it up here are an ugly bunch. They are very close to their goal, but it seems to me there's something about the proximity to the finish that makes them lose focus. They tend to wander off, to break down physically or mentally.

That, I understand.

Dreams burn a wildfire in a body. It's worth it, but there's no coda.

This year seems worse than normal. The AT was officially closed for thru-hiking for the first time in history when the pandemic hit in 2020. I question the readiness of some of the folks out here this season.

You can't get lost on the AT, they all say. But here at the Maine Warden Service, we get several dozen calls for lost thru-hikers every season. Maine is the worst place on the AT to get lost. It's a whole new kind of hiking, more remote than anything that's come before. Not much farther north than where Valerie Gillis was last seen lies the Hundred-Mile Wilderness. At the trailhead looms a sign that reads, verbatim: *Do not attempt this section unless you have a minimum of 10 days supplies and are fully equipped. This is the longest wilderness section of the entire A.T. and its difficulty should not be underestimated.*

Seems appropriate that the architects of the Appalachian Trail put the northern terminus on the other side of these woods. As the hikers say, "No Maine, no gain."

To search is to guess. If the location of the lost person is known, that's a rescue, not a search. A lost-person search begins with a couple of knowns and a whole busload of conjecture. If that sounds hard, it is. I always bear in mind that a century ago, the work I do was conducted with no GPS, no CB radio, no sidearm. Just a couple of guys in beaver skins tramping through the snow.

Here's what we know. On the morning of Monday, July 25,

Valerie Gillis awoke early at Poplar Ridge shelter, said goodbye to two female southbound hikers with whom she'd bonded the night before, and continued her journey north. She had a cell phone and appropriate gear and supplies, and was in a fine mood. There's no cell service on that stretch of trail, but her husband was set to pick her up for resupply at a trailhead the following day. She was almost done with the northern portion of her hike. She smiled for a snapshot just as she turned to leave.

Then she vanished.

The husband waited a day to report Valerie lost. It was common for Valerie to be waylaid at a meetup, so he didn't panic on Tuesday. He panicked on Wednesday. That evening, we send a crew of wardens out to the shelters on foot in the hope that we run into Valerie ourselves, as often happens on a hasty search. Overdue hikers are frequently found trailside dehydrated or with a broken ankle.

We come up empty. All we get on Wednesday is a lead from a teenaged hiker who runs into a warden in a parking lot thirty miles to the north. He says he saw a middle-aged woman sitting on a rock "looking played out" near Spaulding Mountain shelter the day before. Lacking anything stronger, I designate this as our point last seen. We find the two southbound women who saw her leave Poplar Ridge shelter as they are provisioning in town. They give us the photo—perfect. When I get home, I settle at my kitchen table under a cone of light to study my maps of the search area. Only eight miles stretch between Poplar Ridge shelter and the next shelter north, Spaulding Mountain. But because there is no point of exit between the two shelters, the search area broadens to thousands of acres of conifers, fallen trees, rocks, streams, and hobblebush. Numerous unnamed ridges rise and fall like waves with a short fetch. There are no settlements to speak of in any direction for many miles.

HEARTWOOD

It's long past midnight by the time I put away my area maps. I spread my old Appalachian Trail map on the table. The trail is named for the mountains that span the entire eastern coast of this country, north of the Gulf Coastal Plain all the way to Canada. And through this range wends one long, continuous footworn path. Georgia. North Carolina. Tennessee. Virginia. West Virginia. Maryland. Pennsylvania. New Jersey. New York. Connecticut. Massachusetts. Vermont. New Hampshire. Maine. The trail does not follow the low ground of valleys, nor does it circumvent obstacles. Instead, it goes tramping over countless summits, straight across streams; it marches into towns and occasionally humps down highways. The trail moves like a story. Sometimes it makes sense and sometimes it doesn't. The trail wanders like a vagabond. Here it veers toward the impractical, there toward opportunity. How much thought must have been put into its route, and how much agreement. Southerners and northerners clearing a fourteen-state corridor to make way for a humble footpath.

I stare at the map for a long, long time.

Valerie's whereabouts are somewhere right in front of me.

As soon as I hear the first birdsong, I pack a bag and get in my truck.

UPDATE: SEARCH FOR VALERIE GILLIS
Thursday, July 28, 2022

Maine game wardens are seeking information concerning missing 42-year-old AT hiker Valerie Gillis, who uses the trail name "Sparrow," from the hikers using the following trail names: "Strider," "Another Lisa," "Leviticus," "Blister," and "Santo."

Warden investigators would like to speak with the hikers listed above to determine Valerie's point last seen on the Appalachian Trail. Warden investigators are seeking to verify if anyone stayed at the Spaulding Mountain shelter with Valerie on the night of Monday, July 25, or Tuesday, July 26, or if any southbound hikers can ID Valerie from this photo.

Valerie Gillis started her AT "flip-flop" hike on April 21 in Harpers Ferry, WV. If any hikers not listed here have information about her current whereabouts, contact the tip line at 1-800-595-8872.

The Warden Service also wants to inform bear baiters in the search area to be on the lookout for Ms. Gillis.

Dear Mom,

The first thing I should say is that you were right.
    You didn't want me to hike the Appalachian Trail.
    Mothers have a sixth sense. Their love is occult.
    You argued that I'd be miserable. Only one-quarter of Appalachian Trail thru-hikers achieve their goal. What if I made it nearly to the end (you said presciently) and something unexpected happened, like a turned ankle or bad case of giardia, and I had to quit anyway? Thousands of people section-hike the trail, completing a couple hundred miles every summer. Why not me?
    Why not? Because hiking the Appalachian Trail isn't a reasonable thing to do. Anyone who wants to walk two thousand miles in a row does it because they find beauty in the *un*reasonable.
    All that misery, that's the point.
    The high probability of failure, that's motivation.
    You had a bad feeling, you said.
    And you were right!
    You were right, as usual.

People have romantic notions about hiking the Appalachian Trail. *I* had romantic notions about hiking the Appalachian Trail. The truth is, the journey involves a lot of moisture. Always being wet. Mostly in the form of sweat. Damp, rank T-shirts. But also, rain. In June, it rained on us for seven days straight. Rain for a day or two is no problem, almost a novelty. But rain for seven days?

Strange rashes grow in the armpits and buttocks; the feet become pruned and cadaver-like in the boots. Nothing dries. You are trapped in crowded shelters with other wet and miserable beings.

Another form of moisture is tears.

Sometimes out on the trail, I'd get so frustrated and tired I'd just sit down and cry.

My heels were cracked. My knees throbbed, especially on the downhills. Who was I kidding? Those were forty-two-year-old knees. They weren't supposed to be flexed for seven or eight hours straight, all the while carrying a heavy load. Since I'm small, my pack looked unusually large and burdensome. People laughed at it, even after I pulled everything nonessential out. Goodbye, paperback and personal locator beacon. Goodbye, compass.

My trail brother Santo was used to my cathartic crying jags.

He'd just settle down and have a snack or look around.

After I wound down, he'd come and offer me his hand and pull me back up, as huge as I am small.

"C'mon, girl," he'd say.

I'd say, "I'm trying!"

"Do or do not," he'd say in his best Yoda voice. "There is no try."

But every time I was on the verge of quitting, every time I made peace with the decision to quit, to say goodbye to my "tramily" and wish them well and walk away and find some feather bed and be done with it, I'd reach the next shelter just as the woods were growing rosy with dusk, and somebody on the same journey would be building a campfire, the evening air full of fireflies and cricketsong, and I would realize, once again, that the act of walking while carrying the weight of my pack had wrung all the sadness out of me, the sadness for myself and for the world, and that in that moment, I was totally without stress, confusion, or agitation, and that I was perfectly, blamelessly, *whole*.

    The trail transformed me.

    And I can't say, even now, that I regret it.

    After all that I've undergone. All that has been done to me.

"Santo" Live Interview, Bronx, NY, 7/30/22
Recorded by Warden Cody Ouellette

The first time I ever went hiking, I didn't even know what to bring. I knew I needed something to drink. I brought a liter of Sprite. As soon as I started walking uphill, I thought I was gonna die. I was swearing at myself. "You fat piece of shit!" But you know, I'd driven all that way to the trailhead. Almost an hour out of the city. Plus the cost of gas. I said to myself, "Just make it to that spot ahead, Ruben. That tree." And I made it to that spot. "OK, now make it up to *that* spot, that rock." That's how I got uphill.

Fast-forward to me deciding to hike the AT. *Me.* Got a used tent, check. Used hiking poles, camp stove, sleeping mat. But it turns out there's no hiking clothes for someone of my size. I bought two pairs of big-and-tall golf shorts. People wonder why I hike in golf shorts and polo shirts. This is my pops's polo shirt. Dri-Fit is for real. They do not make hiking shorts for fat people. They're like, "Can we all agree we do not want to see fat people in shorts?"

I see fat girls on the trail sometimes. I am like, "Sister, fat girl, hello, I see you." Fist bump. We share a wink.

It's OK with me if you use the word "fat." These skinny people . . . I call them "gazelles." The gazelles just scamper up the mountainsides and disappear over the next horizon. But you know, a lot of those people are down bad on the inside. They *bagged* the Appalachian Trail, they *bagged* the Pacific Crest Trail. They can't stop, because there are so many mountains to crush.

I feel bad for them. You get my 260-pound ass to a campsite, Ima *sit down*.

HEARTWOOD

Sparrow was the same. Just walking. Tramping. Watching some birds. Thinking about life. Waiting to hear a good story. She is what my moms, who is a dreamer herself, would call a poet soul.

Wherever Sparrow was, that's where she *was*, you know what I mean?

(pause)

Sorry.
Sorry.
Give me a minute.

(pause)

What the fuck happened to her? Somebody hurt her?

Dear Mom,

In this small tent, in these huge woods, it's you I imagine on the other end of this letter.
 I write to pass the time. I write to keep my sanity.
 No—I write because it's all I have.
 A notebook, two pens. No more food.
 If things don't work out in my favor, at least I will leave a record.
 I'm writing love letters, I guess.
 This one is for you.

Lt. Bev

THURSDAY, JULY 28. FIVE A.M.
DAY 2 OF THE GILLIS SEARCH.

The mobile command vehicle is already parked in an outer lot of the Sugarloaf Mountain Hotel, engine humming, klieg lights on. Bats are darting in the darkness, fly catching in the umbrella of electric light. I park my truck in the empty dirt lot. I can see Rob moving behind the windows of the black bus.

Rob Cross and I head the Incident Management Team for our district. We've been a team for years. He and his wife and kids include me in almost every family holiday. He's a plainspoken, unexcitable Mainer, husky in build, large in hat size. His big head has gotten us through some very long and difficult searches. Some would say that the operations guy on a search is more important than the team leader. But I'm still the ranking authority and I take the credit and the blame. When I step into the bus, Rob turns to me with his deadpan look, like it's just another normal day at work.

"Sleep much?" I ask him.

"Probably about as much as you," he says.

The Incident Management Team has the following statutory authority per Title 12, section 10105:

> *Whenever the commissioner receives notification that any person has gone into the woodlands or onto the inland waters of the State*

HEARTWOOD

on a hunting, fishing or other trip and has become lost, stranded or drowned, the commissioner shall exercise the authority to take reasonable steps to ensure the safe and timely recovery of that person.

In general, the Warden Service is a pride of the state. We keep the waters stocked, the woods lawful, and we tend to the injured. As for search and rescue, we have a sterling record of finding lost people.

Ninety-two percent of the time, we find lost people within twelve hours of being notified.

Ninety-seven percent of the time, we find lost people within twenty-four hours.

The other 3 percent, we know those stories like scripture.

First mornings of a lost-person search are hell, in a good way. Word travels to everyone involved in search and rescue, professionals and amateurs alike. We're launching the search from Sugarloaf Mountain because that's about as close as we can get to the stretch of the AT where Valerie Gillis was last seen. Headlights are streaming toward us from all over the valley; folks are getting out of their vehicles, cracking sore limbs from the distant drive—everywhere is distant to this mountaintop—filling their thermoses and packs. The colonel sends me thirteen wardens this morning, several from as far away as District 5, up in the Allagash. I haven't met these guys before. They're young and quiet, stretching out their clean hands for me to shake.

A staging area is nothing fancy. In the Gillis case, a dirt lot next to the Sugarloaf Hotel facilities warehouses, with a folding table and sign-in papers that blow away and a couple of cardboard boxes of coffee. When the back of the truck is opened to pass out assignments, the scene takes on the air of a strange concession stand. We fill up the teams on a rolling basis, whoever gets there first, eight to ten volunteers for every warden, then each team leaves for the field. Most searches are dependent on volunteers, men and women who've taken the day off work to hike through the impenetrable Maine understory for ten hours, gratis. Their presence is always sobering to me. What people do for each other. They don't even know Valerie Gillis. She's not from around here.

Despite the greetings and the gearing up and the talk, there's an air of seriousness to the staging area. We know that the probability of finding a lost person drops dramatically after twenty-four hours of searching. We respect that invisible force that knows where she is and how this all ends up. This morning, the sun rises over the great bowl of the Carrabassett valley, the ridgeline of the mountains jagged against the sky, columbine quaking on the hills, and despite ourselves, we whistle at the view.

The hard part is the waiting. It's too early for news. The area where Valerie Gillis went missing is so remote that it will take the teams several hours just to get there. I know that terrain well. It lies in District 7, which is the first district I was assigned to back as a brand-new warden in the early '90s. I was only the second female hired in the history of the Maine Warden Service, and no one knew quite what to do with me. They had to put me somewhere. So District 7 it was, one of the least populated areas midstate, home to fewer than four hundred souls. Days would go by without a single complaint. Patrolling the backwoods, sometimes I hoped I'd catch someone poaching or fishing without a permit. Then at least I'd have someone to talk to.

Rob gets a call from the pediatrician, and I take a moment to step out of the bus into the sun. It's a favorable search morning in Vacationland. The sky is azure blue, with bonny puffs of altocumulus being whisked across the valley. It's good weather both for searching and for being lost. Safe weather.

Search and rescue was a natural fit for me. I love a knotty logistical problem, and I can't turn off the mental mechanism that keeps me trying to put together the puzzle, even while I sleep. I made sergeant in '02, and lieutenant twelve years later. Some high-profile rescues lent my team and me local fame. There was a spread about us in *Down East* magazine. Despite our tremendous success rate finding lost souls under my supervision, my promotion to lieutenant still set the old boys' hair on fire.

"Woman? *Woman?*" my geriatric friend and fellow warden Mike said recently, when we were reminiscing. "We didn't hate you because you were a *woman*, Bev. We hated you because you were an out-of-stater."

Then he howled with laughter.

Unlike most of my fellow game wardens, I was not born and raised a Mainer. I grew up with my parents and two sisters in Leominster, Massachusetts, where I lived and studied until I enrolled at the University of Maine for a master's in wildlife conservation at the age of twenty-five. I'm a New Englander to the gills. But Mainers are still mad about being considered a mere outpost of Massachusetts until being granted statehood in 1820. Out of all the things that could make me unacceptable in the eyes of my community—that I'm a woman, the only female leadership in the entire Warden Service; that I live alone, married (some joke) to the job—nothing is as offensive as the fact that I'm a Masshole.

"Hey, Bev," Mike likes to say, "what's the penalty for drunk driving in Massachusetts?"

"What, Mike?"

"Reelection to the Senate."

There's a ping on my personal cell from Tanya, one of my warden investigators.

Weird vibes from the husband. But he's got good intel. Come see?

I walk down to the administrative outbuilding that the hotel has lent us for the search. Tanya is interviewing Gillis's husband there. I've yet to meet the man, and I am inclined to sympathize. Families of lost persons manifest their stress in strange ways. Besides, we need him. He's been driving alongside our missing person for one thousand miles.

I press through the front doors. The conference room down the hall is closed. It seems quiet within. I knock on the cheap door. After some shuffling and scraping of chairs, Tanya comes to the door, her expression leery.

"Oh," she says. "Come on in, Lieutenant Miller."

I step into the room. Tanya takes her place at one end of a rectangular conference table. The husband, Gregory Bouras, sits at the other end with his hands clasped between his legs, head bowed.

We search twice. We are searching for a body, a physical person, but at the same time, we are also searching for a life—who that lost person is, why they went into the woods, and with whom. Intel from the warden investigators helps us know where to look, what might have happened in the gaps between what we know. My investigators have a strange skill set. They're listeners, but theirs is a dark art. They can hear things you and I can't hear, and don't want to.

"Mr. Bouras," I say, extending my hand. "I'm Lieutenant Beverly Miller, the person in charge of this search."

He finally raises his head and looks at my extended hand. He stands. It always takes men a minute to digest my height. Six feet in boots. We shake hands, then he sinks back into his chair. It's a strangely unceremonious meeting. Most families are desperate to meet me, to question, to share, to plead. But Bouras's gloomy reaction is a new one. Scooting back to her chair behind the conference table, Tanya raises her eyebrows my way.

"Well," I say. "I just wanted you to see my face. So that you know who I am if you need me."

The man nods. "Thanks."

I look to Tanya.

"We're just making our way through the questionnaire," she says. "It takes a while."

Back outside, as I try to figure out what I just saw in the interview room, the sun blinds me, cresting the top of the mountain as I walk back uphill. Sightseers taking the chairlift for a scenic ride sail into its obliterating light. Below, the resort looks like a bustling toy city, golf carts buzzing to and away from the entrance.

Two figures approach, the sun behind them. I shield my eyes.

"Hi," one calls with forced cheerfulness. "Lieutenant Miller, is it?"

One figure has a camera on his shoulder, the other holds a mike. Both smile whitely, reeking of aftershave.

"Any news about the lost Appalachian Trail hiker?" the reporter with the mike wants to know.

"Nothing yet," I say.

"No clues at all?" he asks. "A piece of clothing or anything?"

"We just got started, guys. I will definitely keep you in the loop."

"Super," the microphone holder says. "Can we shoot some footage of you just walking, Lieutenant?"

They trail me as I walk toward the bus.

"How did I do?" I ask.

"You did great," they say.

I take my seat in the bus but feel restless. Rob is regulating all comms, including the statewide police radio, in case Valerie Gillis pops out of the woods on the highway or in somebody's backyard. I flip open my laptop and scan the day's leads for our district, clicking through the usual incidents, complaints, and mysteries that stream into us from all corners on a normal day:

> Raccoon on porch eating birdseed out of feeder.
>
> Man parked car on the side of Rt. 4, then walked away wearing a bathing suit.
>
> Jet Skis on Long Pond harassing loons.

I have little patience for the person who can't solve a two-bit problem by themselves. A raccoon is eating out of your bird feeder? Take down the goddamned bird feeder. I clap shut my laptop and begin a ritual knuckle cracking.

My friend Mike lets himself into the bus, wearing a Disneyland sweatshirt and large wraparound sunglasses perched on top of his lush gray hair. He's retired from the Warden Service and too old to search, so he's come for moral support. In other words, he's come for some intel he can share with the old-timers who like to hash over every noteworthy case that hits my desk. He's brought me a donut. He lays it down in front of me.

"Let me guess," I say. "Boston Cream."

I love it when Mike laughs. For the two decades we worked together, Mike was the only warden I ever felt I could horse around with. Even then, he was mouthy and arrogant and said aloud what everyone else was only thinking. I knew where I stood with him. I know he'd give anything to reverse the gears of time and be reborn as a trainee in a fresh uniform of forest-green worsted. He was a pretty heroic warden by any measure. I admire the crap out of him.

Or—admired. These days, Mike seems to be leaning in to his more juvenile qualities. I think he lost his social skills during the pandemic. He's loud and his jokes have grown moldy. If I point this out, he tells me I'm a snowflake. "Bev," he'll say, "you have zero sense of humor." And I'll say, "Mike, how's this for a deal—you tell a joke that's funny, and I'll laugh at it."

"OK," Mike says now, settling in the passenger seat of the bus. "You ever hear the one about the out-of-stater who got bit by a dog?" Before I have a chance to stop him, Mike says, "You'll like it, it's about your brethren." He winks at Rob and refits his sunglasses on his head. "There was an old Mainer sitting on his porch when an out-of-stater pulled up to ask for directions. Before he got out of his car, the out-of-stater asked the old man, 'Does your dog bite?' 'No, sa,' says the old-timer. So, the out-of-stater gets out of his car, and as soon as he does, the dog *pounces* on him, and *muckles* onto his leg. The out-of-stater howls in pain and *rips* his leg free of the dog and *jumps* back into his car. The out-of-stater screams out of the window, 'I thought you said your dog doesn't bite!' 'He don't,' the old-timer says. 'That ain't my dog.'"

A chuckle slips out of me.

"You laughed!" Mike shouts. "Humorless Hilda laughed!"

* * *

Late in the afternoon, long after Mike leaves, Tanya returns to the bus.

I swivel toward her, and Rob turns down his radio.

"Was that as awkward as it looked?" I ask.

"So many feelings." Tanya sighs. "His own worry plus, well, hostility. He says he doesn't like cops. He, uh, supports defunding them."

A bark of laughter from Rob. "His wife is lost in the North Woods. Seems like the wrong time to pick a bone."

Tanya removes her handcuffs from the back of her belt, sits at the drop-down conference table in the center of the bus, and places her cuffs on the table like an ante. She's dressed in uniform, dark green pants and shirt with her name printed over the breast pocket. She wears two black chevrons on her sleeve, which stands for six years of service. She and her investigative partner, Cody Ouellette, look like brother and sister. Apple-cheeked. The two of them graduated from training at the same time. I claimed them for my team by fiat.

"Valerie Gillis is afraid of the dark," Tanya says, tossing her notebook on the table, as Rob wheels his chair over to join us. "She's got a bottle of Ativan with her. For anxiety. She's a nurse, so she's not squeamish. She's used to crises. She's a brave woman. But she's also afraid of the dark."

"Is she on leave?"

"Yeah. Took five months off. It's been a brutal time to be a nurse. It was supposed to be a hiatus. A break."

"A break? Hiking two thousand miles?"

Tanya's brow pinches. "I guess that's the kind of person she is."

"A lot of AT hikers are 'facing' something, though," Rob says. "For them, that's the point."

"What about him, the husband?" I ask. "Did he want her to do it?"

"Well, he's been her shuttle service for three months and was ready for more after she got up Katahdin, so."

A supported hike takes a huge weight off the mind of the thru-hiker. With someone supporting, the hiker does not need to constantly hitchhike or taxi into towns for resupply. For a solo female hiker, it adds safety and peace of mind. The supporter, of course, is a saintly role. No beautiful vistas. Lots of waiting in your car at trailheads. So why did Gregory Bouras agree to it? Maybe that's a cynical question, and the obvious answer is "for love," but the answer could also be "to keep an eye on things."

"He's given us tons of information," Tanya says. "Exactly what gear she had. How much food. We've got the names of every fellow hiker she ever mentioned. Cody's out talking to some of them as we speak. But Bouras got upset when I asked where *he* was Monday and Tuesday. He got defensive. 'I was in my motel room,' he kept saying. I asked if there was anyone who could confirm that, and he says, 'Why would you need to confirm that? What are you implying?' I said, 'This is just protocol. We ask everybody.'"

We fall silent. The truth is, crime is rare on the trail. Since the completion of the Appalachian Trail in 1937, only a handful of people have been victims of violence. Given the thousands of people tramping out there alone, that's some statistic. The fatalities we wardens handle in general are largely accidental. Flipped canoes, snowmobile collisions, drunk hunting. Crimes of incompetence, arrogance, and bad luck. Honestly, it's my job to assume that Valerie is lost—plain lost. If I started to think about *why* some folks go missing from this battered world, I wouldn't look for some of them.

"What about you guys?" Tanya asks.

Rob and I look at each other.

"Nothing yet," I say. "But the teams are hitting every drainage in the search area. If she followed a stream, then she's riding on the back of someone's ATV at this very moment."

Just then, my radio sounds.

"3321 in Caratunk here. Looking for the lieutenant. Over."

"This is Lieutenant Miller. Do you have her?"

"We—ah—no." The radio crackles. "No. We just located Ninja Turtle." This is the teenage hiker who swore he'd seen Valerie on Tuesday. We all lean in to hear. "We—ah—just showed him her photo. No ID. The woman he saw near Spaulding wasn't Valerie Gillis after all. Must have been a different hiker."

Tanya looks at the floor. Rob toys with the cap of an empty water bottle.

I feel a surge of anger that surprises me.

"Got it, Warden," I say. "Thanks. Over."

I open my laptop and report the note.

Wrong point last seen.

Reconfigure search area to southerly shelter.

I snap my laptop shut loud enough that Rob flinches.

"Great," I say, grabbing the keys to my truck. "Should've known not to follow a lead from somebody with such a stupid trail name."

"Santo" Live Interview, Bronx, NY, 7/30/22
Recorded by Warden Cody Ouellette

People think because I'm a big dude I don't get my feelings hurt. I get my feelings hurt *all the time*. I get my feelings hurt when people don't buy my shit on Craigslist. I'm not thick-skinned enough for this world. All we hear about is men wrecking women's lives. Hands down it's still better to be female. You're allowed to *feel* shit as a woman. You're allowed to *feel*. And even though feelings can press you, women don't have to shoot those motherfuckers on sight.

(laughter)

You know what I mean, Warden? Men are like, "Oh shit—sadness. Better go get my gun."
Right?
Longing: kill it. Need: kill it. Don't ask for no love, kill the asking.
Do I hide behind my size sometimes, when it's convenient? Yes.
I grew up in the Bronx! Why'd I try and hike the Appalachian Trail? I don't know *shit* about hiking. It should have been me out there getting lost.
It's not a bad way to lose weight. I lost thirty-five pounds. I had to keep my pants up with a bungee. I was hungry all the time. But then I got used to hunger. I've gotten used to a million worse things.
It's hilarious though. The looks on the faces of most hikers when I step out of the woods. There's this moment when they literally don't understand, they can't place you. They're like, "Is that a *person of color*?"

(laughter)

Man, do you have to be friendly when you are a Black man hiking. You have to start waving, like, a mile away. "Hey, y'all! Beautiful morning, innit?"

(laughter)

You don't need to write this down, Cody. I'm just fucking with you. I know you don't feel comfortable laughing, but any other *moreno* would find all this hilarious.

I'm fat like my Dominican pops.

He was overweight, Pops. Out of shape. He just sat around on the couch lecturing everybody. Gave him diabetes.

I didn't want that to happen to me—*that's* why I went.

Me hiking the AT seemed like craziness to everyone around me, but it was just me trying to treat my own life as valuable.

Pops thought it was hilarious, the whole idea.

"*Ruben?* My pussy son Ruben, a *hiker?*"

I thought he might come around before I left. You know, say something supportive, at least something serious, like "Good luck." But he didn't.

Last thing my pops said to me before I left was "You look like shit in those shorts."

Cody Ouellette: How'd you get your trail name? Why do they call you Santo?

My trail name? I didn't even know about trail names. I didn't think about it. I knew if I was going to try a thru-hike, I had to do it before I changed my mind or somebody changed it for me.

I started in Harpers Ferry, like Sparrow. But me and her didn't hook up until Pennsylvania. I hiked Maryland in a small bubble of slow hikers like me. We bonded, and I liked them. But then we get into names. I was the only one without a trail name. Other people are, like, supposed to give them to you.

I talked about food a lot, especially about donuts, so I'm like, "I think my trail name should be Donut." And we were all laughing, and one of them says, "What about Chocolate Donut?"

Then everybody starts throwing out Chocolate this, Chocolate that.

I try and get them off the chocolate track. I'm like, "Yo, remember when the door to the privy was stuck outside of Pine Knob shelter, and no one could get it to budge? Then I came over and opened it so easy and y'all were like, 'Thor! Thanks, Thor!' How about 'Thor' for my trail name? Too much?"

And they're like, "Yeah! What about *Black* Thor?"

"Black Lantern! Black Stallion!"

"What about the Dark Knight?"

Then someone calls out, "Bat Hombre!"

Finally, I say to myself, "Ruben, thou shalt taketh no more names from white folks."

And that's when I say, "Santo."

They're like "*What?*"

"Santo. Call me Santo. It's what my gramma used to call me, when I was little."

They're like, "What about—"

And I'm like, "Period. Santo, *period*."

Means holy. Or sacred, more like. Not that I'm holy. But this, all this, is holy.

Me, you, the damn streetlights. That lady walking out of the bodega. That old dude crossing the street. The street, the mountains. All of it.

Tip Line Email from "Sonia," Received 7/30/22

My name is Sonia and I am a professional psychic. I am offering to help find Valerie Gillis, who disappeared four days ago. You may not believe in psychics, but I have personally helped solve many cases via my powers of retrocognition. I have worked with law enforcement agencies here in my home state of Indiana. References are available on request. I do not offer my services for glory or money (although money would be nice!). Ever since I was young, I have been able to use my powers to help others. I do not need travel expenses as I work from my home office. I do need a map at your earliest convenience. I am sorry to say I believe she is dead. As soon as I have a map I can get you the coordinates of Valerie's body. For now, I see a guardrail bending left. A stream is below the guardrail. Look there first.

Sincerely,
Sonia

P.S. I think the husband did it.

Lt. Bev

It's difficult to understand what kind of woods these are until you see them. These aren't your normal woods, with gentle slopes full of filtered sunlight and big hardwoods that create a tidy understory. These are crowded, witchy, moss-dark woods, where root to crown the trees battle for light, everything reaching, even the tiny seedlings sprouting in the leaf humus. These woods are a chaos of rock, dirt, brush, and root. They have a close, almost bloody smell. Searchers don't walk so much as crawl, disentangle, and bushwhack.

In a grid search, a line of searchers moves through the woods within sight of one another. When they get to the end of their pass, the line pivots. One person stays put as the axis; the rest of the line comes around, then spaces out accordingly, ready to walk the opposite way. In open hardwoods, searchers might be fifty feet apart. But in these woods, searchers must stay close together as they swim through the head-high saplings. They vanish to each other.

Searchers are trained to walk slow. If they rush, the probability of detection declines. Space them too far apart, the probability of detection declines. Say you have twenty-five searchers in one square mile. That team will need to make eleven parallel passes to cover the area. This feat will take thirty-seven search hours and 942 man-hours. For one single square mile. In a state with seventeen million acres of woods.

This is what we're up against.

Thursday, July 28. Team Assignment Summary

5:30 p.m., Grid Team 4: No clues found.

5:37 p.m., Grid Team 1: No clues found. Dehydrated searcher returned for medical attention.

6:15 p.m., Grid Team 2: Found an old campsite but no items of the subject. Further searching required.

6:22 p.m., Hasty Team 1: No clues found.

6:50 p.m., Grid Team 5: Single tent pole found. (No match.)

7:17 p.m., Grid Team 3: No clues found.

8:02 p.m., Grid Team 2: No clues found.

8:49 p.m., Hasty Team 2: No clues found. All teams in.

Eleven thirty p.m. I bed down in the mobile command vehicle. I told Rob I'd find a better place to sleep, but that's just a way to get him to go home to the family. The truth is, I want to keep working. I want to double-check everything for the next day, to review assignments, to make sure the GPS units are all loaded, but mostly just to stare at the area map. The cleared areas glow with meaning. I've heard horror stories of search areas being called "clear" while unresponsive subjects groaned in the underbrush. But I can't recheck cleared areas when there are still so many square miles we hadn't gotten to once.

I lower the driver's seat in the bus as far back as I can and try to rest. Out the front windshield, I can see the broad bowl of the night sky through the bus window, an unpolluted snapshot of the cosmos etched by shooting stars.

There's a poem about stars.

HEARTWOOD

*Looking up at the stars, I know quite well
That, for all they care, I can go to hell.*

A lot of folks who get into search and rescue have an early memory of watching someone perish. When he was a boy, Rob's infant brother was washed from his mother's arms in the floodwaters of the Allagash. Cody's sister is a junkie, and as a teenager, he watched her brought back to life by an EMT with Narcan. I don't have such a story, per se. My dad made it into his fifties before suffering a massive heart attack in his desk chair at the furniture store in Leominster. I was fourteen.

I look out at the bowl of stars and wonder if Valerie is looking at the same ones. It's the second day of our search, but the fourth day of her lostness. She has already suffered four sunsets, faced four dark nights, waking at every sound, from the hoot of an owl or the thud of a falling tree in the distance or the terrifying hymns of coyotes, sundered from her people, her species. I think of my mother's face staring out from behind the parted curtains of our brick home in Leominster, the almost waxen and forlorn expression as I walked up the street from school.

In my childhood, there is a before and an after. After is after Dad's death, when Ma kind of lost her handle on things. Before is me in the woods, in cutoff shorts. It was just a couple of acres of woods between the end of our neighborhood and the highway. A dogwood grew in a clearing. A rusted chair, the bitter end of frayed ropes—those woods were full of trash and human remnants. I had read, along with every friendless kid of my generation, *My Side of the Mountain,* a book about a boy named Sam who leaves home to live in a hollowed-out tree in the Catskills with his falcon and his weasel. I read that book so many times I could recite entire passages. In the book, Sam spends a year building fires and rooting through the loam and carrying nuts around in his sweater, until someone finally comes to bring him back home. He was my hero. That kid could forage anything and fix anything. No rabbits in his trap, he'd roast some cattails, or whip up a violet-bulb salad, all the while dispensing friendly advice like "If you ever eat cattails, be sure they are well-cooked..."

Memorial Day, 1976. I was eleven years old. Dad was still alive and the furniture store was decorated with sashes and flags. My sisters were little, just three and four, and Ma was fine. Leominster liked its parades, but 1976 was the bicentennial of American independence, so the town was really in a lather. In the birthplace of Johnny Appleseed, no one wanted to hear your suspicious questions, no one wanted to know how you felt "different." I was out in the clearing. It was early, but I could hear someone warming up his tuba in the distance. In the woods, I was not preoccupied by the sight of my breast buds, one noticeably larger than the other. I didn't flush with shame at my size 9 sneakers. I sat with my back to a tree, watching morning shake the birds from the trees. This memory is one of complete happiness. That's because I have shielded it from the fact that I was being bullied viciously at school. My height enraged the boys, none of whom had yet hit puberty and felt, I could only assume, that I had stolen something from them, that I had questioned the order of things. I regularly found drawings of myself left on my desk, cartoons of laudable skill, with the label "Yeti" pointing toward my likeness. I was strong, but not quick. I can still hear the reverberation in my ears from a blow to the head by the rubber bladder of a dodgeball. When my eyes watered at dinner, and I was forced to discuss it, Ma said, "Oh, Beverly. When a boy teases a girl at this age, it just means he likes you."

I was out there in the woods looking for a sign, you see. I wanted to be called to something. The monk is called, the artist is called. The spring air was cold and clear. I stalked the clearing with a sharpened stick, which I carried like a spear but mostly used for prying old bottles from the dirt. In the distance, behind the massive fallen trunk that formed one boundary of the clearing, I saw the strangest sight—a curl of smoke, rising in the morning air. A mysterious mist, a piece of fallen cloud. A fire? I moved toward it with my spear, imagining Sam saying "If you see a mysterious puff of smoke in the woods, approach with caution . . ." I heard a groan on the other side of the log and the air charged. A full-size doe leaped up from her resting place behind the log, apprehended me with her lucid black eyes, and dodged into the woods in silent, tawny arcs.

I stood there, heart pounding.

You might find them a nuisance—deer destroy gardens; they collide with cars, causing hundreds of vehicular deaths each year; they baffle with their inability to recognize a roadway; evolution leaves them unchanged—but each time I carry one, tag one, protect one, I think, *Breath of a doe*.

That was my call.

Finally, I give up on sleep and go outside in the semidarkness. Soon, everyone will return to the staging area in force. The woods echo with birdsong, but down the hill, the resort is fast asleep. I brush my teeth outside and spit into the grass. I calmly eat my last banana. I don't care that I'm smelling a little ripe, that I haven't eaten a decent meal since Tuesday. If there's news, I want to be on-site. I want everyone to know where to find me.

I know we'll find Valerie Gillis.

We find everybody.

"Santo" Live Interview, Bronx, NY, 7/30/22
Recorded by Warden Cody Ouellette

Pennsylvania. That's what brought me and Sparrow so close.

PAINsylvania. The state motto should be "Why, God, why?"

Usually, the AT is a dirt path, right? In Painsylvania, the trail is made entirely of rocks. Not smooth rocks, not like what you're thinking. Sharp, jagged rocks that you can't put your foot flat on. I think someone came out at night and *filed* those motherfuckers.

OK, I did not have the best gear. You know how much money some beautiful Gore-Tex hiking boots cost? They don't want fat people to hike, but they also don't want poor people to hike. I had factory seconds. I named my boots. I called my left boot "Left Eye" and my right "T-Boz," in honor of the original members of Moms's favorite group, TLC. You ever hear the song "Waterfalls"? You know, "Don't go chasing waterfalls"...?

It's an anti-hiking song.

(laughter)

Anyway, those boots had done pretty well by me. Until we got to Rocksylvania. The pointy rocks started to destroy my boots. I could see my sock through the side of Left Eye. Now sprinkle in some thunderstorms. What is *up* with Pennsylvania and thunderstorms? Once a day, you're just walking along through cornfields and daisies, and you turn around and the sky behind has been, like, possessed by black clouds.

It's evil, man!

But Pennsylvania brought us close, me and Sparrow. We were so slow, we got passed by *everybody*. We walked those miles like two stray dogs. Wet all the time, hungry all the time, but on the other hand, free.

It takes a certain kind of person to laugh. To be like, "What a sad picture we make. Nobody putting our asses on the cover of *Backpacker* magazine."

Cody Ouellette: You probably really get to know a person. Out there for hours. With nothing to do but talk?

Oh yeah. You tell them everything.

Sparrow has such a sweet voice, anyone tell you that? Like an angel. Just listening to it could calm you down. And she *refuses* to swear. Like some chick from the 1950s. She'd fall down a slope—bam, bam, bam, then she'd stand up and be like, "Oh *sugar*."

We sang too. All the time. Hikers sing, and they sing like shit.

What'd we sing? Uh, anything we could remember. Whitney Houston. Christmas carols. I knew a couple hymns in Spanish from going to church with my gramma—those made her cry. Oh—we loved to belt out the national anthem. We'd be going up some steep, ass-kicking mountain, going, "And the rocket's red glaaaaaare!"

No matter what you feel about this country, as it turns out, when you are going up some four-thousand-footer, that's the song that gets you to the top!

(laughter)

And we talked, that's right. I told her . . . I told her things I never told anyone.

The past comes back to you, walking all those miles.

Childhood things. The one trip we ever took to the DR. Watching my father, back then, stepping out of the water in Puerto Plata, with this body like a god. Like a terrible god.

He was a hero to me, for a while.

Silly shit too. We made up games. Word games.

Sometimes hiking the AT feels like being a kid in the back seat of a painful long car ride.

Minus the car.

(laughter)

Cody Ouellette: Sounds like you two were very close.

I don't think I've ever felt closer to anyone in my damned life.

Could *not* have gotten as far as I did. Could *not* have done it without Sparrow.

Cody Ouellette: What about Gregory? You must have gotten to know him too.

Uh ... what about him?

Cody Ouellette: Did Valerie talk about Gregory? Their ups and downs? Every couple has problems. Did she tell you about theirs?

Uh. Man, OK.

Well, look here ...

You recording *everything* I say?

Dear Mom,

All young learn from the mother—the foal, the pup, the gosling.
    I wait for your voice. I wait for you to tell me what to do.
    Hello?
    I poke my head out of my tent.
    It's midmorning. The forest floor emits a musty steam.
    I have the same thought I've had numerous times since arriving to this ridge, which is that I should start a fire. The billows of smoke will be a signal.
    A signal fire.
    I blush. I don't know how! When in my stupid life did I ever make a fire outside?
    I can suture wounds, I can find a vein in a baby's arm, but I can't make a fire.
    Normally, I use my long-stemmed Bic lighter to light my camp stove. I don't like to get close to the gas when I'm trying to heat up water for oatmeal in the near dark. But I didn't bring any of those things on this leg. No stove, no long-stemmed Bic.
    I didn't think I'd be out here long, you see.
    But I do have back-up—matches. I dig through my pack until I locate them inside a tiny green canister. I give it a rattle.
    When I open the box, the matches spill into the dirt.
    Peanuts!
    I tweeze each one back into the box. There are six.
    I stare at the forest. Now what?

Isn't fire-making inborn to humans?

I close my eyes and wait to know.

Then I fall asleep.

Why does mortal danger inspire sleepiness? As a child, I often "fell asleep" to avoid having to go to bed. I'd collapse on the floor, my face in the binding of my coloring book, sure that one night you'd forget that I was there, and a new era would begin—a civilization without bedtime.

It never worked. I was always scooped into the air, obliged to keep my eyes shut as I moved perilously through space, a leaden weight in Daddy's arms.

Then the two of you would begin the same skit: "Where should I put her?" Daddy would stage-whisper. "In the trash?"

"It would be a shame to throw her out," you would reply. "She's not even broken."

"Is she still under warranty?"

"No. And she's not recyclable."

Daddy would sigh, kicking open my bedroom door, saying, "Let's just keep her. We can probably get a couple more years out of her."

Only at the last, after Daddy had left and you had pulled up the covers, would I open my eyes, groggy, pretending to awake. You would smile and stroke my eyes shut. This had the effect of putting me in a temporary trance, just long enough for you to make your exit, leaving the glitter of your absence, a detonated star.

The nightly cataclysm: the mother leaves the room.

Well.

There weren't enough rosary beads in the world, nor numbers to count backward, when you left my room at night. It may be dangerous to be unfathered, exposed on the animal plain, but life unmothered is simply unlivable. I mean, why go on? I held a little funeral every time you left the room. I tried to smother myself with my pillow. I replayed home movies of our lost lives in my head. Then, eventually, I'd start to worry a scab or to scratch my dry legs or count my teeth with my tongue, taking some clinical half interest in my body, waiting for the night to pass. I withstood this agony for at least ten minutes before slipping out of bed to put my eye to the crack in the door. Because the wonderful thing about my bedroom was that it looked out on you. You and Daddy, talking or watching TV. I had you in my sights again.

Sorry for my jealous interruptions! They felt involuntary. I often stood there unacknowledged until you realized I wasn't going away. Then the arbitration phase of bedtime would begin. Two more songs. Three more hugs. Sixteen kisses. You agreed to lie with me for one minute. Then one more minute, until, at last, you fell asleep beside me like a sun-warmed stone.

Victory.

We walked in and out of one another's dreams.

In yours, I was a pigeon. In mine, you were a boat.

Leaves, I think. Leaves, twigs—tinder.

Do something, Valerie! Try something! WAKE UP!

I stomp around my campsite, gathering small sticks and dry leaves. Only the fallen leaves on the top are dry. Underneath, everything is wet. Wet leaves are layered together like phyllo pastry. Below that, a cushion of moist pine needles. The dirt is cold and wet from the recent rain. Lighting anything on fire seems far-fetched. On nice evenings at the shelters, someone young and eager would gather wood and start a campfire in the shelter pit. On other nights, after hiking for miles, no one had the energy, and we'd all collapse by "hiker midnight"—nine o'clock.

I clear a small patch on the ground and push my dry leaves and twigs into a pile.

I strike a match. The tip flares and immediately dies.

Five matches.

This time I crouch near the pile, strike my match, and tilt it downward, touching the flame to the dry leaves. The leaf edge flares. I watch the orange ember travel around the blade of one leaf, then the next.

Then it dies with a puff of smoke.

Four matches.

I hear a chittering and look up to the crotch of a nearby tree. A squirrel is flicking its tail and delivering what sounds like a didactic lecture on what I'm doing wrong.

Shut up, I tell the squirrel. Scram.

Then I retreat to my tent, wrung out from the work.

Water isn't a problem. There's a creek at the foot of my ridge. I can hear it burbling day and night. The music of ongoingness.

All I have to do to get water is climb out of my tent, cross the Green Sea, and descend the slope to the creek. The loam is soft. It sucks on my one bootless foot.

I move slowly, drained of energy. There's no rush. Sometimes I stop to rest my cheek against my Nalgene bottle, or to remember something funny or sweet that makes me smile.

Sometimes I cry too, when I cannot believe what is happening to me. I weep into my own hands.

The creek water is as cold as melted ice. I tip my bottle and water rushes into it. The water smells of moss and sulfur. It swirls with dirt. My fingers grow numb.

I kneel by the creek for a long time. With my eyes closed, the creek sounds like a woman talking. A familiar woman.

Occasionally, there is a consequential shift.

A river stone—after a millennium of gentle pressure—flips.

Back at my campsite, I return to my tent. I'm as tired as if I had just pulled a day of big miles on the trail, when I have only gone down to the creek. The calorie deficit has started to take effect. The fogginess in my thinking. The clumsiness in my fingers. My vitality is being siphoned in vicious little sips.

The trip to the creek has the strange effect of making me glad to be "home."

My world, my tent, my clearing.

Out of boredom and anxiety, I've christened everything in this clearing. For example, Dead Tree. Dead Tree is the rotten monument in the center of my campsite, a broken snag that wears a crown of splinters. Its fallen top half, Rotten Log, lies nearby and now serves as a kind of mothership for numerous insects and ferns. On the other side of Dead Tree lies the Green Sea, where a creeping shade plant grows in an overlapping weft of jungle-green leaves, each one set with a white flower. There are Near Rock and Far Rock, both crusted with lichen. Everywhere else lies the dense, rich disorder of the forest floor, which of late I have taken to studying closely. Seedlings strain upward through the leaf litter and the scrolls of birch bark and broken bracts of pine cones. As for my tent, I pitched that on Moss Mound, a pickle-green mat of moss that is soft to the touch, and which extends to the edge of my clearing, where the infinite bosk continues.

Trees and trees and more trees.

Sometimes I stare at my circle of sky. The fallen crowns of Dead Tree and its several brethren leave a gap in the canopy. Longing has given this patch of sky unreasonable meaning. I stare at it so often hoping for rescue that I've induced a reverse vertigo. When I look down, the ground around me seesaws.

Trees surround me. Endless, numerous, silent trees. Skinny, pin-straight evergreens with no branches. High above, the trees are tipped with green crowns that blot out the sky. When I first stopped here, the clearing appeared large. But today, my clearing seems smaller.

"You silly woman!" I say out loud. "How are the search planes going to see you through that?"

I never really minded being a small person. Of course, my stature greatly influenced my life. I was teased a lot, mostly affectionately. Treated as a toy. Shrimpy, Low Pockets, Tinker Bell. I used to cry about it. But every kid was teased for one thing or another. Rabbity teeth. Ginger hair. I was small, so what.

Small women have to be nice. Not just because we need the occasional assistance in reaching things, but also because we sense the inherent dangers of being easily lifted—well, *seized*.

But now. Now, I would do anything to be visible. To be large.

Not just tall—a giantess. I want to be seen.

I want to be as imposing as a mountain.

I WANT TO BE SEEN.

The truth is, I stopped here because I could go no farther. I was tired of running. I was tired of running and sobbing. I was hopelessly lost and devoid of ideas.

HEARTWOOD

I did not scream. I tried not to make a sound.

Sometimes at night, when I hear sounds in the woods, I wonder, Is that him? Is he back?

I don't know which scares me more—being found by him, or being found by no one.

Lena

Lena Kucharski is a reader. She has been reading for most of her seventy-six years of life. Now, on the balcony of her retirement community, she reads from her favorite new subgenre, memoirs of outdoor catastrophe. Juliane Koepcke's *When I Fell from the Sky*, Donn Fendler's 1978 chestnut, *Lost on a Mountain in Maine*. She reads in waves. For a while she went on a tear of esoteric botanical texts, then seventh-century ghazals, and after that, detective novels from the free-book bin. She learned to read at a very young age. She can remember the expression on the face of her mother, an illiterate cleaning woman, when she found Lena reading Stendhal's *The Red and the Black* in the bathtub at the age of ten. Lena knew that without books, there was nothing but time.

She'd been precocious in all her school subjects. Math was obvious; languages stuck to her like trash in a windstorm. She was at home in the sciences and had to be pulled back from the eyepiece of a microscope.

When she was little, Lena's beloved father, Tomasz, used to tell her that she was "special." It took Lena a long time to understand that the word "special" means something different to an adult than it does to a child. To young Lena, "special" meant "exceptional," "fabulous," "dazzling." Much later, Lena came to understand that what Tomasz really meant was something like "You are an odd and interesting person, an acquired taste, an outlier, and your life will be marked by long doldrums of friendlessness. You probably won't be happy, but on the other hand, you'll be spared the suspicion that you are one of the lemmings of human history."

Lena Kucharski isn't a lemming.

She has been called, in various registers of respect, an "original," a "square peg," and "an acquired taste." She felt no indignation when she'd overheard two fellow residents in her retirement community discussing her recently in the solarium. "I *like* Lena," one had said. "I mean, in the abstract."

But now, after all this, a life devoted to books of all kinds, Lena is occasionally beset by a nauseating transition between the page and the world, as if a decision has been handed down in these twilight years of her life: world trumps book. You can study all day in your sunny apartment in your privileged retirement community until even the neuropathy that makes walking difficult ceases to exist, but when you look up from your book, when you look out the window and see one of your fellow residents jogging unprettily toward the parking lot, breasts swinging, buttocks bobbing, straight into the arms of a woman trying to get out of her car—a daughter, probably, bringing gifts, looks like—your want hurts like an extraction.

You can be a genius, but no matter how much you study life, it studies you back.

How does such a square peg, a skeptic and a prodigal, return to the state of her birth? Maybe the apple does not fall far from the *drzewo*. She was raised nearby, in New Britain, Connecticut—"Little Poland." Life took her here and there, through two marriages, but as soon as her neuropathy worsened, she quietly moved back to Connecticut. To Cedarfield Active Life Plan Community, a "green living space" for "adults fifty and over" where you can join clubs like the Reapers, an advocacy group working to legalize assisted suicide. Lena never intended to live in an institution of any kind. She was born to be alone, and she bears this fact neutrally and without embarrassment. She keeps to the edges of the place. Despite her deep distrust of institutions, clubs, and old people, Lena noticed that she relaxed after moving in to Cedarfield. She slept better, worried less. Not just because the campus was fully wheelchair accessible, but because the scent of the air was so familiar—fresh and mineral, with a trace of river in it—and the birdsong was her birdsong.

Now, she drives down the hall in her power wheelchair with the baggie of candied spearmint in her lap. It's unlike her; she's delivering a gift. To Warren Esterman. Warren is a retired lawyer with a sweet tooth, a flatterer who helps her with her foraging. She first met Warren when she moved to Cedarfield six years ago. His unnerving attention toward her had bordered on inappropriate. After she rebuffed him, she watched him wander around looking for a new fixation. These many years later, seeing his compulsivity has softened Lena. The probation on which she'd placed him has come to term. Besides, Warren is quick to say yes to almost any plan. He's enthusiastic. He doesn't mind mud. That very morning, the two of them had foraged on the border of the campus at a disturbed site with a concrete foundation smothered in regrowth. They'd found wild mint, fresh dandelion, and a basketful of barberries. At her instruction, Warren walks stiff legged into fields and woods to pick the plants and roots that Lena can only gaze at from the road. Warren is her legs.

Something has possessed her to wrap her thank-you gift with a gold foil ribbon repurposed from a Cedarfield party favor. Perhaps this glint is what makes it visible to Bobbi, who sits in the brilliant sunshine of the solarium reading the *Wall Street Journal*. The woman offers her a complicated smile.

"A present for your *inamorato*, Lena?"

Lena says nothing. She motors away as fast as she can.

The long journey to Warren's wing affords too much time to think. The building is so massive. Crammed with people. Four floors, four enormous thetas stacked on top of one another. The first two floors are independent living. The third floor is for assisted living. And on the fourth floor? Hospice. The moment you move to Cedarfield, you've begun your ascension.

And yet. The dying come looking for love. After their husbands or wives depart, within the year, they've re-upped. People pair up in meetings, on van rides to museums; they even pair up in the Reapers. The women form devoted, homosocial attachments to one another. Watching them bent over puzzles in the vestibule, Lena feels a kind of mystification. A fascination bordering on nausea.

You can't love, others have said to Lena. *You don't know how.*

Well, only one other said this to Lena, the most important one.

You're just trying to control me.

Your love is poison.

She has yet to recover.

All she has left is her compliance. If the allegations against Lena are true, then she considers her isolation compensatory.

Poison!

By the time Lena reaches Warren's apartment, she has resolved not to ring the bell at all. She places the baggie on the small shelf outside his door and turns to leave.

Yet somehow, he smells her. His door opens.

She hears, at her back, "Lena!"

She turns her power chair around.

Warren is smiling in the doorway, holding a toothbrush.

"Good thing I caught you," he says, swiping the mint candy

from his shelf. "I was wondering if you'd like to join me and several others for supper tonight."

Lena says nothing. It takes her a second to realize that she can be seen.

"Oh," she says. "No, thank you."

He waits, toothpaste foam ringing his mouth. Must more words be added?

"I have my harvest," she explains. "The dandelions you cut for me this morning. They lose their nutrients within hours."

He nods. "Of course," he says. "Next time."

Back at 2330, Lena sidles up to her desktop and checks again for a response from her friend /u/TerribleSilence. Nothing yet. TerribleSilence has been offline for several days. He often goes out foraging or camping, but this absence is longer than usual. She has missed him.

She found TerribleSilence on a foraging subreddit. He posted frequently, mostly photos of unique, impressive harvests. Handfuls of indigo milk caps. Homemade dandelion honey. The pandemic had been a net gain for foragers and recluses. For many people, the outdoors is a vast sameness. But a forager can see so much. The virus had scared everyone inside just as spring was bursting into life. But Lena had been content to spend cold spring days searching the ground at her wheels. Mushrooms exploded. Fiddleheads straightened. Exotic warblers stopped to rest on the spikelets of cheatgrass.

She knows /u/TerribleSilence by his hands. He's posted so many photos of his hands on Reddit, holding a berry or a bulb. His hands are elegant and long fingered, with dirt tattooed in the knuckle creases. Once, he'd posted a shot of his face in profile, a photo taken by a third party as he leaned in to gaze with pleasure at some redbuds. This photo, she had studied many times. He appeared to be about thirty-five or forty, handsome, with laugh lines around the eyes. With his trimmed ginger beard, he looked a smidgen like the Irish German actor who played Rochester in the 2011 film version of *Jane Eyre*, one of her all-time favorite adaptations of the novel. ("Do you think, because I am poor, plain, obscure, and little, that I am soulless and heartless?") In his thumbnail, he describes himself as a "Forager, Indigent, Wiseass." /u/TerribleSilence has a kind of local fame on the foraging subreddit. He is often the one to reply first with an identification. "Yes that's wild spinach," or "No that's a daffodil, not an onion, don't eat it." Almost a year ago, she'd reached out to him via private mail, and since then they've had an almost romantically constant instant messaging relationship via Telegram. It's hard to describe the commitment she feels toward him. She's different like this, online. Now, he writes.

ROSEHIP. What's good?
Sorry. I been asleep. 😳

> Hello! Good to have you back!
> I had a wonderful haul today.
> Dandelion. Barberries. Wild mint.

What u going 2 make?

> Dandelion salad with lemon.
> I candied the mint. Delicious!

Yum. Post recipe on the sub?

> Will do. Did you see my recipe for candy cap syrup?

HEARTWOOD

>   You didn't comment yet.

My bad.
I see it. 😊
Ooo would be good over some acorn
flour jacks.

    TerribleSilence lives three hundred miles away from Cedarfield, in a town called Bethel, Maine. He's in the process of building a zero-waste homestead in the mountains. He speaks of the moment when he will move into his homestead and go off the grid like a kind of delicious suicide. At night, in the dark, Lena prays he never succeeds.

Got news for you, btw.

>   What is it?

Just passed a sign on Route 4.
MISSING FEMALE HIKER.

>   Have you ever seen a sign like that
>   before?

They only put out road sign when
missing more than 24 hours.
Most lost hikers are found w/in
24 hrs. Longer = rare.

>   Intriguing!
>   Good thing it's July. Lucky for her
>   its warm. Does she have shelter?
>   Backpack, etc.?

Who knows?

> If so, she could survive for quite
> some time.
> Juliane Koepcke survived 11 days
> after falling out of an airplane.

As far as she can tell, TerribleSilence has the manifold skills of the outdoorsman. He can fly-fish, he can rock climb, he has scaled frozen waterfalls with the use of an ice pick. Apparently, he once built a pallet of branches to carry an injured friend out of the woods. Are these things everyone in Maine can do?

Should I join SAR?

> What is SAR?

Search and Rescue.

> YES!

Have done 2 other times.
Found both lost parties.
Older lady with dementia & a teen w/
mental health issues.

> I'm so curious about her now.
> I wonder why she left the trail and
> how she got lost.

Most AT hikers = oblivious.
Don't use maps/don't have
compass.
Lost all the time.
They don't know the basics.
If she'd stayed put or followed a

drainage she'd be home already.
Likely knows zero about survival.

> Poor woman.
> Maybe you'll be the one to
> find her!

    Lena's got routes around her apartment. For short distances, she prefers to grip whatever's near—a chairback, her wooden desk, the doorframe—as waypoints toward the bed or bathroom. She's got a bench seat in the shower and an elevated toilet seat. But the effort to ambulate is tiring and, finally, symbolic. She increasingly relies on her power chair. Now, she stretches up to fill the watering can from the kitchen faucet and ferries it in her lap outside to her tomato plants. She and her friend often stay online while doing other things. This technological togetherness feels as real as any other kind. While she's watering the tomatoes, which are absolutely pregnant with red this summer, she says, aloud, "Search and rescue. Ha. What *can't* you do?" Evening is falling, and she pauses to breathe in the vegetative smell of her plants as a breeze washes up from the valley. As she travels back inside, she hears a ping.

Getting more intel on lost hiker from
listening to the police CB radio.

> Do tell!

She's 42 yrs. Caucasian. A nurse.
I don't have her name yet.

    Lena stares at her blinking cursor. Forty-two. Caucasian. A nurse.
    Lena does not breathe. Something that had been fixed in place comes loose inside her. This fixed weight free-falls; it drops plumb like a stone, then sinks back into silence.

U there?
The nurse part is good, don't u think?
Nurses = smart.

> Why don't they release her name to the public?

They will soon.
I think they have to contact
family first.
Criminal investigation now.
. . .
U there?

> Why "criminal"?

They don't say.

> Don't you know someone you can ask? A warden?

More than 48 hrs.

> What does that mean?

They find most ppl within 48 hrs.
Most ppl after that found dead.

    Dead. Lena pinches her own arm, hard. *Listen up! Not dead. Missing.*
    Lena is rattled by the vertigo inside her.
    She has not felt that particular desolation in years.
    Time passes, one adjusts.
    We think we are so delicate. But we can adjust to anything.
    She needs the lost hiker's name.
    Get her name, that will resolve the matter.

HEARTWOOD

U there?

                        Yes. Why is dying of probable
                        exposure "a crime"?

Guess they think someone/thing might
have killed her.
Or killed self.
. . .
Probably some lunatic.
Anybody could come and slice you
apart in a shelter.
You're totally exposed.
Plus there's other stuff out there.
I could tell you stories.
. . .
U there?
U quiet tonight.

                        I'm here.

Anyway, will find out more on site.
Volunteers invited to gather @ Sugarloaf
Mountain Hotel staging area . . . 6 a.m.
Gotta go get some sleep!
MORE SOON.

    Wait, she thinks. *Don't go yet! Don't leave me!*
    She is typing without knowing what she wants to say, only that she doesn't want to be alone. But in the middle of her sentence, he logs off. She wiggles her mouse.

                        Are you still there?
                        Hello?

Enough time passes that her screen goes dark.

Terrible silence indeed. Terrible, terrible.

As she looks from corner to corner of her small space, her throat tightens.

Dawn is hours away.

At Cedarfield, there are few night sounds. The residents sleep. The traffic fades. Throw open the windows; there are barely any insects in this deforested campus. Lena longs to hear the stridulation of a cricket, the slur of a passing car. Anything but silence.

She wakes to the sound of someone vacuuming overhead. She grabs the armrests of her power chair. She has fallen asleep in her chair. Her blanket lies in a pile on the floor. A pain shoots down her neck as she straightens her head.

She grabs the clock. Seven a.m. Throws the clock on the bed. Warren will be at breakfast. She forces herself to brush her teeth, which she does with enormous hatred for them.

She grabs her lanyard and keycard and flings open the door.

Full speed.

It is such a cliché, but they do—old people walk *so slowly*. She has often wished for a fast lane in the hallway, a lane for scooters and power chairs. What is within the realm of polite to say? "Give way! Coming through! Move!" This morning, she says nothing at all; instead she passes too closely, almost nipping toes. An intake of breath, "My goodness!"

Then a chivalrous bellow: "Slow down."

She finds Warren in the Bistro-To-Go. He is staring at the yogurts.

She tugs his sleeve hard. He jumps back, a startled look on his face.

"Come here," she says. "Come with me."

She doesn't even wait to see if he is behind her. She motors down the hall, smacks the open-door button, and enters the quiet sanctum of the first room she passes. Warren pauses at the door.

"We can't be in here," he says. "This is the meditation room."

"Listen to me," she says. "I need to talk to you about something."

He takes a tentative step inside.

"Come in, *please*."

The door draws shut behind him.

"There's a woman missing," Lena begins. "And I think I might know her." She swallows hard. "I haven't seen her in a while. So, I could be wrong. But I could be right."

"OK," says Warren. "Who is she?"

"She's a hiker on the Appalachian Trail. She disappeared on Monday in the Maine woods and hasn't been seen since."

Warren considers. "I mean, who is she to you?"

For the first time, she feels the loss of sleep in her bones. "I can't say."

Warren blinks. "You can't say?"

"It's irrelevant."

"It's irrelevant that you can't say, or that you—?"

"Damn it!" Lena says, and he flinches. "My daughter! It might be my daughter!"

Warren pauses. "You have a daughter?"

At this very moment, the door breezes open.

"Good morning!" beams a fellow resident, a bald man in a blue tracksuit. "I didn't know there was meditation this morning."

"There's not!" Lena shouts. "Do we *look* like we're meditating?"

The man shrinks backward.

Warren suggests to the man, "You could check the schedule for the next class." He looks down at Lena with disapproval. "I'm late. I told Bobbi I'd meet her at the lecture."

Lena inhales deeply and exhales. She used to say to Christine, when she was two or three and in a snit, *Smell the flowers, blow out the candle.*

"The lost woman is forty-two years old. She's also a nurse. Just like my daughter," Lena says. "What if it's her? What if someone has hurt her? What if I could be of help?"

Warren sighs. "You and your daughter are—no longer in contact?"

"That's correct," Lena says.

Finally, he pulls out a chair and sets it down in front of her. He sits. Now they meet eye to eye.

"This is all very serious talk, Lena."

"I know. I know it's serious."

"Then contact the police. Why are you telling me?"

"Because I don't know what to do!"

"What can you do? You are a disabled elderly woman hundreds of miles away from—"

"I mean with myself. I don't know what to do with *myself*." She rakes at her shirt. "I cannot stand these—*minutes*."

She leans toward him, her mouth open and asking.

But his face is confused, a miscellany of expressions. He doesn't understand.

She is flooded with fury. The incomprehension of others has always made her furious.

She wants to wring his neck. She wants to pound his face.

Instead, she throws her hands to her head and begins to cry.

It had been such a long night. One of the longest of her long life. Her mind was normally a hearthside—a home. Throughout her life, being alone was being intact. She cannot bear the suggestion that her mind is unsafe, a wild place where she wanders, a subject. Her body slumps forward, limp with frustration. She hasn't heard the sound of her own weeping in so long. It is high, strained, like a tone-deaf person trying to sing.

But there had been several shocks in her life, shocking reversals. In her childhood, the vanisher was Tomasz, the man who had raised her. Gentle, amiable, and, as it turned out, a coward. Far worse was the winter evening of Christine's exit. Christine was barely a legal adult—she still used Clearasil, for Chrissake—and it was unseasonably warm, foggy; there was a chemical whiff to the air, the smell of the lives of others; her daughter's main squeeze arrived in a car with flip-up headlights, and against all objections, Christine got in.

Now, Warren stands up. Lena thinks he is leaving too, but instead, he walks around behind her. He places one hand on her shoulder and pats it sympathetically. Her chair rolls forward. She is being pushed.

"What are you doing?" she asks, her face wet with tears and mucus.

"We're going to find somebody to help us."

"No. No. I'm not ready." Lena panics. "Your lecture!" she cries. "Bobbi will be mad!"

He punches open the door and pushes her through. She fumbles for the chair controls.

"Please stop," she begs him. "Warren, please. Dear Warren."

She is finding it hard to breathe in a different way now. Her breath feels agonized. Taken through a straw.

"First let me investigate," she says, trying to turn around and look at him. "I promise I'll get help if I need it. But please, let me do it on my own. There's a tip line. I could call that. Please."

He stops pushing. He is breathing heavily behind her. She has upset him. A risk, at his age, with his heart.

"Please," she pleads, "don't tell anyone what I said. Anything I said."

She reaches backward for his hand. It's no longer there.

She sits in the hallway alone.

Lt. Bev

FRIDAY, JULY 29. SIX A.M.
DAY 3 OF THE GILLIS SEARCH.

Word has traveled to all the amateur search clubs around New England, and eighty-two volunteers show up on Sugarloaf Mountain by dawn light. The colonel sends me twenty wardens today and four K-9 teams. A couple of officers join us from New Hampshire, and a half dozen Canadian border patrol agents come down from Coburn Gore. Lord help anybody else who gets into trouble in the outdoors today.

"Thank you all for coming," I say, standing on the tailgate of my truck to address the group. "This is an impressive crowd. I know a lot of you. But if you don't know me, I'm Lieutenant Beverly Miller. If you've never met me, please come say hello. I'm easy to spot. If you don't already know your team leader, see Sergeant Rob Cross, this ugly guy right here. After reconsidering our leads, we are placing Valerie's point last seen just north of Poplar Ridge. We're imagining she's injured. Maybe she's fallen. If so, could be she's unresponsive. Check every crevasse. Keep your eyes peeled. I'm giving the K-9 teams a head start today to avoid any scent pollution in the new search areas. It's going to be a long one, people. Bring everything you need."

Shouting. Clipboard waving. Engines turning over. Rob starts sorting folks into groups and handing out assignments. The search clubs are easy to spot by their gear—goggles, helmets, rescue packs. They stick together. The overflow are just regular folks in hunting camo, sunglasses, hiking boots. These people are mechanics, trappers, high school teachers. They drive buses in the offseason, lead moose safaris in summer. Some folks search unofficially on their own. Farmers and woodsmen who've hunted these grounds since the Korean War walk outside our search area, scanning the woods for a flash of color in the brush. Like the Amish raise their barns, Mainers search for each other in the woods.

It's what we do.

Dispatch calls me to say that the Valerie Gillis tip line is already flooded. If we want them to keep subcontracting for this search, they might need another hand. I think about which junior warden I could tap to leave his post for an involuntary stint listening to folks sharing their Hollywood screenplay versions of what happened to her.

Missing-person cases like this beat all the frustrated fiction writers out of the bushes.

"The husband did it!" "Bobcats ate her!" "I just saw her in a diner in Pennsylvania!"

Only about 2 percent of tip line calls are useful. But we are desperate for that 2 percent.

The best thing to happen all morning is that Valerie's hiking partner calls us back. His name is Ruben Serrano, and he's living with his mother in New York City. Every hiker we interview about Valerie brings him up. The two of them were apparently inseparable, until he quit his thru-hike somewhere in Vermont. He's very upset and wants to be of help finding Valerie, but he can't drive up. We need somebody down there from our team. I'm not delegating this interview to some local surrogate who doesn't understand trail culture.

Just then, I hear Dolly Parton on the radio, loud. Warden Cody Ouellette is getting out of his truck. I watch him for a moment as he hits the mud off his boots against the sidewall of his tire. I feel about Cody the way I feel about Tanya, which is reassured. I'm going to have to leave this show in somebody's hands eventually. Cody sees me and waves. He's got a sweat stain around his neck, and his hair is pushing departmental standards for neatness. His father is a drunk and a local nuisance, and Cody seems to work twice as hard to make up for the extra admin the man causes us. A father and son couldn't be more opposite.

"Hey, Slick," I call. "I've got something I need your help with."

I'm about to send him six hours down I-95 to New York City to find Valerie's hiking partner. The thing about Cody is, he won't even blink.

"Lieutenant!" The duo from Channel 6 wrestle their way toward me. "Can we have two minutes?" They click on their video light.

"Ha," I say, blinded. "Now I know what deer feel like."

"Sorry," the kid with the camera says.

"Lieutenant Miller," says the other, holding a mike to my face. "Can you give us an update on the search for Valerie Gillis?"

"Sure. We have almost one hundred people searching today. The K-9 teams are out in force. We are feeling very positive."

"Are we still looking at a lost-person scenario, do you think?"

"That is what I think," I say. "We just need to put the right resources in the right place."

I thank them and start to walk toward the bus.

"Can you speak to the fact that Valerie Gillis took antianxiety medication? Do you think she is a danger to herself? In terms of her mental state?"

I stop and scrutinize the microphone holder. I tower over him. "A hell of a lot of people take medication for anxiety," I say. "That's not a scoop. I know you guys want a story. But right now, the story is 'There's no news.'"

One of my three phones starts buzzing.

My personal cell. My sister Kate is calling.

I let it go to voicemail.

An hour later, I'm at a country store outside of Rangeley, getting lunch for the team. I walk down the creaky aisle to what feels like more stares than normal. I pick up our order. Three Italian subs, two black coffees, and a bag of Sour Patch Kids for Rob to take home to the kids. I step up to the cash register. A man about my age wipes his hands on a napkin.

"Any news yet on the lost woman?" he asks.

"No news yet," I say. "But we have great conditions today."

"Helluva place to get lost," he says.

I hand over my credit card, but he waves it away.

"It's on us," he says.

I stand, holding out the card.

"Well, thanks," I say, putting it back in my wallet.

"Channel 6?" Tanya says, slipping into the bus without knocking. "From Portland way? Jesus." She sits down heavily. Rob swivels his chair her way and I join her at the conference table. "I told them no comment. Anything yet?"

I smile stiffly. "Let's start with you."

"Valerie had a personal locator beacon. Guess how I know that?"

"How do you know that?"

"Gregory showed it to me. She took it out of her pack because she couldn't bear any added weight." Tanya removes her firearm and cuffs and leans back against the wall of the bus. She's wearing civilian clothes today—a stiff, lawyerly collared shirt and gray slacks. "Eight ounces," she says, shaking her head. "Eight ounces, and she'd be safe right now, summitting Katahdin."

I grab a Sprite out of the mini fridge and put it in front of Tanya. She just stares at it.

"He cried again today," she says.

"Huh," I say. "What set him off?"

"I was asking him about her survival skills. I wanted to know if we should be looking for a signal fire, you know, and he seemed so skeptical. Hopeless. 'No,' he kept saying, 'no, no, no. Valerie's too polite to start a signal fire.' I mean, polite? I asked him if she knew how to forage. Berries maybe, or even bugs. 'No way,' he says. 'Valerie would never eat *bugs*.' I go, 'Folks can live a long time lost in the woods. They can't live without water, but she's got lots of water sources. People can't live without shelter, but unless she's been separated from her backpack, she's got a tent. Even without eating, there's records of folks surviving for as long as a month ... And he goes, 'Are you asking me if I think Valerie's dead?' And I say, '*I* don't think she's dead. Do *you*, Gregory?' And he just sits there, stony-faced. So I say, 'Is there any part of you that feels like Valerie was at a breaking point? That recent years had been more than she could handle? That she was tired of—I don't know, tired of being a nurse, watching people suffer and die? Do you think she meant to walk away?'"

Tanya traces the cold soda can with her finger.

"That's when he starts to cry. Part of me thinks, 'Shit, Dunning, you're about to get a confession.' I mean, he's really bawling. I tell him, 'Talk to me. I am here for you. Say what you need to say. You'll feel better.'

"But he goes, 'Maybe that's why she doesn't love me anymore.' And I'm like, 'What do you mean? I'm sure that's not true.' And he says, 'She told me so.'"

Rob snorts.

"It was something she realized out on the trail. She was in the White Mountains, walking through the mist or what have you, when she realized that their romantic love had run its course. She felt sad about it. She was still very dedicated to him, she said, but what can you do? She told him as soon as she could. They believe in 'radical honesty.'"

"And he still continued to support her hike? He didn't just get in his car and drive back home?"

"Nope." Tanya cracks open her soda and stares at the wall opposite. "He says he still loves her. Her not loving him doesn't change him loving her."

None of us know what to say to all that.

I picture the man, his trim beard, his ugly European shoes, crying his eyes out. Someone had seen him the previous night at the IGA, buying a tub of vanilla ice cream and a *People* magazine. Could this man have evil in his heart? Could he have wrung the neck of his beloved in a jealous rage and removed her body from the woods? Believe me, I know he could have.

Friday, July 29. Team Assignment Summary

5:44 p.m., K-9 Tracking Team 2: No clues found.

5:57 p.m., Grid Team 3: No clues found.

7 p.m., Grid Team 1: No clues found.

7:03 p.m., DEEMI Team 1: Report of a whistle. Waited but no further sound. No further searching required.

7:14 p.m., Grid Team 8: No clues found.

7:30 p.m., Grid Team 5: Found Eddie Bauer hiking pole. (Not hers.)

8:11 p.m., K-9 Tracking Team 1: K-9 indicated interest along Orbeton Stream, tracked upstream until dog lost scent.

8:19 p.m., Grid Team 2: No clues found.

Nothing.
Nothing.
Nothing.

The worst part of nothing is facing the group. Friday night, I gaze out over the crowd of searchers as they wait for my word. Everyone looks exhausted. Some sit on parked cars. Others stand, legs wide, trying to stay upright. Bleary-eyed, they wear dust and mud, burrs in their hair.

"So," I begin. "It's been another frustrating day. And that's hard to hear. It's hard to say." I catch one or two edgy glances. I know their gist. *What's so hard about sitting in an air-conditioned bus?* "Altogether with the dogs and planes and boots on the ground, we searched over four-hundred acres today. We found some items, but they did not belong to Valerie Gillis. I know how much you wanted this to be resolved today. But that's not the result we got. We did not find Valerie today."

Search-and-rescue personnel often say they treat the lost person as if they're a relation—a brother, sister, grandparent, their own child. Searchers beat sticks against trees, they blow whistles. For variety, they make birdcalls or hoots or bawls, crying as you might for a lost dog. I knew they were out there, screaming her name over and over. *Valerie! Valerie!* Each time, the answering silence put more desperation into the cry. The need to find a lost person starts to hurt. Without a single clue, not one single response to their hollering, soon they'll start blaming somebody— me, God, themselves.

"But there was some good news," I say. "One of the K-9 teams caught a scent north of Orbeton Stream. That's really promising." What I don't mention is that the dog went half-crazy after losing the scent and was taking a couple of days off. "We will focus on that area tomorrow. And tomorrow—" I wait for a moment, hoping folks might look up, look up and see my face, the optimism in it, the confidence in our team. "Tomorrow will be our most concerted, most *important* day of searching yet. We've got perfect weather. It's a Saturday, so our search force will be the largest yet. This is our chance. Tomorrow, each of us has got to give everything we have."

Some of them nod, but it's obvious I haven't given them the speech they wanted.

Rob and I are cleaning up the lot when a car arrives, late. The driver circles the lot, then pulls his aging Saturn into an empty space. Beside him, in the passenger seat, a small woman with white hair sits face forward. We turn to watch.

We know who they are. Wayne and Janet Gillis. Valerie's mom and dad. We were in touch with them yesterday, updating them every couple of hours while they boarded the dog and readied their lives to leave Maryland for Maine.

Valerie's father emerges red-faced and doesn't look at us until he's done helping his wife out of the car. After some agonized whispers, they face us with smiles. My heart slides in my chest like a crate on the deck of a boat. Partly to stifle this sadness I feel for them, I walk right up to them, introduce myself, and stick out my hand.

"Wayne Gillis," he says, shaking my hand. "We drove all the way here. We stopped—what, hon, twice in sixteen hours? This is Janet."

Valerie's mother steps toward me. She is a petite woman in clean white sneakers. Her resemblance to her daughter is uncanny. Short curls, suntanned forehead. A face of health.

"Beverly Miller," I say, extending my hand. "I'm here for anything you need."

"I have to tell you—" the mother says. "I want to tell you—"

Wayne pats her shoulder. "Hon, just take a deep breath."

She grabs my hand and brings it to the center of her chest and does not let go.

"We're relieved to finally be here," Wayne translates. "We understand you have a commendable record of finding lost people."

The small woman reels me closer until we stand there, she and I, like mismatched partners in a dance. Her fingers grip mine. She leans toward me with a craving expression, her eyes welling. The woman is ablaze, her grief one of the brightest things I've ever seen.

"I wish I could tell you how I feel," she says.

"I can only imagine," I say.

"A little of everything. Love, worry. And anger. I'm so *mad*. Is that normal?"

"We couldn't get plane tickets," Wayne says. "None that would get us up here any sooner."

The woman continues, my hand still pinned to her chest. "It feels like outrage. I know everybody loves their daughter. But Valerie is one of the most selfless, empathetic, giving—she's *magic*."

"That's what everyone says about her when we interview them," I say. "Other hikers."

"They do?" Janet smiles, and the tears brim over. "Of *course* they do."

"Don't worry," I say, my hand clasped in hers. "We're still in a good window. I've had several successful searches take as long as a week. It's a little unusual, but there's no cause for despair."

It's the word "despair" that summons a vision of my own mother. What would she do or say, faced with a moment such as this, one that called for almost inhuman strength? After Dad died, it was just her and three daughters. As a matriarch, my mother was gravely miscast. She was delicate and incompetent, blinking out from behind a brunette fringe so long it tangled in her false eyelashes. I was afraid she'd rip, like silk. I felt an intense sense of duty to her anyway. For the longest time, I just thought that was what all mothers were like.

"If she's injured," Wayne says, "she'll make a splint for herself. A splint, a tourniquet, so be it. She can do that."

"I agree," I say. "My belief is that she stepped off the trail, got disoriented in the dense foliage out there, and probably sustained an injury. Those woods are a beast, but we're up to the task." For some reason, I lower my voice so I can't be heard by Rob, who lingers nearby. "We're going to find her. We're going to find Valerie. Don't you worry."

Finally, Janet tips all the way against me so that I am obliged to wrap an arm around her.

I gently pat her back, knowing I have said more than I should. I know better than to promise.

Lena

The hiker's name is Valerie Gillis. On Friday afternoon, a paper in Portland publishes a photograph of Valerie online, taken by a fellow hiker who was the last person to see her alive. Lena sits inches from the monitor as the image loads. Valerie smiles, showing her teeth all the way to the gums. Her face is weathered, makeup free, radiant. Her thumbs are hooked through the straps of her backpack. She wears a hot pink bandana around her neck, tied endearingly at the side in a French knot. Lena reaches up to touch the pixelated face. Valerie is not her daughter, but Lena feels a wrenching intimacy with her regardless.

Lena staggers into the bathroom without using her power chair and hangs over the toilet for a moment. The surface of the toilet water ripples with her spittle. Nothing comes up.

She returns to the desktop.

She reads:

> Valerie Gillis, of Northampton, Mass., 42, has disappeared from the Appalachian Trail seemingly without a trace. Gillis always wanted to hike the Appalachian Trail, a journey that crosses 2,100 miles and 14 states. Gillis was completing a "flip-flop" hike, in which hikers begin in the middle of the trail and reach the northern terminus of Mt. Katahdin before finishing the south half of the trail. She was

only 200 miles away from Katahdin when she left the trail and vanished. A massive search for Gillis is underway.

Valerie, who goes by the trail name "Sparrow," was last seen on Monday, July 25. According to the Maine Warden Service, she left the Poplar Ridge shelter in the morning, planning on hiking that day only eight miles to the Spaulding Mountain shelter in Mount Abram Township. She never arrived there.

Gillis was reported missing after she failed to meet up with her husband, Gregory Bouras, on Wednesday, July 27, where the trail crosses Route 27 in Wyman Township.

Lena begins her research. She examines Valerie's last location on Google Earth. She discovers that there is a forum for AT hikers: 2000milers.net. The forum has lit up with talk of Sparrow.

Missing Person on the AT

Anyone have news of Sparrow? She was last seen leaving Poplar Ridge shelter on the morning of Monday July 25. Please contact the tip line at 1-800-595-8872 with ANY information you might have.

Cherrypie - 07-28-2022, 16:22
This just breaks my heart. She's one of us. I pray for her and her family.

Foresight - 07-28-2022, 17:04
Holy Moly. I hope Sparrow is rescued and home safe soon.

HEARTWOOD

Hill Tramp - 07-28-2022, 17:10
A guy got lost in this exact spot last winter but he was found a few days later because he stayed put, hard as that is. It sounds like Sparrow is an experienced hiker, so I hope she just hunkered down. Fingers crossed.

Foresight - 07-28-2022, 17:15
If one stays on the trail and knows which direction they are headed . . . it's very hard to get lost for long . . . If you do get lost, you use the marker method. Stop and think "I am HERE." Tie your camp towel or something to a tree at your current location. Look for the trail, but *never go out of sight* of that marker. If you don't find the trail one way, go back to your marker and try another direction. I've been lost once or twice when the AT crossed another trail and I was daydreaming or forgot to look for blazes. I got lost once for a whole afternoon. But it's not a big deal. Here I am.

GitItDone - 07-29-2022, 06:37
Yeah it is really & truly hard to get lost on the AT.
But you can't fix stupid.

> **Originally posted by GitItDone**
> *Yeah it is really & truly hard to get lost on the AT.*
> *But you can't fix stupid.*
>
> **Foresight - 07-29-2022, 08:15**
> As other threads on this forum prove, you are no longer allowed to point out stupidity, GitItDone. Even if it could save somebody's life. Better to let someone die than point out that they should know basic woodcraft and orienteering before going on a long-distance hike.

Matt H. - 07-29-2022, 08:19
I'm with you guys. You have to be completely out of your tree to get lost on the trail for long. Or else just a dipshit.

Mudneck - 07-29-2022, 08:40
I expect that most people on this site, including me, have cheated death or mayhem by sheer luck at least once. The thing is, we never realize it was just dumb luck that saved us. Also, I'd like to point out that this is a public forum and Sparrow's family members may read this. Consider speaking with respect.

Cherrypie - 07-29-2022, 14:30
I live in PA close to the trail. I wanted to do something to help Sparrow so I hiked out to the Birch Run shelter and found an entry from her in the shelter log. Can you guys see this **attachment?**

Lena clicks. There they are, Valerie's own handwritten words. With them, the woman herself comes to life. Lena hears the words as if Valerie is standing next to her, reading them out loud:

> *Oh my GOD! I DID it. Slept in my first AT shelter.*
> *Since I started my thru-hike, I've been living the high life at campgrounds and motels with my Treasure Gregory. Why? Because, dear reader, I AM AFRAID OF THE DARK.*
> *(Yes, I need therapy. Yes, I take pills. I'm a cream puff, people!)*
> *But last night, I made it through with the help of new friends.*
> *Especially SANTO who is AFRAID OF SPIDERS.*
> *(HAHA now they know, tough guy!)*
> *It is a beautiful morning. Today is so YES.*

HEARTWOOD

Some people write in these logs. Some people don't.
It's fun to have fun but you have to know how.
Bye 4 now.
SPARROW

Lena reads and rereads Valerie's shelter log. "Since I started my thru-hike, I've been living the high life at campgrounds and motels with my Treasure Gregory. Why? Because, dear reader, I AM AFRAID OF THE DARK." This detail takes on the appropriate cast of tragedy. Lena shudders each time she reaches it.

But how quickly Valerie makes light of her position. ("It's fun to have fun but you have to know how.") Strange choice of quote, yet, like the entire Seussian oeuvre, on the mark. Valerie is a playful woman. And strong. Despite her fears, Valerie Gillis knocked out over one thousand miles of walking.

But what kind of experienced hiker evaporates so close to her goal? A supported hiker, no less. With a husband waiting at the next trailhead.

"Husband." The word has a slippery feel—the *s* that is a *z*. Yet in her entry, Valerie calls hers "Treasure," as if it is his very name. Lena had not had a good experience of marriage until her second try. Lena's second husband was terminally ill when they married. They used to joke that was the secret to a successful marriage—keep it short.

Lena's landline rings. She does not answer.

The husband, though? Too obvious? Lena is tempted to reject it on literary grounds.

She searches the internet for any intel on the husband. After many dead ends, she finds Gregory Bouras in a December 2021 photo caption in the *Daily Hampshire Gazette*. The man is shown in profile, the closest to the camera in a group of socially distant celebrants, looking up into the darkness as the nondenominational holiday lights are switched on by an unseen hand. He wears a placid, somewhat vacant expression and a fluffy scarf. The image only whets her appetite.

At the end of her day of sleuthing, Lena gets into bed and stares at the ceiling. Her stomach makes sounds like a rusty crank. She has forgotten to eat that day. She crabwalks to the fridge, using chairbacks and the countertops, and stands in the revelatory light of the refrigerator. She is highly discriminating with human company, but as a reader, she's a slattern. She read Stendhal as a child, yes, but she also read pulp sci-fi novels and the Tippy Parrish series with equal intensity. It's the same to this day. She's read probably a dozen memoirs of hiking long-distance trails, both here and abroad, some self-published, riddled with crimes of punctuation. In her ambulatory life, she had loved to hike. She had brought Christine up summits in a carrier. As for the Appalachian Trail, who hasn't pondered making the journey oneself? Thousands have done it; thousands more have been humbled. It is tempting to find out what one can withstand. Too late for Lena, of course.

She guzzles a cup of orange juice with a foil lid, a goody from last week's blood drive.

She imagines her friend up in Maine tramping through blowdown, searching the brush for a sign. She prays for his success.

So many things are going wrong at every moment. Wars, brutality, displacement, pandemic, starvation. Hundreds of people on the planet go missing on any given day. But this is exactly why she cares about Valerie. In her Catholic girlhood, Lena learned how to value the symbolic individual. The bigger story is always too big. The crowd is too crowded.

"Save her," she whispers. "Find her."

Dear Mom,

Every time I start to tell you what happened next, I lose the thread.
    I begin the story, then immediately start going sideways.
    If this ends poorly, you'll want to know what happened to me. How I got so lost.
    But it's hard to get there in a straight line. Memories dizzy me.
    I might be a genius, delaying the inevitable.
    But whenever I write to you, I don't feel hungry.
    So, that's good.

One of the first things I did after setting up camp here was to ration my food.
    The two cheese sticks were halved. The almonds were sorted. The chocolate bar was snapped into twelve perfect rectangles, twelve tiny Hershey's bars.
    At approximately two hundred calories per day, I had five days' worth of sustenance.
    That was two days ago.
    I refuse to be sentimental about my own starvation. I know a person can survive for weeks without food as long as they have water. I promise myself that when the late-stage symptoms arrive—the shivering, the nausea, the hallucinations—I'll be able to recognize these objectively. Hunger is a state of threat. It does crazy things to the body and the mind.

The obsessive thoughts about food are much harder to handle than I thought they'd be. As I unfold the golden wrapper of my Hershey's bar to count the chocolate rectangles, I say to myself, Don't you dare. I don't trust myself.

Sometimes I smell movie-theater popcorn wafting on the breeze. It's so realistic that tears of joy prick my eyes. I remember sitting with a bucket of the stuff on my lap, eating the overflowing mound with my face. Extra butter? Yes please.

Triangled wedges of pink watermelon.

Chicken cracklings.

French onion dip.

An erotic nectarine.

I know I need to supplement my calorie intake. I've considered berry hunting, but I'm afraid to stray too far from my campsite. I'm not knowledgeable about plants. I'm a girl from suburban Maryland, for crying out loud. The only foraging I've ever done is finding the cleanest yam at the bin at Whole Foods. I open my tent fly and gaze at Rotten Log.

I approach the decomposing hunk of wood and break off a handful from the top. Millipedes bustle, ants seethe, and larvae of various sizes are stacked in every crevasse. Slugs sleep in rows like students in a dormitory. I select a large white grub. When I hold it up with two fingers, it writhes pitifully.

Sorry, sorry! I say, and put it back.

An ant might be more doable. Something with crunch?

It's surprisingly hard to chase down an ant. And besides, worth it?

How many calories in one ant? I'd have to eat a whole log full.

I look at the grubs again. My gorge rises.

HEARTWOOD

I can't do it.
Oh, if only I were a real sparrow.

I walk down to the creek to wash my lacerated foot.
I watch the mayflies dance over the tumbling water.
I've seen fear in the eyes of more patients than I can count.
But now that I have to nurse myself, I have no memory of what I said to comfort them.

Do you remember the children's book you used to read me, about a moose with no friends? The moose is a real loner. But after a forest fire comes, the moose reconsiders his solitude from the top of a burned and smoking hillside. Suddenly, a now-homeless orange bird falls from the sky—his first friend. Initially, the moose resents the bird, its noise, its chirping and twirling, but day by day, the moose comes to care about the bird very much.
The moose learns how to love.
Then all the bird's friends arrive.
A whole noisy flock!
As a child, I was a flaming introvert. Even when I was little, the rodeo sounds of other children gave me a headache. I wrote pretentious poems and refused to enjoy the rites of childhood, like waiting in a long line for a balloon animal. I was way too philosophical for a child. I'd be sitting on a seesaw, yo-yoing up and down with some other child, thinking, What is the *point* of a seesaw? You and Daddy were always at ease with others. You were good at flocking. All I'm saying is, it was nice of you to read me the book about the moose. I was the moose.
Since then, many of my favorite people have been moose.

I met a lot of moose on the Appalachian Trail, that's for sure. Weirdos. Misfits. Eccentrics of all ages. Philosophers. Survivors. Even the pretties, the bounding young folk Santo and I called "gazelles," broke down after a couple hundred miles, revealing their fascinating compulsions. Everyone seemed to be in some kind of exile or solitary quest. Everybody had a story. They'd been abandoned or rejected or hurt, or they had abandoned or hurt someone else, and they were carrying their guilt like a second pack. They'd been fired or shamed or cast out, or they were coming out of one of those periods in life when you can't catch a break, thing after thing after thing, a backward momentum. Some had survived a literal incarceration, like jail or the loony bin or rehab. And everyone had endured the pandemic. We were all recovered, in recovery, or unrecoverable. A particularly beautiful middle-aged woman sat around the campfire outside of Port Clinton, and when I asked her what her trail name was, another hiker said, "That's Dilly. She's taken a vow of silence."

Listen, no one hikes two thousand miles because they're *happy*. Even the most cheerful or uncomplaining hikers aren't "happy." You've got to have a significant fire under you to slog through over two thousand miles of jagged rocks, rain, and snakes. You've got to have a deep, unshakable point to prove.

Everybody's got a reason to hike the trail.

It's never because they are well loved and at peace.

What was mine?

Well, I suppose it was to heal.

Family lore. I'm two years old. A bird flies into the windowpane of our house in Maryland. I go outside and grab it with one fist. It's a small bird, mortally wounded but alive. We walk into the woods, you and I, looking for a place for the poor bird "to rest." But the bird quivers and dies in my hand. So we sing it a song and you suggest we find a pretty place to bury its little body. But I refuse to bury it. I go to bed with the bird in my hand. You sneak into my room in the middle of the night to unfasten the corpse from my grip.

I was a born nurse. Determined. Unfazed. The opposite of squeamish.

I became a nurse to fix things.

A nurse expects to confront death, of course. I mean, in nursing school, we studied how to help people die. That is, we studied how to read their needs and ease their pain when the end was near. We understood helping people to die with dignity as an honor. Then how does the nurse understand her work when she herself is wrapped in plastic, mouth behind a mask, eyes behind a visor, as the dying person's eyes search for their loved ones, in an absolute vacuum of dignity? When the ventilator rasps, and the nurse, totally aware of what comes next, sees herself for what she is, a kind of terrible handmaiden?

A decent nurse-to-patient ratio is 1:2.

During COVID, we were 1:4. At best.

It's hard to describe how it felt to "work short." Every move I made was a moral dilemma. Could I leave the weeping woman in room 5 to help the frail patient in room 20 get to the bathroom without falling? Could I take a moment to pee or would that be the moment the piano teacher in room 3 died alone?

The sloppiness of the whole operation hurt me. My own sloppiness. The catastrophe of it. The dread of walking through the hospital doors in the morning knowing that at some unpredictable moment that day, the familiar alarm would blare, followed by the robotic chant: CODE BLUE. CODE BLUE. CODE BLUE. Now and again, I'd notice a certain pause in the response to a code. It started to take longer for folks to emerge along the hall. A little less hustle. Because, another one? Already? If a nurse was needed, I was a nurse. If a porter was needed, I was a porter. A scribe, a janitor. An undertaker. And no one ever said, Gee. Gee, this isn't what you signed up for at all. This makes no sense at all. Down is up.

I didn't want to be called a hero.

I wanted someone to acknowledge my moral injury.

Enough.

I turn on my cell phone again. The low-battery icon appears.

No service. You don't say. I throw it back into my pack.

Then I look over my shoulder at Rotten Log.

I take my time sidling back up to it, like it's a bar.

I rip off a fresh hunk of rotten wood. The smell is overpowering. Cedary and strange and off-putting. Citronella mixed with urine.

You really can't gross me out. In the ER, I can be relied on to handle the rankest stench. I'm famous for it. I am not a sympathetic puker. I remember the man who came in to the ER complaining about stomach pain after eating a chicken. An exam showed severe fecal impaction. It turned out, he'd eaten the bones and all. If I can handle a manual evacuation of poop filled with chicken bones, then I can handle anything.

I settle on the grubs. Their creamy white bellies look almost meat-like. Plus, they have the fewest legs. Ants are too fast and too hostile. Slugs are all wrong. Slimy and wet, they seem like something that should only be eaten cooked, like bulk sausage. Grubs. Grubs are larvae of . . . something. Which makes them babies. Great, babies. God!

The problem is getting around the face. That is, getting around the fact that the grub has a face. I can't eat a thing with a face. The face has tiny pincers on it. The face can bite. Which seems fair. Well, tough luck, Val. You get what you get, and you don't get upset.

I realize that if I decapitate the grub, then it can't bite me. Cutting off the head will stop the writhing. I also can't eat food that is writhing.

And I definitely cannot hesitate.

It's like a diving board moment. Like when you're a little kid, at the end of the diving board? Looking down at the pool below?

The moment you hesitate, you're in trouble.

I pull out my Swiss Army Knife and get down to business.

It's like Grand Central Station in there. Insects moving and digging and walking in lines. They do not sense me standing over them. They don't change what they are doing or freeze in alarm. As I sift through the wood shavings, they crawl over my fingers. "I'm a bird!" I shout. "I'm a bird!" I pinch a grub out from its nest and hold it up to my face, where it twists back and forth in terror.

That is to say, I hesitate.

I scream and throw it back.

Monkeyshine!

I stomp to the edge of my camp and engage in some deep breathing.

It's a cruelly beautiful day at my campsite. The wind is gentle. When it riffles through the poplars, the leaves twist. The woods are filled with untouchable silence.

After all that survival, I absolutely refuse to die out here.

I refuse.

I return to the log. I gather a handful of grubs.

I'm sorry, grubs, I say.

I whisk off their heads with my Swiss Army Knife.

Then I eat them.

By the way, it's true, the old wives' tale—hunger *does* sharpen the senses. I've begun to hear sounds that should be inaudible. The whir of spinning seedpods as they fall to the ground. The jaws of caterpillars as they gnaw their leaves. I can smell more too. Where the wind has come from. Boggy and humid is southerly wind. From the north, wind smells white and bears the memory of ice.

So I hear the droning when it's still far away. I hear it, but I can't understand it. I can't square the sound with the woods. Is it a very large insect? I'm getting water at the creek. The sound builds, unbroken, like some rising wind, until finally, I get it. I drop my water bottle and scramble uphill. That's an engine! There's got to be a human being attached to an engine.

I scramble on all fours, as the noise increases in decibels. It radiates from all directions at once. The trees are an unbroken fence.

It's an airplane, advancing through the treetops.

I raise my arms and begin to wave madly as I run toward the clearing.

The sound fills the forest with roar.

"Hey!" I scream. "Here I am!"

The plane's shadow arrives first, streaking across my campsite, like a giant human figure with arms outstretched. The movement dizzies me and I trip, falling to my hands and knees, laughter in my mouth. I'm slow to my feet. By the time I stand, the plane is already in view through the trees, coming up straight toward my ridge, loud and powerful. I reach the clearing just as its belly comes into view, low enough that I can see the rivets on the wings.

My hands seek my neck for my bandana to wave, but of course I no longer have it. Instead, I bounce up and down, flailing my arms and shouting:

I'M RIGHT HERE!
I'M DOWN HERE!
LOOK DOWN!

The plane blots out the sun briefly. It sticks to its course, tracking an unknown waypoint.

I stand in its fading sound, head thrown back. The plane proceeds so neutrally and mechanically that I wonder if it was searching for me at all. The yellow fuselage disappears from view.

I close my eyes. My ears ring.

Sunlight filters into the clearing.

How strange to shout the words "I'm here" and be left with no confirmation.

I crawl to Far Rock and sit with my head in my hands for a long interval.

Mosquitoes begin to swarm. I wait until they land on me, then I smear them each to bloody streaks with my thumb.

I'm furious.

I am furious at the airplane. I am furious at *him*. Mostly, I am furious at the woods, these merciless woods. Beyond Far Rock is Distant Rock. Beyond Distant Rock is simply Beyond.

Beyond Understanding. Beyond Rescue.

Everywhere are trees.

Innumerable, infinite woodland.

Eventually, I stomp into my tent.

I berate myself.

OK, Valerie. What's your PLAN?

Your cell doesn't work. You have four matches. You're wearing one shoe.

What do you plan TO DO?

Are you going to sit here and write in your JOURNAL until you DIE?

But how could I recognize, after all that dying from a virus, new mortal danger?

It didn't look like mortal danger. It didn't look like anything at all.

"Santo" Live Interview, Bronx, NY, 7/30/22
Recorded by Warden Cody Ouellette

Listen, nobody *likes* Gregory. He's like art you can appreciate in a museum but maybe don't want hanging in your own house? Was I, you know, puzzled about what my girl saw in him? Yes.

Puzzled. *Disconcerted.* That's the word Gregory would use.

People love who they love, Cody. If you got a friend like Sparrow—the kind of person who has your back—you accept who they love. Didn't Gregory deserve that respect? He dropped everything to support her hike. To drive hundreds of lonely miles. Wait in parking lots. Didn't blink once when he saw *me* coming. Homeboy could have said, "Hold up, honey bunch. You go into the woods alone and you come back out with *him*? Ho-ho-ho. I find that disconcerting."

(laughter)

He did not say that. He shook my hand. Drove my ass to my first hotel in five weeks of hiking. Where I exercised my constitutional right to cry in the shower. Yes, I did. Cry like a baby. Out of joy, Cody. I was like, "Waaaaater! Running waaaaaater!"

I stood at the sink turning the faucets on and off. Flipping the light switch. Talking to the tiny bar of soap—

Cody Ouellette: So, Gregory—

After the shower, we go to Applebee's. Our server goes, "Would you like to start off with a Kahlúa milkshake? Or maybe a—a passionfruit margarita?" And I was like, "Yes." And they were like,

"Which?" I was like, "Both." "OK. Would you like the—the jalapeño poppers? The mystery nachos?" "Uh-huh, uh-huh." Then I said, "Let's make this simple. Just bring me this whole half of the menu. Everything on this half."

(laughter)

Gregory's a vegan, of course. But me and Sparrow were walking ten to twenty miles per day, Cody. I burned about seven hundred calories *per hour*. Homegirl is eating a tower of grilled cheese and a milkshake. Gregory's sitting there with a seltzer and a side salad. And you know, he could have judged us. But he looked happy. Just sat and watched and listened to us tell stories about the funny shit that happens on the trail. I think he was just happy to be around her.

Cody Ouellette: So, he wasn't possessive? Jealous?

I don't know, man, he knew who he was with.
Sparrow loves the world.
She loves the moon, she loves the wind.
If anyone could fall in love with a stag or an eagle, it's Sparrow.
Can you be jealous of that?

Cody Ouellette: What about her? Did she love him as much as she loved all those other things?

She did. She did.
She was happy to see him. At first.

Cody Ouellette: At first?

Well, you know. At the beginning, she'd meet up with him all the time. He'd be there, waiting, every couple of days. Clockwork. I'd stay in the shelter and wait for her to come back in the morning—

no sweat. But it's strange, man, the bond you form with your tramily. She started to get sad to leave the trail. And it wasn't just me and her that made a tramily. We hiked New Jersey with Strider. We picked up Leviticus in New York State . . .

You go to the trail for the mountaintops. You go to get away from people. But it's funny. The *people* end up being what you remember the most. I learned to stay away from the shitheads. The trail humbled the rest. In the shelters, on a rainy day, all you had was other people and their stories. Man, Sparrow loved other people's stories. They were like food to her.

She didn't have the heart to tell Gregory.

Cody Ouellette: Tell him what?

That she was happier out there.

That she wanted to be with her tramily.

That she had changed. I felt bad for him, how he couldn't understand her experience.

You have to walk it to understand it.

Cody Ouellette: Did they fight?

They bickered. He'd pick at her. Talk down to her.

I stayed out of it. I thought I was just being respectful of her privacy but no, I just didn't want to lose my ride. Let's admit it. I should have told her. I should have said, "Girl, let's just cut loose. We can do this. You're strong enough."

But I just kept quiet.

Yeah . . .

It wasn't convenient for me, so . . .

I kept my fat mouth shut.

Lt. Bev

SATURDAY, JULY 30. EIGHT A.M.
DAY 4 OF THE GILLIS SEARCH.

Day 4 is another clear and clement one, the heavens swept, the winds subdued. Ideal search conditions. One hundred thirty-one souls have joined this morning's search. Wardens from all over the state appear, most on their day off. I see faces from the past. Several retired wardens nod at me solemnly from the crowd, men who had doubted me in decades previous. Mike is there too, wearing a knee brace, winking at me from a distance. A local church has set up a folding table with tureens of oatmeal and coffee. It's not disrespectful to say the atmosphere is festive. If Valerie Gillis is findable, we are going to find her.

Rob catches my eye over the crowd and taps his watch.

"Right," I say.

It's time for our first press conference.

Sugarloaf has donated a conference room in a back wing of the hotel for the growing crowds, as well as a staff dormitory for the team, making it possible for me to effectively be on-site twenty-four hours a day. As Rob and I open the glass doors from the parking lot, we can hear a din down the corridor. We pause at the door.

"Who the hell *are* these people?" I whisper.

The conference room is full. A local rotary club has come with bagels and coffee and is in the process of serving a corps of media wearing button-downs and high heels and press passes.

To the side of the room near the windows, Wayne and Janet Gillis lean against the wall in anguish. Beside them stands Gregory Bouras, looking down into his cup of coffee. When they see me, Janet waves, and Wayne pumps his fist.

"Morning, Little Mom," I say—my new name for her. "Did you sleep?"

"Nope," she says. "You?"

"Not a wink."

"I took a Xanax," offers Gregory. "The stuff is fantastic."

I give them the rundown. "OK, family. This search is in full swing today. We will have more people out searching today than we have had on any other day. We have highly favorable conditions. Clear weather, total mobilization. The searchers are doing what they do best. So—" My radio goes off and I silence it. "The best thing *we* can do is to focus on our chance to talk to the press. I'm going to start with a description of Valerie and an update on the search, then you can issue your statement."

I'm praying Janet will deliver the statement, but Wayne shakes his head.

"Jan doesn't think she can do it," he says.

On cue, tears pour from Janet's eyes.

"She won't be able to get through it," Wayne points out. "She can hardly talk now."

"I *want* to," Janet weeps.

"It's OK," I say, and put an arm around her. "Who'll talk for the family then?"

"Gregory," Wayne says, and I try not to wince. "Gregory will talk first. I'll say something short at the end. We've decided to offer a reward. I'm going to announce a reward."

I nod. "Great idea."

I give Gregory a once-over. He's wearing a long-sleeve denim shirt buttoned to the neck, which looks unseasonal as the July heat climbs. Even as I obviously appraise his camera readiness, he does not smile. The trimmed beard doesn't work. It's not sympathetic. It's not Maine. But Wayne and Janet seem to accept and even love him, which, for the moment, is good enough for me.

I smile at him. "You'll do great. Just remember to address the camera, not the reporters. Look right at the viewers. If people feel you're talking straight to them, they'll take the extra time to think hard, to remember a detail now days or weeks old."

Wayne raises a finger. "You don't really think Valerie left the area, do you? If she did, or if she's in some entirely different part of the woods, how does this help?"

"Wayne," Janet says, dabbing her eyes. "Wayne, we don't *know*."

"At first I thought I knew," Gregory muses. "But every day, I know less."

"Mainers spend more time outside than you'd think," I explain. "Besides, we search on all fronts. We search in every corner. Woods, towns. I can't tell you how important community involvement has been in some of our cases."

"We understand," Janet says. "We trust you."

Talking to the press is not my thing. I'm not photogenic. I have to stoop to reach a mike. My pits sweat. When I watch clips of myself, I see habits I didn't know I had. For example, when I'm listening to a question, I turn my head sideways and bunch my mouth, like a pirate. I am quick in a crisis, and I am sturdy and methodical, I do believe that, but in the lights, I sometimes lose the thread of things, I lose the heft of my title.

Mind you, our "press conferences" are usually a group of two or three local reporters plus a couple of janitorial staff on break. Usually, we're standing in a poorly lit hallway or in front of the state flag. But today, there's a real podium and a real conference room, and the first three rows of chairs are already filled. A dozen other people I don't recognize are walking around getting quotes and shooting video.

This story has traveled.

It's gone farther than Portland. Farther than Boston.

All my insecurities flare. Afraid of the limelight? I'd never even been *in* it before.

I place the blown-up photo of smiling Valerie on an easel beside the microphone. I will stand up there next to it, with Gregory and Janet and Wayne, and we will make a plea to the public.

I step up to the podium.

Tip Line Call from Stacey Sullivan, Appalachian Trail Section Hiker—7/31/22

Dispatch: Good morning.

Caller: Hi. Hi. Is this the right number for—for the hiker who disappeared in Maine? For Sparrow?

Dispatch: Yes, ma'am. This is the tip line for the Maine Warden Service. This call is being recorded. Can I have your name?

Caller: Stacey Sullivan.

Dispatch: We appreciate your call. Please, go ahead.

Caller: So I really don't know what you consider a "tip." I went back and forth on calling . . .

Dispatch: Please, go ahead.

Caller: OK. So. I had the pleasure of spending a night with Sparrow on the trail about a month ago in New York State? In the section just before Connecticut? My friend Jill and I occasionally get away from it all by hiking hut to hut. A girls'-weekend type of thing. Anyways. What a *sweet* person Sparrow is! Such an angelic, unforgettable lady.

    She traveled with a—her main hiking partner was a large—he was an—an African American male. This person seemed very poorly prepared. If I can be honest—can I be honest?—he seemed to be taking advantage of—well, Sparrow was so *sweet*. Is. *Is* sweet. Nice people get taken advantage of in this world. Every hiker is supposed to bring his or her own stuff. But this person—her friend—he was a very large person. I saw him rummaging through her pack once. He had to consume a great deal because he was—because of his body type. I think that's how I'm supposed to say it now.

Also—I got the sense that she wanted to hang out with us but he wouldn't let her. It's like Sparrow was *his*. Yeah. I don't have a "tip," per se. But I just didn't like the *feeling* I got from him.

Dispatch: Was there a specific incident? That you—that gave you—

Caller: Specific? Well. I mean, every time you saw her, there he was. *Bam*. Like a huge, dark shadow.

Once, I tried to bring the subject up. I whispered, "Are you OK? Blink if you need help."

Then *bam*. There he was. All smiles, of course. Everybody seemed to like him. But I didn't buy it.

Dispatch: I will relay your tip to the team.

Caller: Thank you.

I'm just trying to help, you know.

I'm just trying to help that beautiful angel.

Lt. Bev

Post–press conference, I look for Rob. I feel dizzy from the camera lights, almost nauseated. I've survived the jabs from journalists and the quiet sobbing of Janet Gillis. I'm looking for Rob because I'm certain that good news has arrived. Good news has to arrive soon. We are doing everything objectively possible to get it.

Yesterday, when I heard that one of Regina's dogs caught a scent, I said to myself, *Valerie's here.* It was proof. I wagered she'd be back in her mother's arms by the end of the weekend. These dogs have some divine powers. They find people. Police dogs are trained for hot searches, but our teams are different. Our dogs can focus for miles and miles of wilderness, like birds that fly across oceans without resting.

I find Rob in the back of the bus handing out work assignments to late-arriving volunteers.

"How was the show?" he asks.

"Torture," I admit. "But the family did well."

I sit down at the radio bank, trying to get my mind straight. My cell lights up.

It's Arman, our warden pilot.

"We've got something shiny, Lieutenant," Arman tells me. "I saw it with my own eyes. Thinking it might be her space blanket. I've got you the coordinates."

"From the plane?"

"Yes, ma'am."

"Did you circle back and recheck?"

"Yes, ma'am. Saw it clearly. Twice."

He reads the coordinates. Adrenaline courses through me. *We've got something.*

"Rob," I say, as calmly as possible. "Arman's got something." I turn back to the phone. "Well done, Arman. Good work."

"Thank you. We're on the ground here in Bangor. You want us to refuel and go back up?"

"By God yes. Just keep flying over that grid."

Rob hustles to the table and sits at the radio bank. We allow ourselves one small shared smile. It's something. Something shiny. He opens the mapping software and refreshes the map. I give him the coordinates for the shiny object.

"Which team is closest?"

He cross-checks the assignments. "One more second."

"Come on, Rob. Holy crap."

At that moment, someone calls for me on my handset. I hear my call number, clear as day. I tune in, but the voice is inaudible.

"This is Lieutenant Miller," I say. "This is 4006. Repeat."

The reply comes in as static.

I lean hard over Rob's shoulder. "Team number, please."

"Team Two," Rob says, exhaling. "Comstock's team. Comstock."

And that's that. We're able to radio the coordinates of the space blanket to Warden Comstock, who copies. The team moves toward the area.

My head spins.

This is *it*. This is Valerie.

I step out of the bus, turning my handset on and off.

Maybe the person calling me already has her.

I allow myself to practice saying the words: *Good news, Little Mom.*

"This is 4006," I say. "Repeat."

The static answers.

A nothingness that speaks.

Lena

At dawn light, Lena goes foraging by the Memory Center. She knows that reed grass hangs right over the concrete walkways in dirty white tufts. Inside this common grass is a tiny hard grain that TerribleSilence says makes an excellent gruel. Each grain will need to be removed by hand, then crushed. Laborious to others, but not to her.

That's the kind of painstaking work Lena wants to do.

Every human being imagines, but few disclose. Children are quick to share their strangest thoughts and inventions. They cease to do so only after the shaming or baffled reactions of adults, portraits of which the child hangs on her inner walls, until at last, she closes the gallery. What amazing creations she used to make with so little, Christine. She would build tiny worlds inside empty tissue boxes, populated with tiny figures made of trash can twist ties with bottlecap faces. She conscripted armies out of plastic utensils (apparently the next great war would be forks versus spoons). When large packages arrived, Christine would beg Lena to let her keep the cardboard boxes. The child would sit inside those boxes for hours, writing screeds on the interior walls, much as the monk writes his greatest words for God alone.

Christine was brilliant like her father. Lena had met Roger at UConn, where they were both undergraduate students. He wore oversize eyeglasses and walked around like he'd just looked up from his books for the first time in his life. They were instantly attracted to one another, and ecstatic in bed, yet neither one spoke of love or desire for years, until the marriage was hopelessly mismanaged. In the face of conflict, Lena became enraged and inarticulate. Roger's words were halting; they tumbled out in cubes. They were both so stupid when they were mad. Lena was equal parts admiring and insanely jealous of Roger's brilliance. She knew that if she remained silent, her own brilliance could be neither disproved nor verified. He was planning to become a pathologist, which is exactly what he became. Lena was considering becoming a doctor, an ornithologist, an herbal healer, or a professor of literature, and so she became none of those things. No matter. After several years of passivity, she became pregnant before graduate studies might have been undertaken.

None of it ended as it should have. For her generation, marriage and motherhood were absolutes, but as soon as Lena understood the fine print of the situation, which was that she would not even have the time to pursue her thinking life, her eccentricity itself, she ceased to feel any attraction for Roger. She threw her significant intelligence into mothering the baby, a being that rather needed a scientist's attention. How else to interpret the farts and the cries and even the smiles? Her expertise and even her disinterest—what Roger, seeking a divorce, called her "detachment"—actually helped Lena survive long nights of mothering while the important man slept.

God made the sun and sky, and Roger slept.

Rome burned; Roger slept.

The separation was amicable enough. She never once discouraged Christine from seeing her father. She remained proud of his accomplishments. In fact, Lena later took a job at the hospital at which Roger oversaw the pathology department. In the end, she found work that utilized her ability to discern slight differences in two things of the same kind. Her job as a cytologist was to prepare and examine cell material on slides to detect anomalies. The work was akin to art history, except the paintings are cancerous.

Now, Lena draws her hand through the tufts of grasses planted in the Memory Center garden. The garden here is wild and peaceful. In a breeze, the grasses undulate like seawater. She identifies the reed grass, looks around to make sure no one is watching, and cuts a small bushel. She gathers the stalks in her lap like long skirts. The color of the sky this morning is a faint lilac, the color of a mother's nightgown. She motors home around the periphery while trying to keep the grasses from flying away.

And there is Warren, standing in the bright light of the Memory Center.

He has spotted her. He waves. She has to pass him to return home. He falls in step next to her. For a second, neither of them says anything.

"I was wondering. In plant life, is there any equivalent of a familial relationship?" he asks. "Do plants grow near one another out of sheer convenience, or by design?"

She rubs her runny nose. "Are plants attracted to each other? Is that what you're asking?"

"I suppose so."

"Well," she says. "Plants are touching underground, through their root systems. They are highly connected. Trees, also. Listen—" She turns her power chair around so that she is facing him. He stops. "Were you following me, Warren?"

"I followed you here, yes."

"I don't want that, Warren."

"I was concerned for you," he says. "I tried calling several times yesterday, but you didn't answer. Are you feeling better?"

"Better?" she says. "Am I supposed to be feeling badly?"

This flusters him. "Well—the other morning—you were extremely upset. In the meditation room. About the lost hiker. You don't remember?"

She flicks her joystick back and forth.

"Oh, that," she says. "Well, I just got swept up. Carried away by the drama. I know you love drama."

"But I don't. I *hate* drama."

"Listen, forget the whole thing. People go missing all the time. The lost hiker wasn't anyone I know. In the scheme of things, it's piddling. Before we know it, melted ice caps will flood this whole valley, and it will return to the basin it once was. Life on earth is folly. You really can't take anything personally."

His jaw set, Warren turns and begins to walk back to the main entrance.

After a moment, he says, "You are a difficult woman, Lena."

At last, she smiles. "I've been trying to tell you that for years!"

The day deepens, and the grains lie like black-red jewels on the wooden table. After a vigorous threshing, she used a fan to separate the grains from the hulls and flowers. She solved one problem but made another. The floor of her apartment now appears as if under some celestial snow, as if an angel had perched there to molt.

The Telegram window remains empty. Do search-and-rescue teams labor day into night without sleep? Any second, he will report back. Perhaps he has found her.

Or he has already left for his zero-waste homestead and Lena will never hear from /u/TerribleSilence again. She experiments with small doses of exposure to this inevitable moment. Once, she had expressed worry about her friend's plan to live indefinitely on public land, and he'd written back:

Let's not fall into clichés.
I don't want a mother.
I don't want to be "mothered."
Motherhood is a fairy tale. A prison.
I say free all mothers! Free all children!

It wasn't true that the pandemic had been easy for her. The word she refuses to use is "lonely." She wasn't lonely in the way old people are lonely. A reader is never lonely. Besides, she didn't like people, so how could she be lonely for them? But after the lockdown, early that spring, she began to feel a poignant longing, a quickening at the sound of footsteps. Normal comforts couldn't cure this yearning. The foods they brought tasted of sand, arriving with only a knock at the door. Contactless delivery. Parcels of Styrofoam left on her shelf. The waste disturbed her. The place had been advertised as a "green living" community, but now her trash bin was filled with nonbiodegradable containers. If the virus was coming for the elderly, she hoped it would hurry up before her facility alone stuffed the landfill with microplastics.

When management had told them not to leave their rooms for any reason, she cried. It didn't matter that she was free to disobey. She was locked into compliance by the ethics of communitarian life. Eleven people died of the virus in quick succession. Days became the arc of the sun across a cold sky. She spent the time scrolling the foraging archives on Reddit and watching fast-motion videos of seasons changing. In May, management realized the inhumanity of the confinement. Walks were permitted, but only solo. She could see the solitary figures, windswept heads, masked mouths, roaming upon the esker. On the first day they were set free, confused by the signage on the elevator, Lena had shocked herself by turning right around and staying inside.

HEARTWOOD

It was during this time of great discomfort that she had written to the stranger on Reddit.

Dear Sir: I enjoy your posts. I am envious that you've found such a harvest of black locust flowers. I hear black locust emits a heavenly smell. But what do the flowers taste like? I have not seen any here at the 41st latitude. Where do you live? Please forgive this intrusion from a stranger.

After pressing send, she had moved away from her desktop. She hadn't gotten to the kitchen sink before she heard a ping. She had a message on Reddit.

They taste like fresh spring peas drizzled with nectar.
I eat them by the handful like popcorn.
I live in Maine.
Same latitude as Vladivostok and Manchuria.
You?

She beamed. She began to write him back, gushing over his posts, his know-how, baring herself ("I have been foraging for a decade, yet every time I come upon a plant I cannot ID, it is as if I am a novice. Perhaps the impossibility of mastery is what I enjoy most about it . . ."). Again, he wrote back immediately, in his breezy, unedited style. Their conversation was synchronous. It was no less a conversation than had he been sitting there in her reading chair, his ginger hair and beard just touched with gray. Her feelings, when thinking of him sitting in her chair, were not maternal, not filial, and not erotic. He was sui generis. He was the one who chased away the silence of lockdown. It was his infectious foraging spirit that compelled her, in the remnant cold of May, to don her Carhartt knit cap and blanket and venture out with her basket. She snapped photos to share with him on her oversize Nokia cell phone. Her world opened up.

And now, at last, the Telegram alert dings.

And here he is!

I know what happened to Sparrow.

Her heart thrums. She smacks the keys.

                        I can't wait to hear!

Did u know that there is a secret
military training facility along the trail
where she went missing???

                        ??? Do tell.

It's called SERE. Survival Evasion
Resistance & Escape. Its a school
where soldiers and contractors learn
how to be tortured. They deny its
existence but u can see it on Google
Earth. Look at this **map**.

Lena dutifully follows the link to a grainy photo. She must squint: an aerial view shows a fenced area with a gathering of black-garbed figures inside it. Caught in the wind, quite clearly, is the American flag.

But has the Maine Warden Service
searched the torture school property
for Sparrow?
NO. They are not allowed 2 search
there!!!

HEARTWOOD

>My God.
>How do you know about this?

I've known about the place for years.
I used to play out there as a kid. Watched them w/ my own binoculars.
One time I was threatened. This big man, with horns. He told me he'd kill me if he ever caught me there again.

    Lena lets this claim pass. Horns? He must mean a hat or a helmet.

I tried to go up in there yesterday during the search. Team of Special Ops guys searching said I couldn't. I said try and stop me! This place falls within the search area! Them: please leave now. Warden: you are trespassing. WARDEN = COMPLICIT.

>But wouldn't the wardens do anything to find her?
>Why would they omit part of the search area??

A guy posted a blog about his training at that exact same school in the 80s. WHICH HAS SINCE BEEN DELETED. But I found excerpts on Reddit. Listen. The "teachers" pretend to be Soviets that took over Maine. Students are set free in the woods & told to evade the Soviets but they get picked off one by one and taken to a "prison camp." They are thrown in separate cells where wall mounted speakers blare out-of-control saxophone & poetry. This guy gets interrogated by the "camp commander." When he doesn't cave, he gets placed in a 3 x 3 cage with a

coffee can to piss in. Another "Soviet" blows tobacco up his nose till he pukes. They make him dance on the Bible which is the only part of this I find acceptable.
The guy totally breaks down. Starts to believe it's not a training program anymore, but the REAL THING!!! Then he hears gunshots. They have been "liberated" by freedom fighting American partisans hiding in the woods. The American partisans "arrest" the Soviets. They play the star spangled banner and raise the American flag and everybody cries and wets themself.

> Are you joking? This is America!

And get this, this guy loved it. He's pro-military. They only took down his blog post cuz he was giving away torture school secrets. No shit, dumbass. I bet the military wishes they had actually drowned him in a toilet.

Lena cannot believe it. But look, the coordinates of the Google Earth snapshot match those of Valerie's last-known location. Her own grandparents had traveled across the ocean from Poland expressly because people here do *not* get put in three-by-three cages. Also, Lena is preoccupied with a thought that is perhaps off topic: If they torture people with free jazz and poetry, what do they reward them with?

And then, a cold feeling spreads up her spine. A recognition.

> You're saying that someone from this facility knows where Valerie is?

Bingo.
I think she wandered into something

she wasn't supposed to see.
Like I did when I was little.

   The image of a man abducting Valerie Gillis is easy for Lena to conjure. After all, hadn't her own daughter also been abducted? The act of abduction isn't always straightforward. Sometimes a man can abduct a woman with his ideas, his sloppy or wrongheaded ideas, which he presents to a woman with such overconfidence that she forgets all caution. A man who takes advantage of kindness. It's always a man.

The military says the SERE school
exists to help soldiers survive torture.
But it's really cuz everyone is
getting off.

                              This is wrong.
                              Can you go back and demand
                              access to this property?
                              They have to prove they are telling
                              the truth about Valerie.

Not allowed. Was asked to leave
search.

                              For asking questions???

Got in fight.

                              A fistfight?

These people. There is no arguing w/ them.
They are sexually turned on by fascism.

Who?

EVERYBODY.
EVERYBODY IN THIS DOOMED AND
MALIGNANT COUNTRY.
I NEED TO LEAVE.
FOR GOOD.

    There is so much Lena could say here. She could say what others have always said to her throughout her life: "Calm down." "Why are you so worked up?" "It's not a big deal." But when you spend your life in the pursuit of knowledge, knowledge matters a great deal, and mattering is a life force. People were always asking her, "Studying? What are you studying *for*?" The question galled her. "I'm studying because I'm curious. Why aren't *you* studying? Why don't you want to know the name of that raptor in the sky? Why don't you want to taste that dooryard violet?" Her fingers tremble over the keyboard. TerribleSilence is her best friend, whether or not he knows it, whether or not that matters to anyone but her. She doesn't want him to get hurt in a fight or to trespass on military grounds and she certainly doesn't want him to leave, to vanish to her. But for some reason, instead of her own losses, she thinks of Valerie. Because Valerie is still alive. She is sure of it.

    They are onto something.

But what about HER?
Knowing what you know, could you really leave her out there?

. . .

You know that I can't do anything to help.

HEARTWOOD

        I'm useless.
        But you.
        If anyone can find Valerie, it's you.
        . . .
        Are you still there?

A hiker disappears right there near a
SECRET FACILITY with no trace.
Tell me u think = coincidence.

        It's not a coincidence. I believe you.
        We cannot give up.
        We must do something.

Lt. Bev

SUNDAY, JULY 31. DAWN.
DAY 5 OF THE GILLIS SEARCH.

I awake in a strange room. The interval of forgetting is brutally short. I sit upright on the twin bed and comb my hair back with my fingers. I can see myself in the cheap mirror nailed to the back of the door, sitting there in my boxers and T-shirt, like an oversize college student. In the window behind me, dawn breaks over the Carrabassett mountains.

It wasn't her space blanket, the shiny thing we found. It was a thermos.

A stainless-steel thermos some hunter or surveyor left out there who knows when.

Warden Comstock brought it back to the bus himself. Janet, Wayne, and Gregory were waiting. We were all waiting. Most of the teams were in, and the Gillises were passing out cold Cokes from a cooler, thanking everybody. Warden Comstock got out of his truck and the crowd parted and he brought it over to us. Gregory shook his head. He'd never seen Valerie carrying anything like that.

A thermos. Wasn't even hers.

I check my personal cell. A text from my buddy Cath.

I guess it's a no on pickleball?

A text from the pharmacy.

HEARTWOOD

Your prescription LOS is out of refills. Text YES if you would like us to call your doctor for a refill of LOS.

And a text from Kate.

Call me, please. It's about Ma.
It's urgent.

Instead, I call Rob.

"Yep?" he replies, wide awake.

"After we run the assignments today, I want someone to step in to handle comms."

"OK. You want me to go somewhere?"

"Yeah. I want to go out to the field. You and me."

Rob pauses. It's unusual for the search leader and the deputy search leader to actually search. We're the brains of the thing, coordinating the many different arms of the operation. Besides, when you leave the bus, you're turning over operations to some of your junior staff. I trust Tanya and Cody with my life, but a couple of the other wardens hanging around, I'm not so sure. I've never liked Judd Klukey, for example. He's the kind of guy I could see settling into my chair and offering an unflattering impersonation.

"I'll get Mike to come and watch over things," I say. "He can torture everyone with jokes. I want to get out in the field. Walk in her shoes." I let my face drop into my hands. "I need to get the hell out of the bus."

"OK," Rob says. "Then that's what we'll do."

Just after 1 p.m., Rob and I pull up in our ATV to the closest point of entry to the search area, an old tote road that once held a set of tracks for the logging trolleys. Rob's got this idea to leave a VHF transmitter out in the field, like some kind of desolate public telephone booth. He's a communications man, through and through. But this idea of his is a little off. He is feeling the pressure. We all are. He heads into the woods.

One of our search teams is resting nearby, in different poses of exhaustion. Several searchers do a double take to see me coming. I shake the hand of each volunteer as I pass them. "Don't get up," I say. "Thank you for all you're doing. Rest up. Take care of yourself." Warden Bradley not only stands but claps his arms to his side at attention. Rudy Bradley's a young man, a favorite local son, great-grandson of a Penobscot tribal leader. My throat tightens to see his stricken face. I put my hand on his shoulder and we exchange a couple of words.

"We really thought we had something this morning," he says. "We were near a crevasse on the western slope of Saddleback. Who knows how deep it was, Lieutenant? Looked like it went to the center of the earth. I heard a sound. It sounded like a woman's voice. We searched it as well as we could. We called and blew our whistles, we waited for hours, but we didn't hear nothing again."

I nod. I tell him I'm grateful that he took the time to explore the crevasse.

"I know how you feel," I say. "We thought we had her campsite yesterday. A pilot saw what looked like Valerie's space blanket." I let a moment pass. It's hard to drag the words out. "It was just a coffee mug. A chrome coffee mug. Wasn't even hers."

Rudy studies his boots, his face pained.

"You lose a coffee mug, Rudy?" I ask.

He looks up, alarmed.

"I'm just kidding, Rudy. Just kidding."

Standing alone, farther down the tote road, waits Regina. She watches me approach, her expression inscrutable under the bill of her wax-cloth cap. Her German shepherd Badger lies in the shade nearby, his tongue out.

I bend down and stroke Badger's glossy flank. "Good boy," I say. "Good dog."

I stand up and look at my old friend. "I'm getting mad, Regina."

"I'd like to see you get mad, Bev. It would do you good."

"What happened to the scent? You said Badger was certain."

"He *was* certain. He had her scent on Friday. She's out here. Problem is, by the time we get the dogs way the hell out here, it's almost midday."

"And?"

"And by then the air is hot. Rising. The scents are up on the ridges already. Then they get swept away by cooler wind. They can get deposited in ravines anywhere. Even miles away. That's almost worse than nothing."

Regina takes a bite of jerky and shoves it back in her pocket. Even at her age, she's got this long dark hair, which she scents with some kind of rose water or pomade and hides in a bun.

Our bond is deep and strange, me and Regina's. Same age. Some of the same scars. The same crouch you develop when you are so often trying to blend in. She had a long, drifty thirties, then returned to Maine and drove ambulances in Bangor. But her passion was search-and-rescue dogs. For no pay or glory, she learned how to train scent dogs all on her own, and to teach others how to search with dogs, saving numerous lost souls in the process. Off and on, I wondered if I wanted more than a friendship with her. But I decided that what I desired was the feeling of being *paired* when I was with Regina. Whatever we were, we were paired, anyhow, like two of any species—two leopards, two pangolins—kindred.

She shrugs. "If we camped out here overnight, then we could start tracking first thing in the morning."

"No," I say.

"We don't even get to the search area until noon, Bev. Then you say we got to be out before dark. It's not enough time."

"No," I repeat. "That's dangerous for you and the dogs. There's no one around to support you in the middle of the night."

We start to walk down the tote road together. She understands my need to pace. For my part, I am suddenly, urgently in need of a friend. I want to talk, but at the same time, I fear that an innocent inquiry into my well-being might cause me to collapse, like a detonated building.

"I'm thankful no searchers have been hurt so far," I manage. "The only way this could get worse is if harm comes to someone else."

We walk on. It's late July, as hot as it ever gets around here. Badger trails us, tongue out, hips lowered, tail down.

Regina says, "We've never done a K-9 search up here. The ridges are so bad, even the dogs are balking. They're looking at us like, 'Are you kidding me?' Sometimes we have to *carry* the dogs. You can imagine how slow going that is."

I look down at Badger, eighty pounds of muscle and fur. Regina has maybe thirty pounds on him.

When I turn back to her, she's looking at me closely, her expression neutral.

"How you holding up, Bev?"

I have never been a particularly talkative or self-revealing person. There is some latent childhood mortification in me about my size. I trace it back to the year I grew five inches. It happened in sixth grade, the very time I most wanted to go unseen. I grew with such speed that my legs ached. My buttocks rounded and my thighs thickened. My breasts distressed me. They did not look like the two ice cream scoops of the girls in movies, but rather like twin torpedo warheads, with prune-colored areolas. My mother brought home a lace-trimmed bra, held it against me, then returned it. Soon my chest was underbraced by a real beige beauty with six hook-and-eye closures in the back and straps like a butcher's apron. I went to my sixth-grade dance in a frilly peach dress. I remember Ma's face as she finished fussing with the tulle and stepped back. Her eyes darted around my body. "You have such a beautiful smile," she said. By then, I was just shy of six feet, which was where I landed. Later, in high school hallways, in girls' bathrooms, I avoided laughter and gossip, hoping my silence might have a shrinking effect.

"Hello in there?" Regina gives me a small push.

I tug at my vest, which feels unusually constrictive.

Just then, not twenty-five yards away, a group of unfamiliar men part the brush and step onto the tote road. A team of three, all with cropped hair and expensive gear. Guys from the SERE training facility. The facility uses its remote location to run courses for troops and contractors who run the risk of capture in combat. Training of this kind gained favor after World War II, when the military realized it was less costly and more humane to teach downed aircrew how to survive rather than languish in enemy hands. It's brutal, worst-case-scenario training, used to help troops keep their sanity and not divulge too many state secrets. The SERE instructors are trained in every arcane survival skill from sheltercraft to resisting interrogation, which leaves little time for good manners. Badger's ears go erect.

"What the hell are they doing here?" I ask.

"Dunno."

"Are they doing *training* exercises in the search area?"

I start marching toward them. Regina tugs my sleeve. "Bev. Bev."

"Hey, boys," I call. The SERE guys don't look my way. The resting searchers track me as I walk. Rudy Bradley, bless his soul, falls in step beside me.

"*Yo,*" I call.

Suddenly, their indifference seems an outrageous charade.

"Hey," I hear myself bark. "I'm talking to you."

They turn. One of them removes his polarized glasses. He's older than I thought he was.

Rudy and I stop, knees locked.

"Are you boys from SERE?"

"Yep," says the guy with the sunglasses. "And you are?"

"I'm Lieutenant Miller. I'm leading the search for Valerie Gillis. You're in the search area."

My rank seems to relax the man. "De Luca asked us to help you guys today," he says. "Looking for the lost hiker. These are my guys Derrick and Joaquin. Are we in the wrong spot?"

The name Cam De Luca, head instructor at the SERE school, needles me. "It was my understanding you'd search the school property. The restricted area. You're about a half mile east, aren't you?"

"Maybe less," adds Rudy.

"Our bad," the man says, without a hint of remorse. "We'll just take a breather here, then head back." He points to the stream behind me with his expensive canteen. "We're out of water. Mind if we fill up?"

I make an expansive gesture laced with hostility. "It's God's water," I say.

Rob breaks through the understory. He looks from face to face.

I have done everything I can to drown out the fiction writers, the ones who treat these cases as blood sport, the ones who root for us to fail so that they can troll us online. Some redneck sociopath hunted Valerie Gillis down through the woods for fun? Why would anybody living south of the poverty line do that over accepting a $25,000 reward? A rogue trainee from the SERE school suffered a psychotic break and attacked Valerie? That sounds more like a movie plot than a workable search-and-rescue scenario.

Which is not to say we've always had harmonious relations with the SERE school, a twelve-thousand-acre property parked right in the middle of the district. In an effort to simulate wartime evasion scenarios, they guard their "realism" like it's real. They get their backs up if some snowmobiler comes within audible range. I respect their rigor, but their position of nonresponsiveness makes things hard for me. They refuse to help quell the rumors that invariably crop up around their secretive presence. They don't want to "dignify" the chatter. Which means it will spread unchecked through the heads of gossips and gonzo amateur journalists on the internet. Tell me, how does that help Valerie?

The point is, we need everybody's attention on the same thing. Attention is finite. Resources are finite. With every passing hour, her odds get a little worse.

Rob and I are driving back to Sugarloaf in his truck, and Rob is telling some story about a family circus I can't quite follow. The ATV ride from the tote road to his truck felt like forty-five minutes in a blender. I feel a migraine brewing.

"... and then Ry starts to cry. Ry tells me that it was actually *Tig* who searched it up. And Tig was the last one we suspected. That's like hearing that Tinker Bell watches porn."

"Wait," I say. "Tig's younger than Ry, right?"

"Right. There's the baby, then Lou, then Tig . . ."

"What kind of porn was it?"

"I don't know *what* he saw. He's in *second grade*. By this point, Marnie's in tears. She's like, 'I'm gonna homeschool them all!' I don't see how that would help anything."

"No," I say. "The porn's anywhere there's an internet connection."

"It's in 'the cloud.' The cloud rains porn."

Finally, I put up a hand. "Can we just—sorry. I've got the worst headache."

We drive the rest of the way in silence. Silence between us has always been OK. We've probably spent more time side by side in a truck than Rob has spent with Marnie in their house or I've spent with my sisters as adults. But the silence that evening is different, laced with trouble.

My personal cell rattles in my chest pocket. I take it out and check the caller. It's Kate.

I stare at her name until the call goes to voicemail. During a search, you simply have to put the rest of life on suspension. We've all missed weddings, birthdays, the medical emergencies of loved ones. We've also missed many honey-colored mornings in which nothing went wrong. There's nothing to be done about it.

Eventually, we pull up to Sugarloaf Mountain Hotel. Rob turns off his ignition, and we sit there looking at the facade of the resort as Rob's engine cools.

It's a pretty resort. Red brick and green trim, real wooden beams over the portico, it has the whiff of an Alpine hotel. I consider going inside and booking a room. Walking in, pretending

I'm on vacation. It's a Sunday night. People are going in and out of the grand entrance in shorts and dresses, carrying tennis rackets, returning golf carts.

"Damn it" is all I say.

Rob knows what I mean. What I mean is, the weekend's over, we'll have fewer volunteers tomorrow, and the odds are turning against us. I can't think of a search in recent memory that ended in a live find after a week. What I mean is, she's starving. That is, if she is lucky to be alive, she is starving. Her arms and legs are getting thinner, and as a nurse, she knows what that means, and soon, if she hasn't already, she'll stop thinking straight. I mean that the colonel is going to call to ask me what the hell is going on, and I won't know what to say, because all the things that normally work are not working, and I am beginning to suspect that the hundreds of successful searches I've conducted were resolved by sheer luck.

That's what I mean.

Finally, Rob turns to me and sighs.

"When's the last time you were home, Bev?"

"Don't remember."

I stare at the purple mountain beyond, so permanent. I can't summon the courage to meet his eyes.

"Go home, Lieutenant," he pleads. "Sleep in your own bed. Check your property. Bring in your mail. It's just one damned night."

I step out of Rob's truck. I lean down into the passenger-side window, then think better of speaking.

I pat the top of his truck, and he drives away.

"Black Site" on the A.T., by Gareth Marsh

Reporting for the *Portland Packet*
Monday, August 1, 2022

As the search for the 42-year-old Appalachian Trail hiker Valerie Gillis stretches into a new week, the Maine State wardens are scratching their heads over the apparent lack of progress. On Saturday, at a press conference about the search, Lieutenant Beverly Miller promised to provide "all possible transparency" about the massive search and its mechanics. But even as she spoke these words, Miller steadfastly ignored one glaring issue—that the search area encompasses a secretive military facility where trainees are hunted down and tormented in a mock prisoner-of-war camp. Operated by the Joint Personnel Recovery Agency (JPRA) of the U.S. Department of Defense, the facility is one of our country's infamous SERE schools. The acronym stands for Survival, Evasion, Resistance, and Escape—and you can bet some of the students wish they could escape the training itself.

The SERE property borders the Appalachian Trail for several miles near the search area. Any hiker wandering north off the Appalachian Trail in the area soon comes across animal skulls nailed to trees and signs warning against trespass. This is where enlisted fighters from all military branches as well as nonenlisted contractors come to learn how to avoid capture and, secondarily (since none of the trainees do avoid capture), how to withstand the humiliations of imprisonment by the enemy, including interrogation and "exploitation." The war games played at the SERE schools are indeed convincing. Treatment of the trainees includes slapping, sleep deprivation, and being hosed down in freezing-cold temperatures. The program is supposed to push students to their limits—not actually break them. But isn't it possible that a person undergoing extreme stress might forget that the "scenario" is fictitious?

The SERE school's proximity to the spot where Gillis was last seen would appear to warrant further investigation. But for some reason, the Warden Service leaves this massive stone unturned. Apparently, the Warden Service considers the possibility that someone connected to the SERE program could be involved in Gillis's disappearance so implausible that it doesn't deserve consideration. Clearly, they believe it is mere coincidence that she disappeared near a school where disappearing is part of the curriculum.

Neither the DoD nor the Maine Warden Service responded to requests for comment on this article.

Dear Mom,

Like all disasters, I didn't see it coming.

    I was walking on a rugged stretch of trail when I first saw him. I'd only been hiking for two hours Monday morning, just getting started, but I felt itchy and bored. Some days, the redundancy of the action of stepping felt intolerable. Step after step after step, all the while scanning the ground. A hiker looks up at the sky or the woods at her own peril. Roots and slippery rocks command painstaking attention. I missed Santo, whose banter had carried me through hundreds of undifferentiated miles. I missed our singing, our teasing, our games, and our shared pain. Honestly, something vital went out of the trail for me when he left it. Suddenly I saw this kid coming toward me. He was hiking at a clip, urgently. The sun behind him illuminated his choppy brown hair. The light made him look meaningful, interesting. I was very bored and lonely.

    "Are you OK?" I called out as he approached.

    He reached me breathless, his intensely blue eyes full of shock. He was skinny and tall, maybe twenty years old, with boyish and bug-bitten arms. He glanced backward with worry.

    "Come on," he said to me. "We need to get out of here."

    "Why?" I asked him. "What's wrong?"

    With that, he plunged off the path into the understory. I looked to the top of the hill he'd just descended, my heart thudding. His glance made me nervous for him and for myself. Was someone chasing him? I watched his back as he waded through the chest-high mountain laurel, using his skinny arms to swim through. After the briefest hesitation, I followed.

I was worried about him. He didn't seem dangerous at all.

Maybe I was feeling some karmic obligation. The day before, I'd leaped onto a wet rock and slipped, falling on my bottom in a shallow creek, striking the back of my head on a rock. I felt the blow ring in my skull. I lay for a moment in defeat, my shorts filling with creek water, when a young woman splashed into the creek and knelt beside me. "Damn!" she said. "Are you OK?" I was shocked by the sudden fall. Thrown. She helped me up and took off my pack, and she sat with me chatting about stupid stuff for an hour until we were both sure I wasn't concussed. Then she went on her way, braid swinging, like a beautiful scrap of the future.

"Hey!" I called now to this kid. "If you stop and explain, I can probably help you!"

A scramble up the hill, and we were immediately out of sight of the trail. I thought he would stop at the top of the ridge, but instead he kept going, pushing onward into head-high fir saplings. I followed and was instantly surrounded by woods so thick I felt that I was being eaten by them. The foliage was so dense that I could barely see the back of his head as it came in and out of view through the boughs.

"Hey!" I called. "Kid? Wait!"

I lost sight of him.

I paused, a flash of foreboding. That was my last moment to turn around.

If I had turned around, I wouldn't be writing this letter.

I think about it a lot. In this darkness, this aloneness.

How insane it was for me to follow him.

How much trouble my impulse to help would cause me.

Despite his crisis, the blue-eyed boy appeared to know exactly where he was going, as if he had a compass point in his mind. He seemed familiar with the woods. We reached a slope of large rocks. He scaled it with authority. I looked behind me and saw a wall of vegetation that struck fear in my heart. A person takes a couple of steps off the trail up here, and it might as well be miles. I know that now. But then, I thought, Maybe up here is a side trail, or the thing he needs to show me. I'd help him, then we would return to the trail together. I climbed the rocks with a sinking feeling. I felt obliged to help him, but he hadn't given me an ounce of encouragement.

Finally I shouted, "We should stop! I have no idea where I am!"

Ahead of me, he stopped short. He rotated his head slowly toward the sound of my voice, until it locked into place like a piece of ordnance. His eyes were a beautiful blue. He charged back toward me. Given that I stood on a ledge, I braced.

"Wait," he said. "Who are you? Why are you following me? Did they send you after me?"

"What?" I laughed. "No. Who?"

"Are you a *spy*?"

"No! No. I'm hiking the AT. I'm Sparrow. I wanted to see if you were OK. Are you OK?"

"Turn around," he said.

Deftly, before I could even register what he was doing, he unclipped the chest strap on my backpack. He pushed the straps off my shoulders and let the pack fall to the ground, where it flipped end over end down the rocks and back to the base of the ridge.

"*No!*" I shouted. "Why did you do that? I *need* that. That's all my stuff. My food and my—"

"They're tracking us," he whispered. "They're tracking us through *you*."

Sun flecks played on his face as he stared at me with disappointment.

"That's not true!" I gasped. "Let me just go down and get my pack. Then I'll leave you alone and I won't bother you again."

"I can't let you do that," he said. "Hurry."

He grabbed my wrist and gave me a tug. Stunned, I had to hustle to avoid falling into the crisscrossed broken branches of blowdown. I felt a tear along my leg but the pain did not register. He pulled me indiscriminately, straight through obstacles. He lugged me over fallen trees, across false bridges of dried branches that broke beneath us like traps. He pulled me onward even as one leg then the other disappeared into depths of dark orange rot. At the base of the next ridge, we stepped out of the curtain of conifers and down into wetness. Immediately my boots filled with muddy water.

"No," I said. "Now look. Look!"

But he kept pulling, straight through the wet, marshy depression between ridges, pulling me across to the other side, where the land began to rise sharply again, another dark and humid wall of impenetrable understory.

"Let go of me!" I cried. "I want to turn back."

I turned my wrist in his grip, but he held fast. It was difficult to fend off the whipping branches with my free hand as we crashed along. My face grew tacky with sap and spiderwebs. Fighting the forest distracted me from the blue-eyed boy, from the danger of how far off the trail we were. When a branch lashed my eye and I cried out, he glanced over his shoulder, completely incurious, and kept going.

"Stop!" I yelled. "Jesus, stop! Let me go!"

When he and I were partway up the next ridge, I decided to go limp. To collapse, so that he would just leave me there. But as soon as I did so, he tugged harder, like a dog with a rope. I cried out, a stab of pain in the ball joint of my shoulder.

I took orders after that. The pain scared me.

"You're going to thank me," he said. "Wait till I show you what they're doing out here."

With that, I began to cry. I wiped my tears with dirt-covered hands.

Eventually, he let go of my wrist. At that point, there was nothing to do but follow him. How many miles? I have no memory. We walked and we walked. When I lagged behind, he came back and gripped me hard under my arm. I was in shock, I suppose. In a way, that's when I vanished. The only evidence of my existence was the sound of my own panting. I remember the slanting sun. The endless ridges. An inhuman silence after I gave up my voice. I watched his back move ominously through the darkening woods.

At dusk, we came upon a small natural platform in the ridge. There was a small view onto further ridges—a rarity in these woods. A green tarp was tied between three trees at head height. A ladder of twine-tied sticks was propped against another. A bag of supplies swung from a limb.

"Here we are," he said.

He smiled proudly. He had nice, cared-for teeth. Someone who loved him had paid to straighten those teeth.

He lifted the tarp, and I ducked under, stupid with fatigue. In the center of the space was a large flat rock, a kind of table. I felt too weak to stand. I sank to the ground, my vision darkening.

I awoke to dusk, foggy and confused. I watched him like I was his animal, unselfed, my attention glued to him. I was intensely dehydrated. Why else would I have sat there? He lowered his bear bag from the branch and rooted through it. His hands were as dirty as his teeth were white.

I'd done intakes on plenty of people with acute psychosis. The kid was delusional, but he also seemed completely at home in the woods. Maybe he was simply warped by a reclusive life in the wilderness. Had he kidnapped me for company?

I licked my lips. "Can I have some water?"

He retrieved a plastic liter soda bottle from behind a tree and filled my cup. Then he ripped a small white packet open with his teeth and poured the powder in the cup, producing a cloud of chemical citrus. He stuck his finger in the cup to mix the drink, then held it out to me. I looked up at him but had to turn away with nausea, his expression was so intense. Did he have something more violent in mind than company?

I shrugged and downed the lemon-lime concoction while he watched. When I was done, I put the cup down and he refilled it. The drink tasted salty and succulent, with a slight aftertaste of finger. I hung my head for a moment. Then I tried to face him.

"Why are you hiding out here? Who are you hiding from?"

He wagged his head and laughed softly.

"What did they do to you?" I asked. "If you're this scared, someone must have done something terrible to you. You can tell me. Is that why you wanted me to come along? To tell me? You want an ally? Someone to talk to?"

Carefully and without looking at me, he said, "Right on the other side of this ridge, there is a secret facility. Do you know what they do there?"

I swallowed. "No."

"All this time, *your* whole life and *my* whole life, they have been trying to—they have been working on—twenty-four-hour darkness."

I blinked back at him. "Who?"

"A secret branch of the US military. The Night Army."

"The Night Army?"

"Yeah," he said, somehow encouraged. "They've been working on a permanent eclipse. Think how easy it will be to enslave us in twenty-four-hour darkness. The recruits at the compound, they don't realize what they're there for. A lot of guys I know, local guys, they signed up during high school. Just think, some guy sets up a folding table at your high school and talks to you about patriotic service, and you think, 'Adventure!' So you enlist. But they send you to a secret facility that is on no map and they give you a *coffin* to sleep in and simulate drowning you"—he paused, finger to his lip—"so that someday, when everything is in place, you will become hollow-eyed henchmen for the Night Army." His eyes were glassy with anger. "But not me. *Not. Me.*"

I slapped my bare, bloodied legs and stood up.

"I need to pee," I said.

This alarmed him. He rose too, eyes widening.

"Where are you going? They'll see you."

"Too bad. I need to pee."

I took a step forward. He watched me closely, his hands up, as if he were about to catch something thrown at him. I walked another five paces. He followed.

"Well, what good does it do for me to walk away, if you are coming with me?" I said. "Might as well pee right here."

I unzipped my shorts.

I was trying to call his bluff.

Never try this with a madman.

He watched the whole time as I squatted in the moss. My body clenched, and the stream came out haltingly. Bitter tears threatened. I had come so far on that trail. The journey had been hard enough, almost impossible. I'd lost count of the times I wanted to quit. My heels were cracked and wasted. My knees throbbed. My hair was filthy, and a strange dermatitis of the kind I'd treated in homeless people grew on my neck and the backs of my knees. Gregory's voice echoed in my ears. "But you're going slower," he'd said so recently, pleading with me at seemingly every trailhead. "You're run down with the hardest part still ahead of you. I'm worried about you, Treasure." I stayed crouched on the ground, staring into the reddish earth, until I could summon enough defiance to meet the stranger's eyes.

He did not blink. I stood and zipped my shorts.

"What about you?" I asked. "You don't urinate?"

He nodded. He had not thought that one through. He paced one way, then the other, and finally decided to place one hand against a tree and turn his back to me. He fidgeted with his pants. I detected a blush in his ears.

As soon as I heard his piss hit the ground, I ran.

I ran as fast as running was possible in that quagmire. Uneven earth, set with sinkholes, chasms, burrows. Huge fallen branches rose out of the ground like the masts of sunken ships.

My bare legs, lashed with cuts, barely operative, moved nightmarishly slow. I could hear him coming up behind me. Even as I ran, my breath loud in my ears, I thought, What a waste! What a waste of energy! He seized me by my shoulders. I strained forward, going nowhere. He turned me around and shook me gently, the howl still in my mouth.

"We're fighting for daylight!" he shouted. "It's that important."

"That's not true!" I screamed into his face. "I don't even know you! I'm not in your army! I was trying to help you!"

He marched me back to his camp by the wrist. He tossed the tarp back and pushed me under. He led me to the ground, my back against one of the trees. Next he retrieved a length of rope and tied us together by the ankles with an expert knot. He rooted in his bag and withdrew a long bowie knife. He sat back against his tree, placed the knife in his lap, and looked at me with recrimination. We were both panting. His eyes were wide and dilated.

"Great," I said. "I'm your prisoner?"

"You're messing things up."

"I want to go back," I said. "Let me go back and I won't say a word."

"No chance," he said. "Soon, the Night Army comes. I'll take first watch."

Oh, darkness.

Well, you know, Mom, how darkness feels to me.

I don't remember a time when I was not afraid of it.

Most children are afraid of the dark. I just never outgrew the fear. I used to steal into your bedroom and check on you, sick with longing for comfort. Sometimes I even planted a kiss on your cheek. In your nightgown, you were tragically beautiful to me, out on the limb of your dreams. As soon as I got back into bed, I'd miss you again.

As my therapist would say, years later, I was "insecurely attached."

And the moon. Who finds the *moon* comforting? A big rock with a dead man's face on it? The moon is a bystander who never intervenes. How many people have been silenced or violated underneath its helpful incandescence?

Imagine, then, my first night in the deep woods with the blue-eyed boy.

Dusk falls earlier in the understory. Even when the sky retains a pale light, the forest below is already dark. In that remnant light, bushes creep, rocks move.

After he'd caught me and shook me, I refused to speak to him. I scanned the woods for my rescuers, whom I expected shortly. Gregory would alert someone. He would report my absence when I did not arrive at our meetup the next day. Gregory would get help. With their planes and their radar, they would come.

Sleep came intermittently. I had never slept out in the open, like an animal. I wasn't used to the exposure. No tent separated me from the air, no sleeping bag swaddled me. He'd given me his blanket, scratchy wool and mildewed. I pulled it around me, yanked my legs closed, and rested my filthy forehead on my knees. Each time I awoke, I found my captor staring right through me, his lips moving vigorously, his bright knife in his hand. Each time, I retraced the steps that had brought me there. How he had waved me to follow. How he pulled my wrist. My backpack rolling end over end downhill. Each time, the story's conclusion brought a wave of disbelief.

I tried to think of home. I sent Gregory telepathic messages. I told him where I was. I haven't prayed since I was a kid, but I prayed then. What I mean is, I distilled my whole self into a plea and I sent the plea out on the wind. It was pure longing, a kind of homesickness.

No one could understand why, as a child, I was so anxious. I had experienced no trauma to speak of, and neither you nor Daddy had experienced childhood anxiety—the bellyaches, the morbid fixations, the dread of any change or separation. I was simply born that way. Easily overwhelmed. As porous as paper. I had no defenses against the world—*that's* why I was anxious. You were perplexed by me, but patient. You praised my despairing poetry that I wrote at a very early age. When my anxieties were bad, you used to let me sleep with you. We slept together long past necessity.

Eventually, the milky-blue dawn light caused the birds of the Maine woods to chorus.

It was hard to hear the individual songs, there was such cacophony. One of those songs, I thought, one of those songs is the sparrow's.

Lt. Bev

SUNDAY, JULY 31. NINE P.M.
DAY 5 OF THE GILLIS SEARCH.

I'm driving home after parting with Rob when I catch a glimpse of an older woman passing out flyers in front of the IGA, and I realize it's Janet Gillis. She's standing in the brightly lit entry, talking to shoppers coming in and out. I turn my truck around at the intersection and pull into the parking lot.

"Hello there," I say, walking up to her.

"Lieutenant!" she says, flapping her papers at me. "I'm handing out flyers."

A teenager in sagging jeans slinks by. She slaps a copy of her poster to his chest.

"That's my daughter," she tells him. "She's lost. She was hiking the Appalachian Trail. If you see anyone who looks like her, call the tip line! God bless you."

"God bless you too," the kid says. He walks off looking at the flyer.

"Don't you sleep, Lieutenant?"

"Well, I heard there was a—" I glance at the sandwich board propped open beside the entrance. "A sale on artichokes. Here," I say. "Give me a stack."

Janet reaches up and pats me on the shoulder. "Thank you," she says.

A woman in scrubs approaches. Janet steps in her way. The woman looks up from her phone with irritation.

"Are you a doctor? A nurse? Hi. What you do is so important. My daughter's a nurse."

The woman in scrubs glances nervously my way. I'm still wearing my bulletproof vest and sidearm—I seem unable to consider myself off duty—but I smile to soften the look.

"My daughter Valerie Gillis has disappeared," Janet continues. "She was last seen very near here on the Appalachian Trail. She was hiking the Appalachian Trail. This is what she looks like."

"Oh, wow," the woman says. "No, I'm sorry. I haven't seen her, but I can hang this poster up at the hospital. Give me a couple." The nurse stands studying the photo, no longer in a rush. She smiles at Janet. "She's pretty. She looks just like you."

"Watch out." Janet beams. "I'm a hugger."

"Open for business," the nurse said, extending her arms.

It strikes me that as the search drags on and the chances of success worsen, Janet Gillis seems to find fresh strength, reserves enough for everyone. She's stopped crying, at least for now. "Beautiful," "friendly," "a poet soul"—these are words fellow hikers used to describe Valerie. Watching Janet, I see where she got those qualities. Janet isn't standing out here in front of the IGA because she has unreasonable optimism—Wayne, who has some painfully relevant insurance background, has already told me they understand the odds—but due to, it seems, a surfeit of love for her daughter. Dauntless, unending love. Mothers like her will light the last night on earth.

There is a lull in the foot traffic. A pickup spewing vape smoke pulls up, and the kid with the sagging jeans comes out of the IGA and gets into it, still holding the flyer.

Janet and I look out at the night sky. Even with the parking lot lights, we can still see the pinpoints of starlight in the huge black dome above us.

"I don't understand this place," she says.

"The IGA?"

"Maine."

"Yeah," I say. "Me neither."

"It's wild up here. Wild and beautiful, but heartless. Your work is very difficult. I bet your family is incredibly proud of you."

"I'm sure they are," I say. A young father approaches carrying a child in his arms. "We're searching for this woman," I tell him. "Please take a good look and let the Warden Service know if you see anything."

Was my father proud of what I do? Yes. He was a furniture salesman, but what he loved most was fly-fishing on the weekends. I learned to cast on slow water, wading through slop. My father made a spiritual exercise of walking the riverbeds and drawing the whole thing out as long as possible. He was a pretentious fisherman and an absent husband—the man did whatever he wanted—but he introduced me to the outdoors. He embraced me as both son and daughter, kindred and stranger, which essentially trained me for the work I would fall in love with at twenty-seven. My kid sisters Kate and Faith still live down in the greater Boston area. I adore Faith's girls Kelsey, Hailey, and Mackenzie. You'd think, with names like that, they live on the Scottish fen, but Faith's got a place in the 'burbs, not too far from Leominster, actually.

"Are they still living," Janet asks, "your parents?"

"My dad passed away when I was a teenager. My mother is still alive and kicking. She lives in a home near my sisters. I go see her when I can."

Ma was what we used to call a "homemaker." She was as surrounding as air, always near. Despite all that access, it was hard to get her actual attention. As the oldest, I was useful to her, and after Dad died, she often reminded me that I was essential. *I'd be lost without you, Beverly. Sometimes it seems like you're the only one I can count on.* When she was tired or sad, I'd run the laundry or prepare dinner or make sure my sisters were doing their homework. There was one year when I planned Kate's birthday party at the skate rink. She went around and around with these little skinny kids shod with wheels. It was around this time that Ma started taking pills. I made no connection between these pills and her frequent unavailability. Just in the nick of time, Ma would snap out of it and emerge with her hair brushed, and my little sisters would compete for her pale attention. She was a genuinely beautiful woman, with large, emotional eyes. She was very timid. Didn't have a shred of rebellion inside her.

Not long before Dad passed, Ma experienced a religious conversion. She wandered into a church near the grocery store and was overcome by the Holy Spirit. My father and sisters were unnerved by her talk, but I offered to go along with her for company. The church was in a commercial building between a rug store and a diamond seller. It was the kind of church for people who stumbled into churches. There was tinny music playing from a keyboard and folding chairs and no natural light. Some of the congregants were pretty beat-up looking, in bad wigs or blurred tattoos. The minister wore street clothes. When preaching, he'd begin by speaking into his folded hands, as if he were alone, so that when he looked up and saw us, he always seemed so delighted we were there. He talked about hell, he worried for our souls, but his favorite subject was love—the infinite, improbable, no-fine-print love of God for each one of us. One Sunday, he said, "Have you ever loved someone so much that you wanted to be with them all the time? You thought about them all the time, and longed for them when they were away?" I was musing on this question when he lifted his head and fixed his gaze on me. "This is the way God feels toward *you*," he said. I tried to inch down in my chair. Me? I disliked being singled out for any reason at all. But the minister held my gaze. "He hurts when *you* hurt," he told me. "He mourns when *you* mourn. He delights in you. He thinks you are the most beautiful person imaginable. *No matter what you think of yourself.*"

Finally, he looked away, and I glanced at the nodding congregants. Well, I thought, who else but a divine being would feel that way about any of us? My mother beside me—flustered, always on the verge of tears—and I, Amazonian, mute with embarrassment. Yet in my heart, I believed the minister, and I knew what he was talking about—I mean about loving someone no matter how imperfect they were, and hurting when they hurt—because that's the way I felt about my mother.

"Well," Janet says, dusting her hands. "We're out of flyers."

"It's late anyway," I agree. "I think they close soon."

We both turn and look at the bright windows.

"You didn't get your artichokes!" Janet laughs.

Then, without warning, she hugs me tight.

"Thank you," she says into my shirt. "I think you want to find her almost as badly as I do."

Back in my truck, I turn on the ignition and jab the radio channels.

Commercials, sugary songs. I opt for silence.

Finally, I listen to my sister's message on my cell.

"Hi, Bevie. It's me, Kate. So, Ma has taken a turn for the worse. She wasn't conscious at all today and the doc came in and asked about the—you know. Oh, honey, we need to talk. Me and Faith, we need your answer. About the DNR. Faith and I don't want her hooked up to machines. We want to change the directions to do not resuscitate. But you need to agree." There's a pause. My sister sighs. "You're not thinking straight. You can't save Ma this time. Ma's not gonna bounce back. She's not gonna wake up and say all the things you want to hear. You've done so much for her. You've done everything you could. You've done your duty. You gotta let go, Beverly. It's OK to let go now. OK? Call me."

I drive south, underneath another clear sky.

Those stars, those stars that don't care.

I turn south. I'll be home by midnight.

I remember the day I was offered a position in the Warden Service. It was one of the happiest in my life. I wanted to share my excitement with everyone. I got the idea that I should drive down to Leominster and tell Ma.

It had taken years of work to achieve. To gain a position as a game warden, candidates have to pass a physical fitness test first, which weeds out a quarter of each group, then a written test, which disqualifies another half. If you pass that, it's on to the oral board, testing your applied knowledge, including how to ID hundreds of kinds of flies, fur, plants, or scat, how to clean, load, and shoot a gun, and how to use diplomacy so you never have to shoot it. Next is a psych exam, a background check, and finally, the colonel's interview. You pass all those and you may or may not get yourself a chance to earn a modest living saving lives in the woods, which was, when I graduated with a master's in wildlife conservation from UMaine, what I wanted most in the world.

"You'll be one of two female wardens in the *state*?" Ma said, frowning. "There must be a reason there's no other women in that line of work."

Well, I explained. Such work wasn't for the faint of heart,

whether you're a man *or* woman. Not everyone wants to work outside in all weather. Blizzards. Rain. Nor can you be afraid of wildlife. Did she remember, I asked, how I used to catch snakes in her garden and—

"There's want and can," Ma said, visibly distressed. "I know you *want* to do this, Beverly. But will you be *able* to?"

"Why would they hire me, Ma," I asked sincerely, "if they thought I wasn't able?"

She clamped her mouth shut. Then she looked at me and asked, "Do you dislike being a woman, honey? Do you wish to be a man?" She waved away my answer. "Because women are women. It's just so unusual. For a woman to want to drive around chasing criminals."

"That's not—that's not why—"

"It was your father. It was your father treating you like a boy that did this."

"But I'm happy out there," I finally blurted. "I am my very happiest in the woods."

"And I will always love you, Bev. I will *always* love you." She grasped my hand. "You'll always be my special angel."

Then she dissolved into tears.

She was afraid. She was afraid of many things. She was afraid for me. She herself did not know why. She was a conventional woman who aspired to a sameness of days. I was intensely protective of her. Even now, as I voice these words, disloyalty turns my blood cold.

But there was a point, long ago, when I realized that the feeling I had standing atop a mountain, face-to-face with the horizon, or wading in remote rivers, was a satisfaction and a peace beyond explanation.

The backcountry is my mother.

"Santo" Live Interview, Bronx, NY, 7/30/22
Recorded by Warden Cody Ouellette

I'm afraid of two things, Cody. Spiders and hitchhiking. Hopping in a car on remote stretches of road with strangers? That is the whitest idea.

No hitchhiking. That was my one rule. When we needed to resupply, either we met up with Gregory, or we walked. Now, walking an extra two or three miles to get food when you're already beat? Unbased, Cody. Un. Based.

So this one day—we were still in Painsylvania—me and Sparrow see a town in the distance, visible from the trail. White steeples rising into a blue sky. I'll call it Sunnytown. Sunnytown like Anytown, you understand, Cody?

Cody Ouellette: Yep.

By then, Left Eye was holding herself together with electrical tape. Me and Sparrow were hungry and sweaty. Not looking or smelling our best. A car slows down. It's a truck.

Truck is huge. It has those spotlights on top? This truck is an if-you-think-my-truck-is-big-you-should-see-my-gun-collection kind of truck.

There's a white dude in the truck, staring at us.

I try not to look at him. It's a totally empty road, no one else around.

I keep close to Sparrow. But then, on the other hand, not too close, right? Maybe *that's* what Detective Pickup doesn't like, my nearness to a white woman.

Dude leans over and he says, in this gravelly voice, "Hey. *Hey.*"

We stop. There is nowhere to run.

And he goes, "Are you two hiking the Appalachian Trail?"

We nod.

Dude says, "Can I buy you lunch?"

I look at Sparrow. We're like, "What??"

So he starts asking us how our hike is going, how many miles have we covered so far, what was the hardest part of the trail...

Then he hands us each a fifty.

I look around for the cameras. But it's not a prank. He starts telling us about where we should eat. He's like, "If you like pizza, there's Pizza Heaven. If you want a diner, there's Karen's Place. If you want Chinese, there's Bill's Chinese Restaurant..."

(laughter)

Then he goes, "Well, enjoy your time in Sunnytown! Good luck on your journey!"

And he drives away.

There was plenty of pain, is what I'm trying to say, but there was also magic.

Trail magic.

It's *real*.

Get this—we're somewhere in Jersey, and I'm walking toward the trailhead when a hiker passing us says to me, "You left your soul back there." I'm about to agree when I realize they are saying "sole." The sole of my boot is *lying in the mud* behind me. I get a ride to a hiker's hostel with Gregory and Sparrow for a much-needed zero day. I take a shower and prepare myself to find some outfitter so I can buy new boots.

Now, I'm a big boy and so not every outfitter has size 14 shoes.

And if they did, it was not in my budget to pay two hundred bucks for Gore-Tex boots.

It was a problem, Cody.

We're about to leave, but I decide to take a peek at this box outside the hostel. There's always a box for hikers to take or leave shit they don't need. I'm thinking, "Maybe I'll grab some extra protein bars or something."

Guess what was sitting there in that box?

No, really, take a guess.

Cody Ouellette: A pair of hiking boots in your size?

Can you *believe* it?

It was God saying, "Ruben, baby, you fat, you slow, but you gonna make it! I got my money on you, Ruben!"

(laughter)

Cody Ouellette: So, what happened, man? Why'd you stop?

Well, I'm getting to that part.

I have to say it's been a relief talking to you, man. Strangely.

So. Eventually, Sparrow and me made it New York State. New York was a different kind of rocky. Huge, I-hate-it-here boulders and slabs of granite that would be cool if you were, like, a billy goat. In one spot there was an actual ladder. That's the kind of vertical climbs in New York.

But on the plus side, there's lots of road crossings in New York. That means, every ten miles or so, the trail passes near a deli. They call it "deli blazing." You walk half a mile off the trail and there's some neon-lit air-conditioned food utopia. Calzones. Ice cream. Pastrami sandwiches stacked so high they don't fit in your mouth. My home state took care of me. I mean, if you like to eat, you should try long-distance hiking. You eat and eat and eat, and you *still* lose weight.

It's sad now, man. Already I'm putting it back on.

(pause)

I almost quit in New York. There's this place in New York where a cliff split apart and you have to walk through this dark, man-swallowing crack for fifty feet. It's called the Lemon Squeezer.

I looked into that crack.

I was like, "OK, where's the side trail that goes *around* the Lemon Squeezer?"

There's no side trail around the Lemon Squeezer.

I stood there gazing into the nothingness. I couldn't see the end of it.

You really do get to know yourself out there on the AT. I didn't know I had a fear of geological abysses.

So I was like, "OK, I hiked over a thousand miles, I survived Rocksylvania, I even got boots from *God*, but I guess this is it for old Ruben. Nobody's squeezing *this* lemon."

But Sparrow grabbed me and said, "Who's the guy who chased a black bear away from our campsite in Jersey?"

I'm like, "Uh, me?"

"Who's the guy who carried me across the Lehigh River on his back?"

"I guess I did."

"Who's the guy who has hiked hundreds of miles when nobody believed he'd make it twenty?"

"That's definitely me."

She grabbed my hand, and we stepped into the Lemon Squeezer.

We took little Ruben baby steps the whole way through.

Cody Ouellette: That's a good story. I don't like tight spaces myself.

So I get this idea. I want to show Sparrow where I'm from.

There's a shelter in New York—West Mountain shelter—where I heard you could see the city real clear. We got there on a perfect evening. I must say, the view did not disappoint. Down below was the mighty Hudson. Then, at the end of it, thirty miles away, there she was.

Gotham. Full of hustlers. Bright as a galaxy. My home.

One of the hikers was celebrating his birthday with a big bottle of Jameson he lugged way the hell up there. We stayed up late getting hammered. After the party died down and everyone went to sleep, I felt like I could hear him. I could hear him laughing.

Cody Ouellette: Hear who?

My pops! I could hear him in the distance, still shouting about what a stupid idea this was. From the Bronx!

"Who you think you are, *pendejo*? You fat, nature-loving pussy!"

(laughter)

Holy shit.

(laughter)

Yeah, well. I swore that there was no way my pops would keep me from finishing the trail. Well, he finally did it. He found a way!
He got the COVID.
That's what he called it—"the COVID."
Whole fucking pandemic is over, and the man gets COVID.
He always had to do things his own way.
Did he have the vaccine? No. He did not trust the *maldita* vaccine.

HEARTWOOD

He thought he was made of steel. But he was just a fat diabetic.

(pause)

My moms got word to me.
I gave my Sparrow a big hug and I left the trail. Went home.
By then he was on a ventilator and only had a couple days left.
Anyway, that was that.
The end of my Appalachian Trail thru-hike.

(pause)

Guess Pops was right about me not finishing!
Motherfucker always had to be right.

Lena

She works online all Monday and falls asleep too late in the day. She dreams of Christine. In the dream, Christine is a teenager. They sit together in a field, surrounded by chamomile in bloom. Christine leans forward, a soft and loving look in her eyes. She pats her mother's hand, about to say something.

It's spring in the dream. It's timeless in the dream. It's spring forever.

Lena wakes up with a start and gasps for air. She has fallen asleep in her power chair again. The afternoon sun is waning. That morning, she'd been visited by Jodi, director of Resident Services. Lena had forgotten the meeting—a check-in, disguised as a social visit. Lena had smiled stiffly and ignored the seedpod casings that carpeted the apartment floor and the maps and printouts of *Boston Globe* articles that littered her desk and the sweatpants knotted on the unmade bed. Jodi chatted, showcasing her white teeth and large, strigiform eyes, but Lena understood her mistake. The only reason Lena had gotten this choice apartment was because the previous tenant had been deemed non compos and was involuntarily relocated one floor up to assisted living. She'd rather die.

"By the way," Jodi had said, rising to leave, "I'm going to send housekeeping in here, OK? You could slip on that stuff on the floor. It's a hazard."

"OK," Lena said meekly.

"There'll be a charge on your bill."

"Understood. Thank you."

When she closed the door, Lena had to catch her breath.

And now, seeing Christine in the dream upsets her in a related way. Because sometimes, of course, her powers of observation had failed her. For example, the measuring game. When she and Roger first separated, Lena was surprised by the new intensity between her and her daughter. It was as if Lena, a woman who was barely competent in one role, was now expected to excel in two. For a time, she made valiant efforts toward some kind of maternal-scientific compound. They took the normal markings-on-the-wall ritual a bit further, and little Christine laughed as her mother measured her cranium, her arms, her shoulders. Lena jotted down the numbers, thinking—what? That Christine would later cherish this kind of metadata? Over the years, Lena continued to use a notebook, making neutral observations, somewhat like field notes. "C making repeated coughing sounds but is not ill. Nervous tic?" "C has trouble with fractions. Grades dropped. Math quiz with 70 found in the trash."

Lena had considered herself vigilant, constantly scanning the horizon for potential threats to Christine—to her body, mind, or heart. How did such effort lead so disastrously to *him*? He was five years Christine's senior, twenty-three years old. A grown man. They met in the hardware store where Christine ran the cash register after school in her senior year. He was a high school dropout. Nobody special. And yet, magnificent Christine fell into a consuming rapture over this man. The world moved in his hands. For him, she eschewed childhood, her future, her neighborhood, her friends, even her country, for he swept her off to Canada, where he had some kind of work visa, during which Lena engaged in an extended, activist letter campaign to bring Christine to her senses. The marriage lasted a surprisingly long time.

Now, the sun turns the bricks on the wing across the courtyard vermillion.

It takes Lena a minute to hear the Telegram ping.

She is slow to react. She pulls herself away from the dream toward her computer screen.

I found a source.
A guy who is on retainer at the torture school.
He plays one of the partisans that captures trainees.
We meet tonight.

Lena fumbles with the keyboard. The day has left her disoriented.

> A torturer?
> Are you meeting in public, I hope?

Bar.
I know him.
We went to high school together.
Guy's an idiot.
Not surprised he likes to abuse
people as a job.

> Please be careful.

Here they are, in the midst of Operation Sparrow, and yet she's not sure if they should be. It feels good to do something to help Valerie, but this? She feels disconnected from TerribleSilence, even as he sends her more missives than ever. With confusing directives like this:

Obtain SERE court martial records.
What is behind military firewall?

Or worse:

HEARTWOOD

IS VALERIE INSIDE THE COMPOUND?
Possible SERE grounds stakeout.
Night vision goggles, etc., look for any
suspicious movements or activity.

    Now, Lena writes:

                  Don't you think the wardens saw
                  the article in The Packet?
                  It backs up our claim!
                  "The SERE school's proximity to
                  the spot where Gillis was last seen
                  would appear to warrant further
                  investigation."
                  Don't you think it will force the
                  wardens to reconsider this lead?

No. Why not? Because the Warden
Service is IN BED w/ military.
If we lived in a country where the
military never lied to the public and
covered up crimes then sure, lets
believe the military!
But that is an IMAGINARY NATION, friend.
. . .
Besides. Do these douchebags really
inspire confidence in u?
Didn't u hear that bozo in charge on TV?
"This one has got us all stumped."
Gee whiz! We're stumped!
Here's the **link**. I just posted it on
Youtube for all to see.

She should be ashamed to call herself
a Maine warden.

                        I could call the tip line.
                        Tell them our theory.

Sure, knock urself out.
But who are we? 2 voyeurs. Wackjobs.
. . .
Did u know that if you call a tip line, u
can become a suspect?

                        You can't be serious.

Sometimes perpetrators call tip lines.
For fun.
That's why.

    Lena wrings her armrests. Agitation mounts. Legs, legs are useful, but what she wishes for is wings. She wishes to go to her balcony and push off into the air, soar north over the thickening forests. To leave Cedarfield Active Life Plan Community behind. Forever? Fine. What tremendous grace it takes to move into a place like this, knowing you will not leave alive. She would give her last breaths for this stranger. What use are they to her?

Psst.
I did something I shouldn't have.

                        What?

I took a souvenir.

                        What is it?

You want to see?

                        Of course I want to see!

HEARTWOOD

She waits, bent over almost entirely, face inches from the monitor. His message lands. A photo. In the photo, her friend grips a metal sign.

WARNING
MILITARY TRAINING FACILITY
NO ENTRY BEYOND THIS POINT

Adrenaline courses through her. The sign is bent, having been wrenched off a post or tree. In the photo, he holds it with the same intelligent fingers that had proffered so many fascinations for her, wrested from woods she couldn't enter. He wears a brightly colored bandana wrapped around one wrist.

You didn't!

They'll be furious!

I'M furious. I'm furious that my tax
dollars are sponsoring a torture school!
Spreading death.
Spreading darkness.
In our name.
I cant live w/ that.
Can you?

She rubs her face vigorously, then wheels away, silencing him, until she is staring out at the dark sky. Can she live with that? Yes or no, she is and always will be an observer. It's not the wheelchair. She watches from a self-imposed distance. Always has. What has it mattered, honestly, that she was so knowledgeable? What has she made of it? Her mind was like a cat, appreciating the brindled scapulars of a bird it is stalking. Many times, she had wanted to hold Christine, to tell her that she, too, remembered the horror of her first period, the pierce of adolescent betrayals, the shame of failing a test in school, but whenever she got within arm's length of the girl herself, fellow feeling withdrew. It was as if she feared that compassion for her daughter would crush her. She was a survivor. And, well, she chose herself.

Her nose begins to run. It's the stress.

She returns to her monitor and clicks on the YouTube clip that TerribleSilence posted.

She presses play.

A conference room. Limp flag. Podium. A tall woman in a green uniform with handsome cheekbones is bending down to speak into a microphone. Beside her stands a poster of the photograph of Valerie smiling with thumbs hooked into her straps. Lena turns up the volume meter.

"Yes, that seems like a reasonable conclusion to draw," the warden is saying to a questioner outside the range of the microphone. The woman's face is glistening. She seems uncomfortable. When she lifts a hand to shield her eyes from the lights, Lena leans in. "Yes, this is highly, highly unusual," the woman is saying. "We've searched three hundred acres thus far. Valerie is *nowhere* that she's supposed to be. We're—well, we're stumped, is the word. I guess I probably shouldn't say that, but it's the right word." Apparently, the word "stumped" irks someone in the unseen audience, and the warden nods, listening for what seems like a brutal interval. "Absolutely. Everybody is cooperating," the warden stresses. Then, "I can't comment on that." Later, with just a touch of impatience, "If I knew that, then Valerie would be standing right here next to me, wouldn't she?"

A beefy man in the same forest-green uniform steps up and

whispers something to the woman at the microphone. She nods and points to the poster beside her. "Anyone who has information can call the tip line. This line is monitored twenty-four seven by a live—by a person. This is not an extension that sends callers to a voicemail. We want to hear from you. And I want to thank our warden investigators who have—who are working day and night. I want to thank, most of all, Valerie's family—" The warden stops midsentence and puffs out her cheeks. Lena puts a hand to her own face. The warden is trying not to *cry*. The awkward silence is palpable even virtually. It's unprofessional, it's embarrassing, it's *female*. But to her surprise, Lena flushes with sympathy.

"Keep talking," Lena urges her. "Breathe."

"Valerie's family, who—who are here in Maine now and who—desperately need the help of the whole community to—to find their daughter." At last, the warden resets and continues in a mechanical tone, "Thank you for your time and your cooperation. Now we're going to hear from Valerie's—Valerie's, um, husband. Gregory?"

The husband steps into the frame, sad eyed, slope shouldered, shorter than the towering woman who now retreats into the background. Lena is immediately skeptical that this man is remotely capable of hurting Valerie. Not because he didn't want to—she isn't speaking to his purity—but because of his lugubriousness, which reminds her of the old-world Poles complaining in the living rooms of her childhood. He holds his notecard with two hands, as if it's heavy. There's a reward—that's good. That might convince somebody to break his silence, maybe the very source her friend is meeting in a bar at that moment, somewhere along a moonlit road in Maine.

The clip ends.

* * *

At sunup, Lena throws open the door to her outside patio and gulps fresh air.

Is there a word for the nausea induced by too much blue light?

Her patio is on the second floor. It's just high enough to be hidden from passersby below, but low enough to hear their conversation.

A shadow flickers across the patio. Lena looks up.

The bird circles the sky slowly, without moving its black wing tips. Such a large, silent bird. Vultures do not call or sing. A vulture has nothing to prove, no territories to claim.

The vulture does not rush.

Dear Mom,

I'm now drawing tally marks inside the cover of my notebook.
    So I don't lose track.
    One, two, three, four, five makes a set.
    Plus three more. Eight days lost.
    Hunger undresses me.

On the second day of my catastrophe, I awoke to rain. Raindrops drummed the tarp and snapped back the leaves around the campsite, sounding like the second hands of a thousand clocks. I pushed myself to sitting and scanned the woods. The forest was quiet.

    The rope was still knotted tightly around my ankle, but the other end lay loose on the forest floor. The blue-eyed boy was nowhere to be seen.

    I straightened my legs. Pain traveled up my spine. I rolled onto all fours and stood up. I pushed back the tarp, which was heavy with rainwater.

    The woods were empty.
    The pines stood uninterrupted.
    He had fled. He'd left, he'd been eaten—I didn't care.
    I laughed, staggering out into the rain. He was gone. Crazy kid, he'd left to go conscript someone else. I began to run downhill, dragging my leash, back toward the never-tiring trail and its white blazes, toward safety and maps and protection and sanity, toward you and Daddy, and toward home and my friends and my

loyal Gregory! All of these things were as vivid as daylight to me when I broke through the grillwork of sticks and belly flopped into a deep hole. The fall did not hurt, as the pit had been dug in soft earth, but it knocked the wind out of me.

I rose to my elbows, dirt in my mouth.

I'd been snared again.

I buried my face in the earth, and raged.

Later, the kid and I sat in the same confrontational pose beneath the tarp, almost knee to knee, staying clear of the sides, where water dripped down in sheets. He seemed like a different person, duller, less confident. Moments after I'd fallen into his trap, his face had emerged at the opening. He peered down into the hole, perplexed. Like he couldn't understand why I kept doing the wrong things.

Water bottles sat on the rock table with several water purification tablets disintegrating inside. Bits of vegetation rotated in the tea-colored water. Everything about me was wet and dirty. My hair dripped water down my neck and into the sleeves of my fleece. My legs cried rivulets of dirt. To add tears to this would be redundant.

I kicked his leg and he startled.

"Hello," I said. "I'm hungry. Do you have any food?"

He dug in his pack. He placed a lovingly wrapped sandwich on the rock table. Mayonnaise and frilly lettuce and a pink layer of baloney between Wonder Bread. He poured me a cup of water.

I stared at the sandwich. I had not eaten in over twenty-four hours. I grabbed the cup of water and threw it back. This was nonnegotiable. I'd be rescued, I was certain, before my bowels could be destroyed by whatever bacteria he had failed to kill. In the short term, I simply had to stay alive. He settled across from me and looked at me intently. I devoured the sandwich.

We sat in silence, my intestines puzzling.

I said, without thinking, "Someone packed your lunch, didn't they? That looks to me like a sandwich a mother would make."

He grimaced and looked into the woods.

"These woods used to belong to everybody," he said, his expression darkening. "Then they put up their warning signs and claimed twelve thousand acres." He laughed bitterly. "There's really nobody good, no fairness. No goodness. The only reliable person is a newborn child. And him only for one day."

A memory resurfaced, something I noticed several miles before he came running toward me on the trail. An animal skull nailed to a tree. A warning sign. NO TRESPASSING. I went cold with fear. Was the boy right? Was there something out here besides him to be afraid of? I tried to restore my confidence in reality by picturing Gregory waiting for me at the trailhead. Gregory would alert someone. He'd get help.

"Listen," I said. "I need my backpack."

The boy gazed out at the rain as if he had not heard me.

"It was wrong of you to separate me from my backpack. Do you know where it is? Can we please go back and get it?"

I nudged him again with my one boot. His mad eyes sharpened.

"I need my backpack," I repeated. "I have medication in my backpack."

"Medication?"

"Anxiety," I said. "I take medication for anxiety."

He shook his head. "Don't take that stuff. You don't know what they put in there. They say it makes you better. 'Take this,' they say. 'It makes you better!' They mean 'It makes you just like *us*.' It makes you obedient. They don't know me. I'll do this on my own, thank you."

I drew a breath and let it out slowly. "So . . . you were on medication before. And you've stopped taking it?"

He blinked his eyes so slowly it seemed he was falling asleep.

"I need my backpack," I said, louder now. "It's *mine*. I need it. I need my toothbrush and my pills and my journal."

"We can't have that here. It's bugged. I told you."

"But I need it. I just told you why."

Suddenly, I leaned toward him, emboldened.

"How long have you been out here, anyway? No fire. No shelter to speak of. No sleeping bag. What's your goal? What's your *point*?"

He spoke carefully, as if I were an imbecile. "My point," he said, "is daylight."

"Right," I said. "Right, of course. Daylight. But isn't daylight a force of truth? Shouldn't you be telling the truth? If what's happening out here is so terrible, shouldn't you tell everyone about it?"

He blinked again, as if in psychic pain.

Then he reached around for his backpack and took out a rifle. I shrank back.

"Extreme emergencies trump rules of good sportsmanship," he said, laying the gun on his lap. "We can hunt game with this. And a Maglite. We can blind deer with the light, then shoot. Cut the meat in strips. Make jerky and pemmican. No fires, though. They'll see. You can dry the jerky on a sunny rock. Fish is good raw. There's lots to eat out here. I'll teach you." He'd perked up, now that he was back on the plan. When his mood brightened, he seemed totally sane. "You think there's no food out here, but there's tons to eat. We've got cranberries near the bogs. That's why they're called bog berries. Blueberries. Lowbush blueberries mostly grow between boulders. They've got that white bloom on them, rubs off, that's how you know they're not nightshade. Nightshade is poisonous and pretty. Don't ever eat anything that grows on a red branch . . ."

The rifle made it hard to focus on what he was talking about, which appeared to be his plans to live here together indefinitely. My windpipe narrowed to the size of a straw. Fear, oh, Mother. My earliest memories are filled with it. Premonitions of extreme weather, rattling windows, prosaic dangers—where *were* you? When I was older, when the old fears roared back, pills helped. But these days, I mostly carried them for reassurance. One thing I loved about my job was that when I was too busy, too needed, my fears faded and had no power over me.

He slung the rifle over his shoulder and rose to his knees.

"Ours is a doomed and malignant society," he said. "FUBAR. Fucked up beyond all recognition."

I groaned. He looked over at me, angry.

"I mean, I don't disagree with you," I said. "It is a pretty broken world."

He paused and fiddled with his rifle.

"Do you want to have sex?" he asked.

"Oh God," I said. "No!"

My stomach turned. I had to breathe deeply not to vomit.

"Do you know how old I am?" I cried.

No. No, no, no.

For dinner, cold chicken drumsticks. I couldn't afford to refuse. The rain lifted at dusk. He retrieved a pair of binoculars from their hook on a tree, and he spent the remaining daylight hours scanning the forest and sky.

Who was I kidding? When I failed to arrive at our meeting spot, Gregory wouldn't find that unusual. I was always late, for one reason or another. At the beginning of my hike, we'd had arguments about my unpredictable timetable, until finally, at my insistence, he gave over to it. He'd go back to his hotel and sleep deeply. We loved each other, and we were always going to be friends, but my thru-hike had changed me—no, shown me to myself. I'd been honest, very honest. What had happened to my feelings for him, how they had changed, was certainly hard on him. Who would blame him if all this had cooled him a little, made him feel, well, less attentive?

I watched my antagonist. So. He was just a kid who wouldn't take his meds. His desire to hide out in the woods wasn't crazy in itself. Plenty of people bought freeze-dried rations and rain barrels and ammunition and seeds for the end of days. I myself had undertaken a solo hike in the woods, a decision rooted in the same desire to slip away, just for a little, to hide from everyone and everything, to be unfindable.

Darkness ebbed in. He hung his binoculars on the tree.

Something in me said, Talk. Let him get to know you.

"I miss my sleeping bag," I said. "More than my toothbrush or my pills or even fresh clothes. Though I do miss those things." I sighed. "Don't you miss creature comforts when you're out here? I don't even know your name. My name is Valerie."

He did not reply.

"I can't believe I've made it this far on the trail. I'm a slow hiker. I get distracted, is the thing. The way the sunlight makes a pattern on the ground, or, you know, I'll watch an airplane, high up. I'll watch the thing cross the whole sky. Birds. I get very distracted by birds. Especially birdsong. My mother taught me the songs of birds. Which humans give funny translations. For example, the robin says, 'Cheerily, cheerily, cheer *up!*' Or the owl goes, 'Who cooks for *you*, who cooks for you *all*?' I mean, *I* don't think the robin sounds like it's saying 'Cheerily, cheerily, cheer up.' But the words do help a person remember—"

"I have to tell you something," he said. He stared at me, eyes wet, jaw clenched, as if tasting something bitter.

"OK," I said.

"I can't understand why I've been chosen for this. The odds of success are impossible. Traitors are everywhere. I'm going to fail. I'm going to fall on my face. Soon, it will be dark all the time."

"You just need to see a doctor," I said gently. "The things you hear, they will torture you."

"They *do* torture me," he said.

"I'm a nurse. I can help you. Let's leave, together. Let's find help."

Tears began to pour from the outer corners of his eyes. "The problem is that they know my weakness. A darkness in me calls out to them. Something nocturnal in me howls back."

I licked my lips. What to say? He was in agony. It was true, to him.

"No," I said. "You'll never join the Night Army. Not you."

"I *want* to, sometimes. It would be a relief."

He began to cry hard. Ugly, loud tears. He did not hide his face nor wipe the tears away. He cried looking straight at me, as if he were speaking his most honest words.

"Shhh," I said. "It's OK."

I unknotted my pink bandana and slid it off my neck.

"Here," I said. "Here. This is what I've used to dry my tears on my thru-hike."

He looked back and forth between me and the bandana.

"Take it," I said. "Maybe it'll help you too."

HEARTWOOD

He took the bandana and buried his face in it. I watched him, his long dirty legs bent like the hind legs of a cricket, boots untied. Everyone I'd met was grieving. After six million people die from a virus, the concept of twenty-four-hour darkness claims a kind of deranged feasibility. I watched the woods darken with less panic than I had the night before. Darkness doesn't really *fall*. It rises. Shadows fill the woods first. The pale sky darkens last. After a while, his breathing grew even.

He scrubbed his eyes with the bandana. "I have to go talk to Bill Burns," he said. "He thinks the interrogation program ended in 2007. But it's alive and well up here. They're using it as a cover. The Night Army. They're lying to Burns, you get it?"

"Yeah," I said. "I get it. I won't get in your way."

We both squinted out into the darkness.

"I'm sorry you fell into the death pit," he said.

"The—oh. That's all right."

"It wasn't meant for you," he said.

"Oh, I know."

"There are five of them," he said. "Be careful."

"OK," I said. "Thanks for telling me."

That night, I slept. The wind masked the sound of his leaving.

In the morning, he was gone again.

A note was tacked to the tree: "Back soon. Your watch. Stay vigilant."

I was untied, alone.

At my feet was my backpack.

Lt. Bev

MONDAY, AUGUST 1. SIX A.M.
DAY 6 OF THE GILLIS SEARCH.

I meet my retired buddy Mike at Melby's Diner outside Waterville. The place is already humid from the frier. Mike breathes in the scent of bacon grease like it's aromatherapy. He's already been up for several hours, waiting to meet me. He doesn't have a lot going on.

Today, he looks focused. The old Mike. "Your search is going like shit," he says.

"Thanks," I say. "I didn't know."

"I've been trying to think of other cases like it," he muses. "I remember the skier lost out that way last winter. The moose hunter lost seven days back in '08. But those were experienced woodsmen. This subject, she doesn't know the area, and she doesn't have the skills. Odds are, she's dead." I wince, though this is based on fact. "However. People beat the odds all the time. That's what separates us from other mammals—our ability to be surprising." He taps two packets of Splenda into his coffee. "Now, why do you think she hasn't set a signal fire?"

I shrug. "I don't know. Lack of skills, as you say."

"Or she's scared, yes? To do so. Why? Either she doesn't want to set the whole woods ablaze and barbecue herself, or because she doesn't want someone *else* to see her fire."

I tuck my hands under opposite armpits. "Mike," I say. "Don't tell me you're falling for online conspiracies. Please. Not you."

Mike looks at me closely. "What's going on with you? I've always admired your open mind. No one knows the variety of lost-person scenarios better than you."

"This case is like none of them. She's nowhere she's statistically supposed to be. She's either down some deep crevasse or she traveled in a totally atypical way. And *far*."

I take a scalding swallow of coffee.

"So has Cam De Luca been cooperative?" Mike asks. "Has he shown you his maps?"

"His search maps? No. He *teaches* how to search."

"No, he teaches evasion," Mike clarifies. "SERE. Survival. Evasion. Resistance. Escape. I don't hear the word 'search' in that."

I signal for the bill. "I need new ideas, Mike."

"I don't feel heard," Mike says.

"Those men are some of the best trackers in the world."

"They're also the best evaders."

"My dad served, you know," I say. "Reserves. So I know that those people at the SERE school are not out there for fun. The training is excruciating. They're doing it in case they have to lay down their lives for their—"

"You *hate* Cam De Luca. He's stonewalled you for years. I don't know what's wrong with you, Bev. Why are you being so polite? I've seen you wrestle armed men to the ground."

Gretchen brings the bill. I don't storm out. I finish my coffee, feeling my stomach twist. The old shame. In 1992, when I joined the Maine State Game Warden Service, I entered a world of men. Apparently, the leadership was worried about being penalized by the Feds for not hiring enough women. When the colonel at the time decided to hire me, he announced, "Well, if we have to hire a woman, might as well be this one." I arrived to my induction in my ill-fitting green worsted to a silence thick enough to cut. Polite? Half the time I was so polite as to be incorporeal. I knew I had to earn my space. My fellow wardens seemed to split into three equal groups. There were those who accepted my presence, those who rejected it, and those who were waiting to see which way the wind blew. Each passing day went on the scale. The first body I recovered. My first arrest. Moments of triumph were often cut short by some interaction in the woods with outdoorsmen devoted to the same behavior as my detractors. *If I tell you you're pretty, will you still give me a ticket?* Deep in the backcountry, men with red eyes muttered, *You shouldn't be out here in the woods alone, honey.* And, well, you know the story. The one who has the most to prove works harder, works until she bleeds, works all day and night, takes every call, dispenses with the weekend.

The fact is, throughout most of my life as a warden, I remained at arm's length from almost everyone. When I sat at bars or ate at lunch counters, I inspired whispered conversation. Folks didn't feel at ease to joke around with me the way they did with the male wardens. At the same time, they felt more entitled to complain to me. I lost count of the times somebody approached me during my off-hours asking, without pleasantries, "When do the fines come off coyotes?" or "Why do I gotta buy a ticket to shoot a turkey?" It's better now, with more female wardens by the day. But for many years, as a tall, quiet woman with no children, a female keeper of the woods and waters, I felt a little hypothetical, even to myself.

Mike slides the bill off the table. "Why didn't you call me earlier? You always call me when you're in a bind. I've been waiting by the phone like a teenage girl."

"Now you know how it feels," I say.

When I walk into the conference room, the team is assembled: Rob, Tanya, Cody, Arman, Detective Matt Milkovich from the state police, and Cam De Luca from SERE. Cam is sitting with his musclebound arms crossed. He doesn't look too happy to be there. He isn't a meeting type of guy. I know he's searched hard for Valerie. He suspended programming so that his faculty could comb the place looking for her. But it's a new week, and his men haven't found so much as a boot track. Maybe he wants to turn the page. He won't look at me.

Rob projects our master map on a screen, and there it is, our searched areas. A big brain of trails and grids, snaking and overlapping. A map like this could make you feel one of two ways: either reassured that we are searching the heck out of those woods, or silenced by the huge swaths of uncleared forest on all sides.

Me, I feel the latter.

"It would be good to see your maps, Cam," I say.

Finally, he looks me in the eye, surprised, and I see it, what Mike talked about, that flash of hatred I have ignored so many times. Don't I understand I am being barely tolerated? He wants credit for it.

"I know you've searched the heck out of your property," I say. "But every acre? We haven't done that on our end with twenty times the manpower."

"We've gotten pretty damned close," Cam whines.

"I don't want close."

"It's more an issue of our boundary," Rob clarifies. "Between your searches and ours, did we leave any unsearched land between us? We don't want to lose her because we've got too many agencies on the case."

Cam's jaws clamp shut. The effort not to tell me off creates some complicated movement in his trapezius muscle.

"Fine," he says. "No sweat. I'll get our maps to you today."

Then he sinks back into resentful silence.

I turn to the investigative side. "Let's hear from you, Wardens Dunning and Ouellette."

Tanya flinches. Bright as she is, I can see a familiar pallor when her name is called. She's got a handful of female wardens coming up with her, enough to flock. I've seen them huddled over bright blue drinks through the window of Applebee's.

"Cody just got back from New York," she says.

"Yeah," Cody says, refitting his sunglasses on top of his hair, which has grown more mop-like since I saw him last. "OK. I spent most of the day on Saturday debriefing Valerie's hiking partner at his home in New York City. This man, trail name 'Santo,' had to leave the trail for personal reasons in Vermont. Valerie probably wouldn't be in her current situation if Santo had been able to stay on the trail with her." We agree with a somber silence. If only. "The portrait Santo paints of Valerie is consistent with what everybody says. She made friends at every shelter. She's a slow hiker. A dreamer. Santo said that her relationship with Gregory Bouras was positive, but there were signs of strain."

"You've done a background on the husband?" Milkovich asks. "Anything funny?"

"I've been with him on and off now for days," Tanya says. "He's pretty devoted to her. He gets along well with the parents. But it looks like they were on the verge of breaking up. Valerie, um, had come to that conclusion during her hike. That her feelings for him had changed."

"And she told him?"

"She told him."

"How did he take it?"

Tanya makes a sympathetic face. "Unusually well. He took the high road."

"It's lonely on the high road." Milkovich taps his pen, smiling at Tanya. "Not much traffic. Can I talk to him with you? Work him over a little?"

"Please do," Tanya says. "You can tell me if I'm missing something."

"Great," I say, flushing with impatience. "But I want to hear about *new* leads, Wardens."

Here, Tanya goes pale again, and Cody frowns at his notepad. Rob is glancing back and forth at me and the team, worried, maybe, that I lack the grounds to be bullish at the moment.

Tanya, to her credit, pushes back. "We have followed up on over one hundred tips," she says, "and they are still coming in. Very few are credible. Several female hikers had complaints about male hikers who they felt harassed them. We're looking for those guys." She looks at me now. "Mostly, we've gotten a load of personal opinions and armchair experts. Several people claim to have had visions. Psychics. Honestly, Lieutenant, we've even followed up on those. The last one gave us coordinates where she said she was sure Valerie's body was. It was the eleventh hole on a golf course."

Milkovich laughs. The others at the table know better.

"We've gotten contradictory leads. Did Valerie make it to Spaulding shelter? Some hikers say she did, others say she didn't. It's hard to get a full picture. It's like a game of telephone out there."

She's right. There are a hundred legitimate reasons we've been so far unsuccessful. My investigators, overwhelmed with tips, have been delegating leads to a growing and unmanageable set of surrogates. Can we be sure these novice wardens and trail maintainers and searchers are asking the right questions? No. None of us can know everything or be everywhere. Worst of all, our most credible leads have turned out to be the least helpful. We'd spent the first, most important day of the search using the wrong point last seen from a stoned teenage hiker who couldn't tell one middle-aged lady apart from another. And yet I do not want to hear about it. I do not want to hear excuses, no matter how valid.

"Hold on," I say to everyone at the table. "I do not want to hear how hard this is." I thud on the table for emphasis. "I do *not* want *anyone* to waste time explaining how hard this is."

The room falls silent.

"You know what's hard? Being lost with no food left. Shivering uncontrollably day and night. Watching your body consume its own muscle. Feeling godforsaken." I stack my papers in the quiet. Nobody moves. Outside, someone drives by the window, radio blaring. "Tanya. The hiking community is playing out the scenarios in the chat rooms, right? Let's comb through those again—*again*—no matter how crazy, let's consider every angle. Everybody. Everyone. Keep your mind open. Eyes open. Arman, no more flyovers. Let's just use the chopper. Let's get lower. Let's look closer. The answer is right in front of us, but we aren't seeing it." I stand. "And, Cam, if you've got anyone missing, anything doesn't smell right to you, you've got until the end of the day to tell me."

"Or?" he says.

"Or I send a hundred pissed-off Mainers right past your bullshit signs."

* * *

HEARTWOOD

That night, I drive out to the IGA to pick up some food for myself and the team.

When I get back to my truck with my groceries, a note flutters in the breeze on my windshield. I tug it out from under the wiper.

DO YOUR FUCKING JOB YOU TWAT.

**Gregory Bouras, Live Interview,
Sugarloaf Mountain Hotel, ME, 8/1/22
Recorded by Warden Investigator Tanya Dunning
and Maine PD Matt Milkovich**

Warden Investigator Dunning: How are you doing this morning, Gregory? You sleep OK?

Gregory Bouras: No, I did not sleep OK. I was awake most of the night as usual. And you are?

Detective Milkovich: I'm Detective Matt Milkovich, of the Maine State Police. I'm the police liaison on this case. I've been pursuing leads in the greater area. Keeping an eye out.

Bouras: A cop.

(inaudible)

Milkovich: Well, we don't need to be friends, Greg. I'm just trying to help find your wife.

Bouras: Thanks. But she's been lost for a week, so I'm wondering why you're only showing up now. By the way, she's not my "wife." We don't use those terms.

Milkovich: OK. Your partner. Can I call her that?

Bouras: I use the term "supporter."

Milkovich: We should call you her "supporter"?

Bouras: Yes.

Milkovich: OK. Should we call her *your* supporter? Or partner?

Bouras: You can call us both, either one.

Milkovich: But not "spouse." Can I use the word "spouse"?

Bouras: I prefer not.

Milkovich: No to "spouse." No to "husband," no to "wife," and no to "spouse"?

Bouras: Yes. No.

Dunning: OK, guys. Let's not get—let's not get stuck in the weeds. Gregory, you were Valerie's supporter in several senses of the word. You'd been following alongside Valerie since April 21, when she started off from Harpers Ferry.

Bouras: We called each other Treasure, actually. Almost all the time.

Dunning: OK . . .

Milkovich: Should *we* refer to her as your "Treasure"?

Bouras: No. It was a private term.

Milkovich: A pet name?

Bouras: That phrase is pretty offensive, don't you think?

Dunning: It's an endearment.

Milkovich: Were you *her* pet?

Bouras: What's that supposed to mean?

Dunning: Hey, so. Guys. I think we should proceed, OK? We can just—bumble through.

Bouras: Great. So we're going to find Valerie by "bumbling through"? That's the game plan?

Dunning: That's not what I meant. Could you shut that door, Matt? Thanks.

Bouras: I mean, how am I supposed to have a frank conversation with you people, when you are *sitting* there with your laptops and your walkie-talkies and your *guns* with your—your attitude of total omniscience?

Dunning: OK, OK. Let's reset. Gregory. Matt. Let's reset. We truly want and need to hear your reflections. I can just—I can take notes in my notebook, OK? Matt, could you remove your firearm from the room?

Bouras: Can he remove his entire self from the room?

Dunning: All right. That won't be necessary, Detective. What is our common goal here? We have a common goal, Gregory. To find Valerie. Right? Right?

Bouras: Sorry. I'm sorry. I apologize. I'm sorry. I'm so tired. I feel like I've been waiting here at this hotel for *generations*.

Dunning: The hours go by so much slower for you.

Bouras: I tried to get her to quit.

Dunning: Tell us about that.

Bouras: Most hikers get faster as they go. Not Valerie. She was getting slower. But she still insisted she was going to finish this season. She was going to return to Harpers Ferry and hike south. At that pace, she'd be hiking into freezing temperatures, into winter.

But it wasn't just that. As the months wore on, she was starting to seem—I don't know—disoriented. Once, I brought supplies out to them at the trailhead. We sat and talked and had lunch. And then—ask Santo!—Valerie stood up, put on her pack, and started walking the *wrong way*. South.

Some hikers say the White Mountains do strange things to your head. People die up there all the time. Tourists and day hikers with no coats, yes, but experienced hikers too.

Dunning: The Whites *are* dangerous. Beautiful, but eerie.

Bouras: Well, they lay ahead. I knew I wasn't going to be able to help her out there. I tried to mentally prepare myself. I tried to—let her go.

Milkovich: But she came through. The Whites didn't break her. Gregory?

Bouras: She met others who helped her through the Whites. Everyone she met, she was, you know, enamored.

Milkovich: Enamored?

Bouras: I mean. They were all so bonded. Everyone out there. Everyone except me, it would seem.

Milkovich: So, she's out there, in some dangerous conditions. Bad sense of direction. Enamored with everybody and everything. You asked her to stop. But she didn't listen.

Bouras: I told her, "I can't keep supporting this. I support *you*, but

I want you to stop. Stop. Your heels are bleeding and your knees are swollen and the hardest part is still ahead of you."

She shrugged. She said she was going on with or without my support.

She thanked me for my concern.

(pause, muffled sounds)

What was she *thinking*?
Why did she need to do this so badly?

(crying)

I didn't *really* think she would try to hike the entire two thousand miles!

I thought she was just making a *statement*.

Dunning: It's OK—it's OK. Can I get you a—here.

Bouras: God, I'm tired.
I can't sleep.
I've gone through the most gruesome scenarios in my head.
In my head, I've seen her bludgeoned by a rock. By a stick. Bludgeoned by a bludgeon. I've watched men rip off her clothes and violate her. I've imagined big dirty hands around her small wonderful neck wringing the life out of her. I've seen her dragged by the foot through the brush, over stones. I've heard her screaming my name from far below in a dark cave. I've watched her bloated body float down—

Milkovich: Gregory. Gregory—

Bouras: And some people think I had something to do with it! I *know* what they say.
I'm being trolled. Mocked. Photographed.

As if I don't already loathe myself enough.

Dunning: Try not to torment yourself.

Bouras: Why? Why shouldn't I torment myself? I'm sitting here in a—in a *ski resort*, talking to *you guys*. And she's absolutely alone! She was *terrified* of being alone! She's more alone than she or I or you have ever been! I think tormenting myself is a pretty reasonable response.

And yet you guys can't find her!
With all your radios and planes and intel!
How can it be *this hard* to find her?

(pause)

I've been sober for nine years. Ever since I met Valerie.
She took me to my first AA meeting.
The reason I agreed to drive along in the support role, if we're being honest, is I didn't think I'd stay sober without Val.
That's my motive for tagging along.
Not support, really. Just need.
There. That's the truth.
Nine years.
Jesus Christ. What I wouldn't give for a drink.

Tip Line Email from Leeanne Bright, Received 8/1/22

Dear Maine Wardens,

I have been holding this story in my heart for several days. It may seem unlikely at first but all I can say is it is true. I was at the Crystal Nail Salon in Frederick, Maryland, on Friday. In walked a petite woman in sunglasses. She sat down to get her nails done, and I commented to my technician (whose name is Perri), "That looks just like a girl I went to high school with. What was her name? Oh, I remember. Valerie Gillis."

I smiled in her direction, but something kept me from saying anything. We both graduated from Frederick High School (class of '98) and of course we both moved away since then. Valerie had always been friendly. She was smart and nice. But something about the way she carried herself said, "Not now."

"Well," I whispered to Perri, "Valerie Gillis. She looks better than ever."

Later, after she left, I googled Valerie's name. I was looking for a photo to prove to Perri that I was right. Then I saw the headline. Valerie Gillis was missing.

I ran out to the parking lot. I looked around for her everywhere. I went into stores. I asked if anyone had seen her. I showed everyone her photo. I looked into cars. But she was gone.

I have been crying ever since. I wish I had said something.

HEARTWOOD

I wish I had said what I wanted someone to say to me when I was in trouble as a kid. My whole life would have turned out differently if one person had just said to me "Do you need help? Tell me what's going on. I will help you."

Thank you for your time,
Leeanne "Loli" Bright
Taneytown, Maryland

Dear Mom,

Out here, boundaries fade—hour to hour, day to day.
    Each day tells its tale to the next.
    The gray end of night is borrowed for dawn.
    According to my markings, it's my ninth day lost.
    There is a moment, halfway between dark and half-dark, when the birds sing from all points. They sing from the trees, the floor near my tent, from the sky itself, so loud that I can barely stand it. I stuff my camp towel in my ears.
    All this time without human voices has made my ears delicate.
    Birdsong floods my brain.

I want to write to you, but this morning, my right hand refuses.
    I can't grip the pen anymore.
    But I still have more to say.
    So I am going to finish this letter in the quiet of my heart.
    Mother, mother.

What happened next?
    He left me there. Crazy boy, he meant what he said. It was as if his sole function was to separate me from everyone and then leave me utterly alone. Aside from the note, the tarp, and the pair of shattered binoculars hanging from a branch, he'd taken everything with him.

It was as if I had dreamed him up.

I grabbed my backpack and unzipped it. My belongings were as I had left them. Hard stuff sack of fresh clothes, a roll of socks, headlamp, pills, toothbrush, my meager but crucial provisions, my journal, my things. I raised my head and looked out at the forest. Trees, and more trees, a boreal hall of mirrors, an unknown, unaltered wilderness where at night predators sang their discordant hymns, and trees collapsed, and the wood and the flesh and the husks were humified by an impersonal savagery.

What should I do?

I walked to the edge of his camp and found the first trap—the one I'd fallen into—and skirted its edges. Moving carefully, I tested the ground. I knew he might step out in front of me at any moment, holding his blade, changing the rules. What if this was a test of my loyalty?

Then I heard your voice.

Run! you said.

I tried to quiet my terrified heart.

And then, Mother, I ran.

I could not have stopped running if I tried. I had begun to go crazy myself. A state of panic, I guess. Crazy with lostness. Ugly running, half stumble, half crawl. Loud running. Sticks and branches snapped beneath me. Loose rocks made resonant knocks when I stepped on the high sides. My consciousness was turned inside out, rendered on my skin, in my deranged senses. Shadows felt heavy. Rounding one bend I smelled hamburgers on a grill.

I ran with a wail stuck in my throat. It was ridiculous, it was all ridiculous. Not just him, not just this—all of it—*life*—to be afflicted with the endless urge to survive. It turns out, there's almost nothing you can do to stop trying.

I stepped into wetness. A stream. I remembered a rule, a rule about following streams because streams lead to rivers and rivers lead to—somewhere. I gripped the straps of my pack, exhaling with each step, whispering, Help, help, help. Only once I left him was I afraid of him. I pictured him on his hands and knees, studying the shape of my boot print in the mud. I dodged back and forth across the stream, trying to hide my tracks. Tears streamed down my face.

The slope flattened and the stream turned into a small creek. Ahead, a pool of sunlight caught my eye. I pushed through the wall of woods until I stood at the edge of an open space. Such spaces do not exist in these woods. A clearing. From which I could signal for help. From which I could be seen.

It took a half dozen steps to realize I was sinking. I looked down. A tea-colored water seeped around each boot. I stood marooned on a sun-bleached hummock. Below me was water in all directions. The mat of dried grasses on which I stood began to bow. The surface was a false surface, a floating sponge of moss and peat and entombed trees. I lunged forward and plunged into muck, grabbing the mat in front of me as if it were a beam from a shattered ship, my body weight discharging the bog's sulfurous vapors. Panic overcame me. I stabbed for the bottom of the bog with my feet. I could stand. The bog terrified me anyhow, in its suck. Hauling my waterlogged pack, I fought my way through water and matter back toward the rim of the bog, the surface sloshing around me like a waterbed. On half-solid ground, I wrenched my legs out. One was covered in black muck, tipped with a white sock.

My foot hung aloft while I registered the sight.

The bog had stolen my boot!

Searching for my boot in the muck, I felt sharp shapes under the surface. Broken branches that felt like the horns of beasts. Head wrenched back, I grasped what felt like a shoelace and pulled. When I stood, a long, glistening worm writhed between my fingers.

A crash in the woods. I froze.

Around me, dragonflies browsed serenely.

Nurses are supposed to save people. All those people I had mended and touched over the years—broken bones and lacerations, holding closed the bleeding organs, clearing vomit from the throat, thwarting death—I would have betrayed all that and defended myself to the death against him if he made me stay here one more minute. I stopped struggling with the bog. I accepted that I would not find my boot in this death-haunted material, these stinking clots of suspended matter.

Then I heard something new. A nothing that was something. An observing silence. With muddied hands, I covered my ears. I crawled toward solid ground in terror, a terror that was not about him. Was I going to die out here?

Run! your voice rang out on the wind.

I grabbed my pack straps and began running again, running differently.

Every other step was pain.

The day dragged on as I tried to run back the way we'd come. At first, I traveled with flashes of recognition. A boulder looked familiar. A ridge. A bend. Yes, I'd been here before.

Hadn't I?

But gradually, I fatigued. I staggered with less direction,

running with a limp, deeper and deeper into my lostness. I walked uphill and downhill countless times, stuck inside some great terrestrial ambivalence.

Mom, I was ridiculously human.

I had no plan, no pattern. I was walking myself to death.

A gust of wind racked the trees, shaking me back to consciousness.

Was I passing the same woods on a loop? Was I walking in a circle? The same armies of skinny firs. The same ridges that never peaked, only unraveled. I climbed them until I descended them on some pointless far side, bringing a cascade of earth and rot with me as I fell.

And I fell a lot.

As for my socked foot, it was less of a problem than you would think.

I no longer felt it.

Then I saw a white blaze, lit with late-afternoon light.

An Appalachian Trail blaze. Someone had painted that. A living person!

The blaze was visible through a stand of trees on the opposite downslope. The marking was not like the patches of pale lichen I often mistook for blazes in my trail life. This was a bold, white Appalachian Trail blaze. I laughed out loud, jogging forward. I tried not to take my eye off the mark, but the chaos of the forest floor had to be constantly navigated. I lost the blaze for a moment between the ever-shifting trees. My socked foot fell though the root masses and rot, and I had to struggle to get my leg back.

When I arrived at the tree, the blaze was gone. I scanned the area, sweeping to one side, then to the other. I marched in a wide circle, hoping the forest that took my lifeline away would give it back.

I searched for a long, long time.

Much later, in the waning light of day, I stopped and opened my pack.

I drained my entire bottle of water.

I spread out my provisions, the bitter end of a supply only meant for three days.

Two string cheeses.

Two energy bars.

A Ziploc baggie of almonds.

A Hershey's chocolate bar.

I tore open an energy bar and devoured the whole thing.

Time passed. Spears of light streamed down on me as the sun shied behind a ridge. Halos of light lent the scene a holiness. Spiderwebs electrified. Motes sailed like comets across this last light.

I watched it like a suicide.

Maybe I was waiting for your voice to blow my way with the warm updraft of wind, calm as when you used it to coax me out of my childhood anxieties. Not the real you. The remembered orientation that borrows the word "mother."

I looked over one shoulder. Looked over the other.

The woods were washed with shadow.

Paper birch. Quaking aspen. Ranks and ranks of pine.

The infinite bosk continued.

Lena

Lena does not emerge from her apartment Tuesday or Wednesday.

She messages and she waits. She sits vigil by the Telegram window.

She has sent TerribleSilence over twenty messages.

> Dying of suspense.
> How was the meeting with our source?
> Are you there?
> Are you OK?

On Thursday, it begins to rain.

Warren calls three times, until she is driven to answer.

"I'm terribly busy," she says. "Besides, it's raining. We can't forage in the *rain*."

"You need to eat," he says. "Come to the dining hall tonight. As you say, you can't forage in the rain. My treat."

She watches the cursor of her blinking screen.

"Lena," Warren says. "Don't become obsessed. It's not good for your health."

"I'll call you later," she says.

> Please send news.
> Just a thumbs up or thumbs down.

HEARTWOOD

> Very worried now.
> I have put our work on hold until I receive further direction.

Waiting in agony will do her no good. But honestly, what would she even wear to dinner? She idly swipes through the blouses and sweaters in her closet.

None suffice.

Hours pass. She's looking out the window at a family of five trying to walk up to the Cedarfield entrance in the pouring rain, clustered under one umbrella. It's funny—when one member of the family yanks the umbrella over them, another is exposed to the rain. When a correction is made, a different family member is soaked. But they don't mind. They are laughing.

One reason Lena never goes to the dining hall is because she does not want to be asked about her "life story." How do you tell your whole "life story" on command? How long should you make it? What should be left out for the sake of politeness? What if the parts of your life that interest you the most are the least interesting to others?

She can tell her "life story," sure.

For her, it would go something like this:

A century of plunder by their three largest neighbors drove waves of Poles to immigrate to the US throughout the 1900s. Some of them settled in the small city of New Britain, Connecticut. My mother and father were two prototypical Polish Americans raised in New Britain in the 1950s just as it transitioned from a haven to a slum. Little Poland, they called it (and still do). An American city with a Polish heart, New Britain is a place of parades and bakeries, a place that still supplies Connecticut with many of its cleaning ladies. After my mother was discovered to be lying about my paternity, she became one of those cleaning ladies.

The word "Connecticut" derives from the Mohegan word "Quinnehtukqut," which means "beside the long tidal river." The Poles liked the Connecticut River because it reminded them of the Vistula. We all know what happened to the Mohegans.

The end.

As the dinner hour approaches, Lena begins to feel a sense of inevitability. She had promised Jodi she would "extend herself."

Miserably, she goes to her closet, seeking a clean blouse. She holds one up to her chest in the mirror. Her baby-fine straight silver hair is combed and pinched back at both temples with a bobby pin.

Soon, she's dressed. Her glasses are clean and she's draped a scarf around her neck. At 5 p.m. sharp, she emerges into the hall and takes the elevator down one flight. When the doors open, she drives forward slowly.

At the entrance of the dining hall, her pulse begins to race. It's only 5:05, but almost every seat is full. She can see the slender bottles of wine on the tables, jars of pink roses for each centerpiece.

She drives forward, until she is close to Warren's table.

Seated are: Warren, Juanita, Bobbi, and a new arrival she's not yet met. They are at a five-top, thank goodness. One of the round tables near the dining hall entrance.

They all turn to stare at her.

It is immediately obvious to Lena they had no idea she was coming.

"Why, *hello*," Bobbi says, hand to heart. "What did we do to receive the honor of your company?"

Stiff necks crane around them.

"Good evening," says Warren, too formally.

Lena clears her throat. "Is this seat taken?"

Warren looks between her wheelchair and the chair-chair that sits empty at the five-top. Finally, Bobbi stands and pulls away the chair-chair. Lena pulls up to the table.

"Thank you," she says to Bobbi.

Warren flushes red to the roots of his hair.

"Nice to see you, Lena," says blind Juanita.

Lena says, "You too, Juanita."

She turns to the New Girl. "And you are . . . ?"

Up close, the New Girl is rather beautiful. The apples of her cheeks are smooth. Her hair is white and airy as smoke. But she does not style it in the stiff bobs of most of the women at Cedarfield. This woman wears her hair loose. It falls past her shoulders. She wears heavy rings on several fingers and is otherwise dressed simply, in a linen tunic.

"I'm Clara," the New Girl says, accented.

Ah, a foreign-born. From where? The name is pervasive. Austria? Czechia? France?

"A pleasure to meet you." Lena shakes out her tented linen napkin. "How is everyone this lovely evening?"

Bobbi guffaws. "Lovely evening?"

Willow branches stick like dirty mops against the wet windowpanes. There is a well-timed boom of thunder.

"I never see you in the dining room, Lena," says Juanita.

"In fact, I haven't been here for years," Lena says.

"Years? How is that possible?"

"I grab things from the Bistro-To-Go all the time. It's convenient when I'm busy. And of course, before that, the dining room was closed to us all."

Juanita says, "True. I'm just glad it's open, after eating alone out of Styrofoam containers in our apartments for a whole year."

"Lena likes to cook for herself," says Bobbi. "She's a real individual."

Lena looks at Bobbi with the respect an enemy deserves. Then she shrugs. She isn't yet clear on why she never comes to the dining hall herself. It's hard to feel welcomed with all those tables surrounded with chair-chairs. Not one single gap set for a wheelchair. But that isn't all. Her aversion also has something to do with the food. Copious amounts. Clusters of pie slices and cake slices and coupe glasses of puddings. The dining room—its candlelight, its loveliness, and most of all its bounty—makes her deeply uncomfortable. She doesn't deserve it. None of them do. Why did some of them slip through the jaws of death in the last several years and some of them didn't? It was hard to avoid thinking they had been gathered at this pretty place to make it easier for the virus to kill them. They had lost eleven people in the early months. She looks anew at Bobbi. Hadn't her partner been among them?

But Warren intones, "We were talking about presidential biographies. Our favorites. Mine is Robert Caro on Lyndon Johnson. But Bobbi insists David McCullough on Adams is better. She's got me there, haven't read that one." Warren is still blushing. He looks ecstatic. He loves her, Lena sees. "Juanita's partial to anything by Ron Chernow. Which got us to whether or not it's a fair question. Meaning, do we judge the biography by the writer or the subject? For example, Adams was such an interesting *figure*. Nixon too."

"Sinners make for better stories," says Juanita. Lena nods. Juanita had been an Episcopal priest before retirement.

"I remember when the point of a biography was to praise a person," Warren says.

"I don't miss that," says Bobbi. "I don't miss all that sanctimony."

Lena clears her throat. All four look at her expectantly.

"So, do we serve ourselves or . . . ?"

Her partners explain. It's a sit-down dinner tonight. They will be served at the table. Lena is saved from the awkwardness of waiting while others rise for the buffet. Lena steals a glance at Bobbi. She is oddly touched by Bobbi's caring. What's she working at? The woman is like sandpaper.

Lena reaches for the wine at the center of the table. The others smile.

"Oh," Lena says. "Does wine cost extra?"

"It's mine," says Juanita. "I'm the only drinker at the table. Join me, please."

"What kind of wine do you like, Lena?" booms Warren.

"I like the kind with alcohol in it," says Lena.

They bring the food.

Fifteen minutes of banality pass. Beside her, she can feel Clara's shyness. An openness to talk. But it's been so long since she has attempted to get to know someone, she isn't sure how to dive in. Meanwhile, Warren and Bobbi scrutinize Ron Chernow's *Alexander Hamilton*. Of all the genres to discuss, they've picked the one in which she has zero interest. Lena feels oddly disappointed that they haven't asked her about her life after all, her past, her secrets, about Little Poland, which is a piece of real, living history not very far from where they are sitting right now. Such insular communities are full of sin, full of good stories. She could tell them stories they wouldn't believe. Her own mother was the belle of Little Poland when she was brought low by an older man. Impregnated at eighteen. A younger man was found and a wedding ensued quickly. Eight years later, the identity of Lena's biological father was revealed. He was not the soft-voiced blond man who had raised her. Her real father was the revered priest of the Sacred Heart parish, who'd recently set off a newer scandal by scrambling down another female parishioner's fire escape.

Clara touches her arm. When Lena turns, she is once again startled by the woman's face. The evening light turns Clara's eyes into sea glass.

"You haven't touched your food," Clara coos.

Side by side, they cut their chicken Dijonnaise. The meat oozes a rich oil. The mustardy sauce awakens a vicious hunger inside Lena. She stabs a morsel and eats. The feeling of the woman beside her also induces a sense of well-being. Lena wants to ask her questions. She glances over. Clara glances back.

At last, Clara leans over. "Do you know what surprises me the most?"

Lena waits, with a faint smile.

"How much *sugar* they put in ketchup," Clara says. She shakes her glorious head, but says no more.

Lena returns to her chicken. Automatically, she cuts and eats.

Ketchup? Such an ethereal woman, and ketchup is what surprises her *the most?*

Lena grabs her wine and drinks deeply.

Perhaps Lena is meant to be dead already. She is still alive due to some clerical oversight. She lingers in a fading body, one that is being erased unevenly. She still has her bowels, her grievances, and her obsessions. But she no longer has her legs, nor any fellow feeling, no patience.

"Well," Lena says, after another fifteen minutes, backing up from the table. "It's been a pleasure."

They gape at her. It's not even dessert yet.

"I am in the midst of some important research," she explains. "That is," she admits, "important to me."

"Tell us," Warren pleads. "Tell us about it."

Bobbi turns and gives him a sad look. "Lena is busy, Warren. Didn't you hear her?"

"Nice to meet you," Lena says to Ketchup. And to the table, "Thank you for sharing this meal."

Lena speeds down the hall to the elevator. She presses the button, then looks down into her hands, which are oily with butter. She waits.

She can still feel her father's touch where he blessed her forehead at Mass. This man had guided the huge Sacred Heart flock for two decades. He had baptized or buried almost every Pole in New Britain. He was also famously learned, spoke a dozen languages, and wore tailored clothes from Warsaw. Of this, Lena was defiantly proud.

The rest, less so.

Despite the fact that her biological father was apparently trying to personally repopulate Connecticut with Poles, everyone made excuses for him. After he left Sacred Heart, having been called back to Poland to assume some elevated position there, it was Lena's mother who was shunned.

Kindly Agata.

Called a whore.

The man that Lena called her father left. (Tomasz, how she had loved him.) Lena's maternal grandparents returned to Poland, and she no longer saw Tomasz's family. Her cousins, aunts, and uncles disappeared. Her mother lacked the smarts or the vengeance or the grit to acquire help or mercy. There were entire years when food was scarce, which made the absence of love or affection or community seem like a secondary loss. The two of them moved as far away from Little Poland as they could without leaving the state of Connecticut—to Torrington, the ugliest town in the prettiest corner of the state. Clearly, her uneducated mother never quite understood the concept of "states." The woman would have considered a move to Iowa or New Jersey an act of immigration. Lena's mother grew old, promiscuous, forgetful, but she was loyal to Lena until the day she died—too young, Lena was only twenty-four—of emphysema.

The elevator pistons sigh.

Ping.

The doors part.

It would not have made for a good dinnertime story anyway.

Lt. Bev

WEDNESDAY, AUGUST 3. FIVE A.M.
DAY 8 OF THE GILLIS SEARCH.

I've been so grateful for the clear weather that I didn't realize how low the rivers have gotten. Streams have slowed to a trickle. In the unseasonable heat, there's a die-off in the resort's man-made pond, where a hundred silver fish bellies float.

For us, August is the beginning of a transition. Back to life as it was. Smaller town. Mostly locals. Purple aster blankets the hillsides. Gardens swell with sunflowers, summer's farewell flowers.

When the colonel calls, I'm not surprised.

I dread it, but I'm not surprised.

"As much as we hate to say it," he says, "this search is going unfavorably. You and everybody around you is running on fumes. I'd advise against a ground search today, Beverly."

I've moved into the hotel-staff dormitory. I'm sitting on the edge of my twin bed, dressed but not really awake. Valerie Gillis has been missing for ten days.

"Yeah," I say. "I understand." I do understand his reasoning, but I disagree with his characterization. I still have fuel. Plenty. No one on my team has complained to me, so is the implication that others have gone around me to complain to the colonel? Who would do that? Rob, Cody, and Tanya are just as willing to drive themselves into the ground as I am.

"Let's take our own zero day," he says. "Order some air searches if the planes are available. Use this day to plan for one more large-scale search effort. Take your time, plan it right. Give it everything you have."

All I can manage to ask is, "Is this a downgrade?"

"No. Not a downgrade. Not yet. A postponement. Hard as it is. To hear what they are saying about us."

"Yes," I say. "Hit pieces. I don't linger over them."

"You shouldn't."

"Thank you," I say. "For more time. Because I know we are going to find her."

"You shouldn't say that either," the colonel says.

I hang up and go outside. It's humid already. The temperatures are predicted to hit ninety. That will turn the bus into an oven. I walk to the upper parking lot, the bus gleaming black, no other cars around it. It won't be too hard to call off our volunteers today. I only had ten signed up to come. A formation of geese passes silently above. Rob's truck approaches. I can see him looking at me through his windshield with concern.

To tell a family that a search is going unfavorably is the absolute worst part of my job. At 9 a.m., I walk downhill toward the resort, sick to my stomach. I don't know how this sounds, but occasionally, I'm not averse to giving myself a good crack in the face. A fast, open-palmed strike that hits out drowsiness or complacency. I sneak in a hard slap. *Goddamn you, Beverly.* Then I stop and take a couple of deep breaths before entering the building.

Other family members have joined the Gillises in recent days. They fill the spacious conference room. Janet's sister and brother-in-law have come up all the way up from Raleigh, North Carolina. Valerie's younger brother arrived over the weekend with his wife and their toddler, who runs around holding a dirty panda bear. I'm grateful for the sound of his prattle. Otherwise, the atmosphere is subdued. Each day after the teams are out, one of us stops by the conference room to touch base and answer questions. I'm early. So when I enter the room on Wednesday, the small crowd turns at once.

"Good *mor*ning," I say, with too much enthusiasm.

Except for the little boy, who is driving a toy truck along the wall, the family is gathered around the food table, looking out the picture windows at the hazy blue sky. In each face I can see their varied expectations—that I'm bringing wonderful news, that I'm bringing bad news, that I'm bringing more of the same, nothing, nothing, and nothing. Wayne raises his coffee cup.

"Lieutenant?" he asks. "Coffee?"

"Yes please," I say, heaving a sigh. Janet steps toward me, wearing a new sweatshirt from the Sugarloaf gift store. She flashes her stoic smile and opens her hands, as if to convey that she's ready for whatever I'm about to say.

Dear Jesus. How to begin?

"Sit, Beverly, sit," Janet says to me. I do as she says.

"Well." I raise my hands. "In coordination with my supervisor and my own team, we've decided to postpone a large-scale search today." I feel Janet wince beside me. "We are *not* giving up, even for one day. But the reality is that many of our volunteers have been here for days on end and have been out of work. So, we—we're facing a lower number of searchers. It doesn't make sense to produce a search that is ineffective just so that"—just so that what?—"without regrouping first. With each day, we cover more and more territory. After searching the areas bordering the trail, and all the drainages, we are now expanding the search area and searching the ridgetops. But why can't we find her? By God, I wish I knew."

I wait for someone to interject with a question or an accusation, but no one does. The Gillis search is a career anomaly, but in my time, I'd met plenty of people awaiting the discovery or retrieval of their missing loved one. Most family members start out with confidence in their loved one and in our search team. They worry, but they believe. But when a search drags on, they can abruptly switch modes and presume their lost one dead long before we do. Their questions become morbid, awkward to answer. My theory is they just can't stand it. Their flailing minds want resolution.

"We're preparing for another major search," I say. "Today, Sergeant Cross and I are putting together a list of every search club coordinator, trail manager, border officer, dog handler, every retired warden, every woodsman in the state of Maine, to plan our next search operations. If we wait until Saturday—"

"Saturday?" Bouras raises his head. "Three whole days of doing nothing?"

"No, we'll keep searching in the meantime. With small targeted search teams of wardens only."

"If we wait until Saturday—" Wayne prompts.

"We'll have a much better chance with a bigger group of rested searchers."

"Beverly," Wayne says. "Our odds of finding Valerie have, what, decreased? By how much?"

I swallow. "We've searched over four thousand acres so far. At about five thousand acres, give or take, we start to get into what's called ROW. It stands for 'rest of the world.' It's where, based on the area searched, the likelihood of finding Valerie a half mile out of the search area is the same as finding her fifty or a hundred miles out of the search area. Which means, statistically, she could be anywhere."

The group falls silent. The little boy, sensing a bad turn of events, crashes his truck onto the table, making a siren sound.

"*Wee*-ooo-*wee*-ooo. Rescue Mission reporting," he parrots. "What's your emergency?"

"Riley," his father says. "Hush."

Mystery is fine in heaven and in poetry, but on earth, mystery signals human failure.

Someone has failed to understand, to master the unknown. This is unacceptable.

There is something too mortal about unknowing. It smells like rot.

That day, I stay and talk with Wayne and Janet for hours. Nothing else seems more important. They start to tell me stories. Stories of Valerie's childhood fascination with droppings and dead animals. Stories of how she dressed up her little brother as the sister she'd wanted. At my suggestion, the other family members head off to a nearby lake for the afternoon, taking the little boy, his truck, and his dirty panda. The simple act of packing up for a swim lightens the mood. Valerie's uncle makes edgy jokes about drowning. Valerie's brother carries his little boy like a machine gun, shooting bullets out of his head, while the child howls with laughter.

Life goes on, it just does.

After they clear out, we stay. Janet blinks the tears from her eyes. "The worst part is the reruns," she says. "I mean, going over what I should have said and what I should have done. As a mother. Going back to some stupid little incident. Decades ago. How crestfallen she looked when she overheard me joke to another parent after ballet class that we weren't going to get rich off her dancing."

"She was a terrible dancer," Wayne says, leaning against the plate glass window where he stands, as if he might be closer to his daughter there. "She really was."

Janet laughs. "But she was a born poet. She would say the most beautiful things as a child. They'd just fall out of her mouth. Once, when she was trying to describe how sad she was—we were leaving the beach cottage we used to rent, remember it, Wayne? Anyway. She was sad to leave. I said, 'I'm sad too. I have a pit in my stomach.' She said, 'I feel a pain in my back where my wings were.'"

"Wings." Wayne shakes his head.

Janet blinks back tears. "She was wide open. She was so *sensitive*. She had to be talked through her anxieties. That's why we appreciate Gregory, don't we, Wayne? He's not perfect, we know that, but he is so patient with her. Just as she was with him, with his sobriety. I'm a doer. I didn't always have the patience with little Val. Did I, Wayne?"

"No mother in the history of the world has been perfect," I say. "And no daughter either."

"I was against her taking this hike," Janet says. "I believed she was underestimating how hard it would be. I just wanted—after all she's been through at the hospital—I wanted her to rest. We fought about it. She said, 'You don't think I can do this.' I said, 'No, I don't.' What I meant was 'Please don't.' But I was playing tough. I didn't mean it. The comment seems unforgivable to me now."

Janet lowers her gaze to the table.

It's been a while since I've made it to church, but in my heart, I'm still faithful. Because of this, I do not believe in such things as "unforgivable mistakes." God knows you are a broken sinner and loves you anyway. If I didn't believe that, I don't know how I would have endured being myself—a girl-monster in a peach dress, the only female in the law enforcement training program, the one who left Ma behind in Massachusetts even though I knew she depended on me, the lady warden eating solo at the two-top.

God loves you anyway. God hurts when you hurt.

But the nonbeliever is in a bind, because without God, who forgives? Human beings are pretty unforgiving. The law certainly isn't forgiving. Forgiveness needs a messenger.

Some folks say, "Forgive yourself." But who the hell can do that?

It's a goddamned conflict of interest.

"Janet," I say. "Somehow, despite the agony you all are in, you still manage to be kind. You *are*. To me, the team, and to one another. Look how your son plays with his boy. Look at this table of food you keep full. For us. Even in this situation, you worry about others. That's incredibly rare. It takes a very special person." I squeeze her hand again. "This is a somewhat awkward confession, but I have thought, more than once, how nice it would have been to have you for a mother."

I gesture for Wayne to sit, and I put a hand on his shoulder. "Listen. There was nothing either of you could have done to prevent whatever happened to Valerie. If she fell, if she's sick or injured, or just lost to the degree that she is, there is no way such a thing could have been foreseen and stopped. Do not fault or blame yourself in *any* way."

Wayne nods, maintaining his expression of rational neutrality. Then, as if a curtain has dropped, he starts to cry. They lean toward one another like two trees bent by the wind.

"Santo" Phone Call, 8/4/22, 9:30 p.m.

How's it shaking, Warden?

I know it's weird for *me* to call *you*.

I don't have anything to report. I just—thought I'd—

Cody Ouellette: I'm glad you called. You can call me anytime.

You know, I had to look up what a "game" warden is.

First I thought, "What a fun job. Games!"

Well, let me tell you, I did not know there were cops in the woods.

Might have made me think twice, Cody.

Cody Ouellette: Ha. Yeah. We're watching you! People call us all sorts of things. Deer cops. Fish cops. Dickheads . . .

Well, people are always happy to see *me* coming.

"UPS? Hey, honey! Yoo-hoo! Over here!"

Suddenly, everyone's home.

But—but—

But recently, it's been hard to motivate myself. Just to get up and get to work. I can't think straight. I've got to talk myself through the most basic tasks. Like I'm a little kid. "That's a toothbrush. Pick it up. Put some toothpaste on it. Good job."

Things feel wrong.

I eat, and I eat, but I don't feel full.

I stand in front of the fridge at night . . .

Yo, Cody, if you're not supposed to eat after 8 p.m., why's there a *light* in the *fridge?*

(laughter)

You know I'm just fucking with you.

Cody Ouellette: I know.

So there's really no sign of her yet?
   Nothing?
   No clues at all?

Cody Ouellette: I'm sorry. I wish I had better news. We can't understand it either.

We're still searching. On Saturday, we're going to have our biggest search yet—

I know you're trying.
   And I know how much trail there is. Believe me.
   But I feel like—I feel like—
   I can't believe she's out there by herself.
   I shouldn't have left her there.
   I shouldn't have left the trail.

Cody Ouellette: Ruben, no. You had to leave.

Oh yeah? I did? For what? For the funeral of a man whose favorite hobby was tearing me down? I leave my loving friend alone in the woods to go pay a tribute to a man who never showed up for me once?
   He did, however, do an uncanny imitation of me laughing . . .

Cody Ouellette: It's not your job to find Sparrow. It's ours.
   She just got lost. It's no one's fault.
   Besides, thank God you were hundreds of miles away, man.
   Think about it. If you were anywhere nearby, who would everybody be accusing?

If I were nearby, she'd be safe!
We kept each other safe.
We were *partners*.
We kept. Each other. Safe.

(pause)

When you're in the backcountry, you can let down, you know? Rocks don't comment on what you look like. The sky doesn't care how slow you hike. No mirrors out there either. Your body matters, but not how it looks.
It was a gift.
I wanted to tell all my people, my Bronx people, "You gotta come see this! These woods are ours too. These woods are *everybody's*."

Cody Ouellette: You can go back and finish. When you're ready, you can get back on the trail. You don't have the finish the AT in one—

I know. But there's a problem now.
I miss her. It hurts. I feel that hurt.
Missing her shows me that I don't miss him.
I don't miss him. Pops.
You know why?
I never had him.
I can't miss him because *I never had him*.

(pause)

I have this crazy theory about why y'all can't find Sparrow.
What if she's changed shapes? Like, transformed? Into an actual bird. All those people out there searching for her, and she's flying above them.
And she can see everything.
And she can understand everything.

Cody Ouellette: Are you all right, Ruben? Do you have someone you can talk to down there? A minister or a counselor?

I *am* talking. I'm talking to you!

Tell you the truth, man, I feel like you know me pretty well. Nobody ever sat around interviewing me, Cody. You brought out all my deepest, darkest shit.

I'm not stupid, though. I know it's your job, man.

Cody Ouellette: It's more than that. It's more than a—

All right, all right. Get a hold of yourself now, Warden!

Don't lose your edge. The woods will be lawless. Those deer will be gearing *up*. They'll be like, "We are here to cull *you*, motherfuckers."

(laughter)

It's all right, really. I'm all right. I'm going to be fine.
I am fine!
Now go save somebody, please.

Tip Line Email from "Cold Pop," AT Hiker, Received 8/5/22
Shelter log entry found at Morgan Stewart shelter, Holmes, New York.

"Ode to My Spork"
by Sparrow

(for Santo)

O spork! With your spoon face
And your spiked lips
You are the centaur of utensils.
What's for dinner?
Never fear.
Spork: you scoop AND spear.

Brave, useful spork!
Backcountry soldier,
Stalwart, winner.
But like a lot of us,
You are a freak in the front country,
Where no one invites you to dinner.

Lena

The heat arrives on Friday. Much discussion has been devoted to the heat wave. For days, Lena heard people talking about it in the hallways and common spaces. Residents have been advised to stay inside. But Lena is developing an aversion to her own apartment, where her cursor blinks, her computer screen stares. She believes both TerribleSilence and Valerie Gillis to be in grave danger, and yet there is absolutely nothing she can do to help either of them. Uselessly, she cruises the hallways. Down in the lobby, the old people watch the landscape as if they might *see* the heat rolling up, like tidewater. When a face turns idly her way as she passes, she nods. But to a one, each fellow resident knits their brow and turns back to the window.

Whether out of pride or exhaustion, Warren does not call or visit.

Lena reads on her balcony. Her scalp sweats. Occasionally, a dry breeze gusts like the air out of an open oven.

At the dinner hour, two teenage girls, slouched like tulips, stroll up the Cedarfield walkway. They both wear oversize sunglasses and cheap dresses. Somebody's grandchildren, joy of joys. Or high school kids doing community service.

Lena herself was a horrible teenager. Christine was much nicer to Lena than Lena was to Agata. Christine was—is—always was a nice person. Not nice as in "bland," but as in calm, understanding. Everyone liked Christine—teachers, other children, her stepsiblings, cashiers, wildlife. Lena smiles, remembering the child staying out for hours collecting quarters for UNICEF, the cardboard box heavy as a barbell.

When puberty came, Lena's notebook revealed the normal developments: "Breast buds visible through shirt, trip to JCPenney suggested." "C buys feminine products w/ own money. Keeps it secret. Period 12 yrs. 5 months." Christine remained an innocent, in many ways, a nice girl, even after she achieved sexual maturity, which occurred around sixteen years of age. At that point, it was *Lena* who felt racked by change. Her emotions took the course of a six-seater airplane in a headwind. Nauseating changes in altitude. When Christine asked to go out with friends, Lena often acquiesced. But more times than not, Lena would end up driving around looking for her. Casing the houses where Christine had said she was going and where it did not appear that anyone was home. When Christine came home at night, Lena would analyze. A long subtle sniff of the coat. Observation of the walking. Lena stood and watched while the girl drank a glass of water. Why so thirsty? Conversation was strained. Lena never came out and accused Christine of the betrayals of which she began to suspect her.

All that changed when she met *him*. Emboldened in her attitude, lazy with her lies. Came home smelling of pot smoke, hair mussed. She met Lena's evaluating gaze, a flint in her eyes.

Christine was only eighteen when she informed Lena that they were going to elope. The same damned age as when Agata met the priest.

Legally, there was nothing Lena could do to stop them.

But, oh, she tried. Oh, the words Lena had said.

Vicious words that set them all on fire.

Conveniently, she only remembers Christine's:

If I have to stay here one more day, I'll die. Your love is poison.

Lena only met him once, the day he came to the door to get Christine's things. Tall, slender, sallow, tricky looking. Denim jacket, faux-fur cuffs. Shit car, flip-up lights. It was in this chariot that her daughter was taken away. In the moment when Lena might have said goodbye—the girl was leaving, bags in the car—Lena went into her bedroom and closed the door.

It was a cold comfort that Lena was right; the marriage crumbled. Christine returned to the States a decade later, a childless divorcée and a trained nurse. She took a job in New Hampshire and began to see a therapist. Lena encouraged it. She herself doubted the merits of therapy, but she recognized that some people enjoyed unburdening themselves. Why, then, when Christine was free of her marriage, a self-supporting grown woman, did she begin to say crazy things?

I don't want to talk about that. I have a right to my own privacy.
I am not an object for study.
Maybe you should start examining yourself instead of me.
You could ask yourself, "What part did I play in all this?"

Christine started to employ psychobabble.

Jung said that until you make the unconscious conscious, it will direct your life and you will call it fate.

Lena shouted, "Don't *quote* at me. I am an educated woman."

The implication infuriated Lena, that there was a fatal flaw in her significant intelligence.

"Here's a theory for you," Lena had said. "*Omnis cellula a cellula.* It's Latin for the theory of cellular regeneration. 'All cells come from preexisting cells.' The prince you married? He was a replica of the others. Tomasz, the priest, your own self-obsessed father. I warned you. And you walked right into it. Shame on you."

Christine didn't call for a while after that.

Not long after, the axe fell:

I would like to suspend contact for a little while.
I know that makes you feel bad, Mom.
I am not a bad person for asking for what I need.
I have a right to ask for what I need.
"This is ridiculous!" Lena laughed. "I'm your mother!"
Lena disregarded the embargo. She called frequently.
For years, she called.

Hello?

A ping from the desktop. At last! Telegram!
Thank God.
Lena goes to her desktop, heart pounding.
She straightens her hair, as if TerribleSilence can see her.

>THERE YOU ARE!
>Where have you been??
>I've been out of my mind!!!
>Are you well?
>What happened at the bar?

I don't know who you are.
But you seem like a friend to Daniel.

Lena's hands freeze above the keyboard. She does not know how to respond to that.

If you are truly a friend to Daniel, you
will understand that he cannot write to
you anymore.
He is not here.
Please have mercy and understand.

HEARTWOOD

Lena hesitates to believe this voice. She types.

> Where did he go?

He went to get help.

> For Valerie?

Who is Valerie?
I don't know what Danny told you.
He's not well.

But this is senseless. Not well? Who even *is* this person, this euphemizer, this invader of privacy? This person who has clearly hacked into her friend's Telegram.

And what of the timing of this interference? Days after a secret and dangerous meeting? Wouldn't the military like to shut him up? Shut them both up?

> I'd like to interface with him directly,
> if possible.

You can't. Given his condition, these
messages upset him.
They are bad for his health. He's being
treated now. He's getting help.
Please. If you care about Danny, do not
contact him again.
Please find it in your heart.

> I think there is a misunderstanding.
> Look at his Reddit page. He has
> numerous images of his foraging
> work. He just posted last week.

Oh he knows a lot about the woods.

AMITY GAIGE

And computers.
He's a brilliant young man.

                Is he at his zero-waste homestead?

You mean his campsite out near
Black Nubble?
No he's not there.

    Lena pauses. "A lot about the woods"? TerribleSilence can tell a wild carrot from hogweed, a true morel from a false one. He *is* brilliant, the hacker got that right. She thinks of the photograph of him pointing out redbuds in the spring. His trim ginger beard, like that Irish German actor who played Rochester in the 2011 version of—

                Are we talking about the same person?

My son's name is Daniel Means. He's
21 years old. He's struggled with mental
illness his hole life. In the pandemic things
went downhill. We had to keep him at
home. We lost touch with his doctors. He
sometimes stops his meds.

. . .

But he's at Dorothea Dix Psychiatric now.
We did it for his own good.
We're worried about him and that he's
going to hurtt himself or someone else.

. . .

I know that you don't know me, but you
will have to take my word for this.
I love my son and I need to protect him.

HEARTWOOD

Lena laughs shrilly and grabs for her tea. She upsets the cup. Tea goes running off the side of her desk. She watches it for a moment, her cursor speechless.

I'm sorry for whatever Danny said or did
or whatever promises he made to you.
He's just a kid, forgive him.
I am sorry.
Best wishes.

Lena stares at the window of blue light on her desk. She toggles to his Reddit page—Danny's page. She scrolls through his posts, seeking confirmation of her rightness even as she experiences the inarguable knowledge of a breach of faith. Were these not real photos of real mushrooms? "I don't want a mother," he had written. "I don't want to be 'mothered.'" Of course he didn't. His mother was right there, worrying herself sick. Rapidly, everything starts to evaporate before she can separate it, everything adjacent to him, including herself with him. Truth is the bird on the high wire that you didn't notice. She finds the photo of him and his redbuds. What stupid, sappy affections she'd attached to that face. That borrowed face. A real face, but someone else's. If she looked hard enough through the internet, she could find out who the face belongs to. Perhaps it *is* the Irish German actor who played Rochester in the 2011 film version of *Jane Eyre*. Is the actor, in fact, the person her imagination had supplied this whole time, whispering to her across her desolation?

He's just a kid, forgive him.

As if by an impersonal force, the mug she uses for pencils goes flying across the room and breaks in half at the foot of the patio door. Next, the burl of a tree that she uses for a paperweight. She swipes all the papers off her desk with her arm. Maps and diagrams and handwritten pages flurry to the floor. Grunting, she pushes the books off the desk. They land in inarticulate thumps. Curiosities found foraging smash to the floor. An oriole nest threaded with horsehair. An old Coke bottle filled with quail feathers. She rocks the desk but cannot tip it. Finally, she seizes her keyboard. She heaves it at the wall behind her monitor. It crashes cheaply, spraying letter keys, then hangs from the back of the desk, swinging by its cord.

Lena rolls over the disorder. Out to the patio. She sucks air in and out. *Smell the flowers, blow out the candle.* The hot breeze rises. Red taillights. Guests leaving, staff leaving, everyone leaving. In her near view, two women laugh under a cone of streetlight in the parking lot. Darkness falls before she trusts herself to go back inside.

I am now a connoisseur of the eye level.

The forest floor outside my tent flap is a miniature world. Seedlings spread their threadlike rootlets through the dark soil. Beetles trundle between the tiny trees. There is another world below me where the trees spread their taproots for miles. I imagine a hammock of root hairs holding me up.

I'm eleven days lost.

Moss! Have you ever looked closely at the stuff? It paints my clearing ancient green.

How does moss thrive in these shadows, this diffuse light?

Nothing reaches it directly. Not even rain.

Moss drinks vapors from the air.

When I grow up, I want to be a moss.

Sometimes I brave the mosquitoes and I pull myself out of my tent just to knead my lush moss mat. Such colors. My moss is a juicy emerald green, but below Near Rock, there are tufts of yellower, pickle-colored mosses. In my wanderings, I have seen mosses bright as turquoise. Rocks covered in blackish, peppercorn moss could pass for heads of human hair.

I know, I know. How strange, to focus on the beauty of this place.

It can't be a good sign.

Sleep comes easily, often.

    In the middle of the night, I hear another search plane.

    But when I wake up, a mosquito whines in my ear.

    There's one square left of my chocolate bar.

    I've saved it. To show myself my own willpower.

    I hold the morsel in my hands like a holy relic.

Cold, cold, cold, I'm cold all the time.

    I've got both my sweaters on. Both pairs of socks.

    I shiver constantly. I can't tell you this.

    What's going on metabolically is invisible but I know. My body gnaws on itself. First it consumes stored fats and proteins. Next it will break down muscle for fuel. My arms have grown skinny, strange to my own eye. When I reach for things, my arms seem to belong to someone else.

    And eventually . . .

    Well, the heart is a muscle.

I've been thinking about Halloween, strangely. Near my tent, I hear squirrels kicking in the leaf litter. It's the sound of Halloween. Children dragging their robes and capes and funny shoes through the crisp October leaf fall.

    You'd think an anxious child like me would hate Halloween. But Halloween was the one night I *wasn't* scared. I'd hear those footfalls in the leaves, and I'd squeal. They're coming! The trick-or-treaters are coming! Filmy ghosts blew like molted skin from the trees. There was a graveyard for every house.

    From the upper window of our house, I could see them walking through the dusk, in reverse birth order, babies first—the pumpkins, the mice, the Pooh bears ... Next, the robots, the Supermans, the prepubescent witches. It would be another hour before the older kids came out, their faces hidden behind rictus masks, eyes swimming behind the rubber eyeholes—gorillas, disgraced politicians. I'd be safely inside before they walked down the middle of the streets howling.

At Halloween, I was only Scooby-Doo scared. Meaning, the terror would be relieved with a flourish of meta-knowledge.

It was all lights and mirrors!

You rotten kids!

I am standing in the middle of the Green Sea looking up at the sky when I hear your voice, Mom!

Look down! you say. *Eat!*

(You sound like birdsong. In fact, you may *be* birdsong. Sometimes you squawk. Sometimes you sing.)

I look down at the thick carpet of plants that cover the Green Sea.

I think, You want me to eat those?

Then I kneel down and feel around in the thick, glossy leaves.

Berries!! There are berries hidden underneath the white flowers. A cluster of three juicy drupes under each flower. I drop to my hands and knees laughing. I rake through the plants in my slow, goofy way.

The berries are delicious and creamy and faintly sweet.

The seeds are tiny. I crunch them up. I harvest the entire crop.

Then I sit against Dead Tree, legs out, almost—

Sunday summer drives, is that a thing anymore? Drive far enough out of any American city and you'll find fields of undulating rows. Corn, hay, tobacco. Fragrant hills dotted with shadow-casting bales. Shop signs hung crooked. Jelly glasses filled with cut flowers for sale by the honor system. Orgies of ants crawling over an overturned ice cream cone.

It all seems kind of beautiful now.

In the back seat I used to try and keep up with your grown-up conversation, but it seemed so trivial. I felt bad for you adults. Your talk was filled with inanities. You ate your breakfast fast, like dogs. You were married to clocks. Work relieved you. When I left for school, I pictured you and Daddy standing on opposite sides of a featureless wasteland with all my friends' parents, breaking rocks into smaller rocks all day long.

But there was nothing more comforting than listening to you prattle on from the front seat, while I in the back seat, staring at the mesmeric yellow lines and the rise and fall of the horizon, went limp in the arms of the world.

Does it bother you that I never wanted children of my own? Maybe in private moments you think it speaks poorly of you or of your mothering. But the opposite is true. My choice reflects my awe of mothers. After all, as an anxious child, I understood the masochistic level of exposure a mother takes on the moment her child is born, how agonizing her position. Your response to life's chaos was to over-function. You were a taskmaster, a list maker, a toer-of-the-line. Like mothers the world over, you labored simultaneously on multiple fronts, clocking in at work while still managing a family. (Sick child/flat tire/dirty grout/empty fridge.) Thank you for being conflicted. Thank you for how godawful you looked certain mornings. For your occasional deranged soliloquies of resentment. Honestly, they made me love you more.

Thank you also for playing make believe. For allowing me to think that the universe was hospitable, and people decent, and death distant, even when you knew that someday I would consider these ridiculous illusions.

Your love dug me a kind of trench, a groove in the universe where I still go to mourn.

It's hot this morning. I wake to the smell of pines in the sun.

I poke my head out of my tent.

Is the creek quieter? I can't hear it.

I've waited too long to leave. Let's face it.

I cannot imagine leaving my tent.

Besides, I've grown attached to my creek. Its sustenance and its sound. It makes me happy that the creek runs all day and night, constant, carrying old rain.

I reach for my water bottle—empty.

No problem, I say. I reach for the other.

But that bottle is empty too.

My clearing looks different, paler. I reach out to touch my moss mat and I recoil. The soft fronds have crispened, brittle at the tips.

Have I been asleep for days?

I rake my fingers through the dirt of the forest floor.

Dry dirt, like tailings from a mine.

It does not rain and it does not rain.

The moss looks disappointed.

Almost as I watch, the tiny leaves retract, folding inward. The moss readies itself to wait for the rain's return, however long that might take. The moss is suspended. Suspended life.

I remember reading somewhere that dried mosses can be revived with a sprinkle of water after years in a specimen closet.

I smile, imagining the first drink after years of thirst.

I lay back down in my tent. My haunt. My den.

I feel like I am living inside an orange uterus.

My eyelids grow heavy. I am lulled by a feeling of cosmic indifference.

A desiccation.

That's when you start screaming like a harridan.

STAND UP!

GET UP, VALERIE!

STAND. UP.

GO GET WATER.

SAVE YOURSELF.

OK, OK, Mom, I say. *Jeez.*

I promise you that I will. I mean it at the time.

Lt. Bev

SATURDAY, AUGUST 6. SIX A.M.
DAY 11 OF THE GILLIS SEARCH.

Today marks the largest search force in Maine Warden Service history. Eight K-9 teams. Six horse-mounted searchers. Three aircraft. Two hundred sixteen souls. Most of them are standing in front of me, backlit by headlights under the dawn sky. I'm standing on the rear bumper step of someone's truck. My dirty hair is pulled back. No hat, empty hands. I can still make out the faces in the crowd, and I can see the first streak of dawn as it bores through the darkness. I don't say anything for a moment as they talk and jostle. I'm taking them in. Ask any of them about the probability of finding Valerie Gillis today. They will say 100 percent. On one level, they are right. We never give up. If we don't find Valerie today, we will never stop looking. We will look for her remains with the same dedication that we looked for her living body. I have spent the last two days awake, discussing search assignments with my team, my ear glued to my phone confirming volunteers. But suddenly, I have no interest in rousing speeches. I don't believe in 100 percent. I've lived fifty-seven years, long enough to know.

Rob clears his throat. The group has fallen silent.

"Well," I say, as my breath boils in the headlights, "I've stood up here before. Exactly one week ago, I stood up here and I told you we were going to find her. And we didn't. We had perfect conditions, favorable chances. But we didn't find her." I shove my hands in my jacket pockets and shrug. "We didn't find Valerie using some of the best search clubs in the country. What could I say now that would really sound true, you know? Another kind of person might give you some kind of battle cry. I don't know. That's not me. We don't have favorable chances."

I look down at Rob, who looks dismayed. He screws up his face as if to say, "What the hell are you doing?" A geared-up volunteer says something to scattered laughter. I keep my eyes fixed on the rear of the crowd, on the seam of the tree line against the sky.

"But I have studied lost-person behavior for my whole life," I say. "Some of the people I've searched for were experienced outdoorsmen. You know the kind. That crack bowhunter, the guy who can snowshoe for miles, or who can free-climb a wall of ice . . . But sometimes, even those guys don't survive getting lost. Those guys, I've found them drowned from crossing a river with too much gear. I've seen them travel directionally right across roads that would have taken them home, just out of pride. It's not always who you'd bet on that makes it." I shake my head. Rob is now shifting nervously from foot to foot, scanning the crowd. For some reason, they're still with me. A couple of volunteers are nodding. "Some lost people don't have the skills but instead they have something else. I don't know what to call it. Heart. They survive because of their love of life or of the dear ones in their mind. They stay present. They keep their eyes open. Often, when these people are rescued, they report feeling a sense of wonder out there. For the moments they had left. For the privilege of being alive at all."

A breeze crosses the crowd. Leaves whiffle. It is quiet.

"And *that's* who you're looking for," I say. "*That's Sparrow.*"

"That's right," someone says in the rear.

Another voice whoops. The crowd shifts.

I see Mike in the crowd. When our eyes meet, he gives me the Vulcan hand signal. I see Cody, his cap pulled low, his eyes wet.

"Sparrow is waiting for you," I say, shrugging. "So go find her."

The day is now bright, and Wayne and Janet Gillis are passing out hot oatmeal and coffee to late arrivals. Gregory Bouras is standing beside them. He's been requesting to search in the field for days. He wants to see the terrain himself, to understand how Valerie could be so lost. Finally, I relent and put him on Rudy Bradley's team and tell Rudy to personally watch over the guy. "Don't let him out of your sight," I say. "Else we'll be searching for him too." As Rudy gathers his things to lead the last team out, Gregory stares at the outdoorsmen in his group with the big sad eyes he must have used to win over Valerie.

We don't know Valerie, but at this point, we feel like we do. We've heard so much about her. I glance over at Rob, who is surrounded by Bradley's team, describing the boundaries they're to follow. In some ways, I know Valerie Gillis as well as I know Rob. I know that Valerie has a high, sweet voice, almost that of a girl. I know she was sweeper on her high school soccer team in her boring Maryland suburb. I know that she has a weakness for white chocolate and country music. I know she's afraid of the dark.

Suddenly, I feel a chill in my scalp, like I do before rain, a kind of physical fragility that augurs poorly. I fight off the feeling. I'm the search leader. You don't send 216 people out to cross rushing rivers and hike ankle-breaking terrain for a lost cause.

"Rob!" I whistle over the remaining handful of volunteers waiting for assignment. He looks up. "I'm going to go patrol Route 27. Back in a bit."

HEARTWOOD

I get in my truck, turn off the radio, and drive in silence.

Most bodies cannot handle this work past sixty. For me, that's three years away. As a lieutenant, I don't have to hike long miles. But my presence is still often required in remote places. It would be a source of lasting shame to swamp my boat or break an ankle or have a heart attack while I'm out in the field. Every warden dreads the moment when they're the nearest law enforcement officer to some domestic dispute that comes in over dispatch while they're in town. You haven't fired your gun in years, but if you're there, you go.

Retirees get a pension, about half a paycheck. They cover the rest by taking up a new career. Some folks get their pilot's license, but I have zero interest in taking to the skies. On the other hand, I'd rather die than strap on a Walmart bib. Old people stay tough in Maine. I want to be one of those ninety-year-old women I drive past in the backcountry, stacking wood, living off crab apples and grouse parmesan. I figure that because I'm tough, because I have been tough and hardworking since I was a kid, I can just go on being tough, because being tough has gotten me this far. How does a warden age? My single predecessor moved to Florida the minute she retired back in the aughts. I've got no women ahead of me to say.

I drive fast, scanning the blurred woods along Route 27, my heart skipping a beat whenever boundary ribbons flash between tree trunks. Those ribbons are the same color as her bright pink bandana. I keep almost seeing her in the woods.

"Keep it together, Beverly," I say through gritted teeth.

I drive south, long beyond the search area, until I'm just driving, driving through Maine, like any neutral visitor, in and out of the village of Kingfield, New Portland, past Maggie's Moose Lodge, Nowetah's Indian Store & Museum, past Gagne & Son Masonry

Supply (NOT ALL CONCRETE IS CREATED EQUAL!). I finally pull into a convenience store and ask if they've got any cases of cold soda in the back. Then I turn the truck hard back Carrabassett way, the soda beside me. An hour later, I pull into the Appalachian Trail parking area on Route 27. I back my truck in so that I face the tunnel of trees hikers pop out on before crossing the road, the same view Gregory Bouras had as he waited for Valerie many days earlier. I sit there in a state of near lunacy, daring her to emerge.

My personal cell starts buzzing. I look at the caller. It's Kate again. I decline the call and tuck the phone back into my cup holder, but it immediately begins to vibrate again.

Finally, I answer.

"I know, I know," I say. "I'm terrible. I owe you a call. But today is the very, very worst time—"

"She's dying," Kate says. "That's all I want to tell you. They say tomorrow, maybe the next day. I understand you might not make it here to say goodbye."

"Wait. Ma's dying?"

There's a pause. "Yes, Ma. Our *mother*. Didn't you—haven't you at least listened to my messages, Bevie?"

"I did. I have. But I had to put it off my mind. We've got—we've got the biggest lost-person search in Maine history going up here today."

"I know how needed you are," Kate says. "The good you do. That's why I can never be mad at you. I'm not telling you to come home. I mean, it's like she's already gone. She wouldn't even know it was you. But it felt wicked shitty not to let you know. Not to even *call*."

"You were right to call. Thank you. I want to come say goodbye. But it's not going to be today."

"And what about the DNR? They need to know."

I stare out the windshield at the tunnel of trees before me, the poplar leaves flashing their silver undersides at the slightest breeze.

Ma was a good person. Just lost. I never wanted her goodness to be measured by whether she was good to *me*. As a teenager, I was disappointed about the pills and how I couldn't count on her. I understood that if others knew about her helplessness at home, they would think poorly of her. And if they knew, I would die from the unwanted attention. Worst of all, I would have to admit that much of what I'd gotten from her wasn't really goodness as much as postures of goodness. Her well-groomed cameos, her empty questions. I guess I'd always known that what I was protecting was a kind of cliché, a wish worth a penny.

Tears brim over my eyes. I dab them with a Dunkin' Donuts napkin.

"I'm sorry, Kate."

"Sorry about what?"

"I'm sorry I've been hiding. I've been hiding from myself, not you."

Kate is silent.

"I love you, Kate."

"I love you too, Bevie."

"And of course—yes. Yes to the DNR. Whatever you and Faith think is right, I stand behind you. You're the ones down there. I agree that Ma's pain has gone on long enough."

Was her life one long stretch of misery? Maybe. Did I help? Not much.

"Oh, Bev. Are you going to be OK?"

For some reason, I think of Naukeag Lake. Movie night at Naukeag Lake with Ma before it became members-only. We used to sit there on a blanket on the hard sand watching some Gene

Wilder vehicle with the other locals. I was maybe six or seven, my sisters not yet on the scene. We both loved that stupid lake. It had terrible circulation and was riddled with nuisance algae even back in the '70s. Dragonflies buzzed around the duckweed, laying their eggs, their bodies brighter green than beetles, brighter green than June itself. I remember Ma's delighted face in the projector light. Happiness—rare as it is, fragile as it is, its sightings achieve a kind of private fame. Look, here I am, still talking about it.

Lena

The next morning, as promised, the heat worsens.

The cooling system strains to reach the bodies on all four floors.

The apartment is still a wreck. Lena cannot clean it herself because she cannot get down on hands and knees with a dustpan. Nor can she ask for help. Jodi will send her straight to assisted living if she sees this place. She rolls over her printouts and maps and skirts the larger objects. Her wheels crunch over the deconstructed curiosities. The broken keyboard pieces bring home the memory of yesterday's betrayal, as if the scattered letters spell out his name. She's still wearing what she wore yesterday. She avoids the mirror.

The injunction to stay inside remains, but she has a constitutional freedom of movement. She won't be able to stand a day trapped inside. She must go out. She grabs a floppy hat but brings nothing else with her. No key card, no water. As if she does not plan to return.

She waits by the elevator, braced. When the elevator door opens, she sees that it is occupied. In fact, it contains a person Lena actually likes—Juanita. Lena hesitates to address Juanita. The moment passes, and she tucks her chair in the opposite corner. The bell dings, the doors slide shut.

Juanita sighs. "Hi, Lena," she says.

"Hi, Juanita." Lena laughs edgily. "How did you know it was me?"

"You're the only one who tries to hide from me."

"Well," she says. "I should know better."

The elevator descends.

"I'm going outside," Lena says.

"Stay cool," says Juanita. "It's going to be a hot one."

A long moment passes.

"You know, Lena," says Juanita. "Every time I see you, I get a little mad at you."

"Oh?"

"Sometimes it seems as if you think you are the only one around here with grief or pain. Is that what you think?"

The elevator stops but, as if it itself is old, pauses before opening.

The doors wheeze open.

"That's not what I think," Lena whispers.

In birdsong, regional dialects exist. The crow with the southern drawl. The wren with a brogue. The white-crowned sparrow in this part of Connecticut sings a distinctive local song, one that diverges from accepted recordings.

It sounds to Lena like: "Don't *for*get yesterday-day-day."

Quite beautiful.

She sits by the feeder in the courtyard, in full sun, next to the empty bench. The heat is immediately oppressive, like a physical weight. She can feel her skin recoil, her heart strain. Lena disapproves of bird feeders. They are not only a health hazard to the birds, but also a trope of old age. And yet. A goldfinch balances on the rim, his bright back emblazoned. Below him, mourning doves peck at the fallen seeds, surprisingly beautiful birds, pearlescent as seashells. Why shouldn't one lure birds in order to see them up close?

Seeing. Looking.

She spent much of her adult life looking through a microscope. Gradually, this action had honed her ability to detect tiny differences in almost any category. Handwriting analysis, bryology, mycology, birdsong. She had watched her daughter with the same practiced attention. She *saw* Christine. Then, to be told she had *not* seen. That she had *not* loved.

Besides, it's unfair that people think of science as cold, predictable, or cut-and-dried. It can't be, when its subject itself is glory. The natural world is fecund. Excessive. Unnecessarily ornamented. Even cells are beautiful. Luminous membranes, some furred, some smooth, some trailing flagella.

The extravagance of creation is what motivated Lena's entire life of study.

Look at the ants. There, at her wheels. Tiny empires. Miraculous collaborations. How they pile their excavated sand into pyramids. Why march to the top of the pile with your single grain instead of scattering it? The same reason that the mockingbird sings his amateur operas with no mate in sight. The same reason the puffer fish creates his seafloor mosaic.

Because beauty.

Lena begins to cry outright.

She cries audibly and does not try to hide under her hat. She cries with true grief, grief as simple as soap is clean. Her tears mix with sweat. She grows even hotter from the output, but she does not leave her spot in the sun. She cries on, dragging her forearm across her face like a squeegee. She is aware of the presence of others, that she can be seen and heard. Concerned voices murmur behind her on the veranda. The birds scatter. Her crying perplexes them. Yet who comes hopping back first, cocking her dun-colored head? Of course, the sparrow. The great avian improvisor. The one who makes her nest in cold chimneys and tailpipes and ruined foundations, the one who has learned to concede the ideal. And for this reason, she is everywhere. Sparrow is everywhere and always will be.

A body lowers itself beside her on the bench.

A hand rests upon her arm.

"Lena," says Warren. "Lena, Lena. Poor Lena."

"It's so hot," she says. At last, she takes off the hat and fans herself with it.

"It's hot as a motherfucker," Warren says.

Lena chuckles. He passes her some Kleenex.

"Someone said, 'What's that person doing sitting out there in this heat?' And I said, 'It's Lena. She's probably conducting an experiment.'"

Lena blows her nose. She puts her hat back on. The sparrow sprints into the woods.

You can certainly blame yourself for not seeing, but the truth is, it is painful to see. Once you see the ants, for example, once the life underground and nests in the trees are visible to you, you are all the more devastated when an acre is scraped for development, or the dry hills go up in flames. Once you see that your daughter suffers, you must acknowledge that you are impotent and perhaps even insufficient as her mother and protector. There have been studies of blind people who, after their sight is medically restored, beg for their blindness back.

"But now I see that you are just sitting here, crying," Warren says. "Is she dead, your hiker?"

"What?" Lena looks at Warren. He's got a hat on too. His bright blue eyes are rheumy and his wide nose sweats. He gazes out at the view. She once read that the sense impressions of one-celled animals are not edited for the brain. This means only the simplest animals perceive the universe as it is.

"Have they found your hiker?" he repeats, louder.

"No. No, they haven't found her." She clenches her fists. "But I think she's still alive. I do. I really do."

"Why are you crying, then?"

Lena's face contorts. Mockingbird operas. Puffer fish mosaics. All she says is "Ants."

"You are crying about ants?"

She nods. Fresh tears fall.

"What happened between the two of you?"

"Me and who?"

"Your daughter."

"I—I really don't know." She looks at him full in the face, straight into his weepy eyes. "Well," she says. "Many things."

Warren sighs. "Seems to me children are nothing but heartache. Even when everything goes right."

She considers his implication, then looks away.

"Good you didn't have any," she says.

"What?"

She raises her voice. "It's good you didn't have any children."

He shrugs. "Maybe. Maybe not."

They both sit with the truth of this.

The heat is bending the air over the valley. The sky is pale gray and empty.

"So how do you know your hiker is still alive? Hm, Detective? It was on TV. Everyone but you seems to think she's dead."

This befuddles her too. How *does* she know? Sparrow, mockingbird. Sparrow, mockingbird. She's heard mockingbirds in the throes of logomania, running through their greatest hits, strangled imitations of hawks, cardinals, and jays. She always felt a little pity for a bird cursed with no inborn song of its own. The mockingbird gives her an idea.

"I have an idea," she says.

"You don't say. Lena Kucharski has an idea."

"I have to get to work," she mutters. "I have an idea. A hunch. Can I use your computer? I destroyed mine."

She powers on her chair and drives it hard back uphill.

"Be careful," Warren says, jogging alongside. "You'll bust your motor!"

Lt. Bev

SATURDAY, AUGUST 6. TEN P.M.
DAY 11 OF THE GILLIS SEARCH.

You lose some. You lose sometimes. I remember the drowned boy I recovered, that first summer of COVID. A boy visiting from New York City. He'd just gotten a new iPhone and took it out in a kayak he didn't know how to use. The kayak must have tipped over in the chop, and no one saw. We found him without needing the dive team. He'd washed into the shallows. It was clear to us that he'd drowned trying to save the phone, which was still clutched in his hand.

I open my laptop and write the day's report.

Saturday, August 6
6,905 vehicle miles, ATV miles, and foot miles logged.
268 overtime man-hours.
No sign whatsoever of Sparrow.

The least you can do for a mourning mother is give her a body. The mother of the drowned boy wailed. I'd never heard a sound quite like it. Her grief sounded right. It sounded perceiving.

"You haven't touched your pizza," Rob says, pointing at my paper plate.

I blink and return to earth.

Tanya, her hair loose and lank, looks up from her cell phone. I can hear the beeps and chimes of a video game. Her under-eyes are dark. It's late.

"You should eat," she says, thumping my arm. "Or else Robus Maximus will eat the whole thing."

Earlier that day, when almost every searcher in the state of Maine was out looking for Valerie Gillis, a lost-person call came in from Belgrade. A five-year-old girl had gone missing from her parents' camper. All the K-9 teams in the state were out on the Gillis search, so it took us three hours just to pull a team and get to Belgrade. Little kids have to be found more quickly than adults due to their low body weight and susceptibility to exposure. We'd found her at dusk, under an overturned rowboat, mere steps from deep water. She'd wandered out of the camper at night and her brother sleepily got up and locked the door. The Gillis search was starting to endanger other lost people.

There's a knock on the bus.

Gregory Bouras sticks his head inside. "Anybody home?"

"Gregory," I say, wiping my fingers. "Come on in."

He climbs the steps and rests a canvas duffel bag at his feet.

"Going somewhere?" I ask.

"May I sit?"

"Of course," I say. "Want some cold, terrible donated pizza?"

"No thanks. But thanks."

Rob scoots over and wipes down the plastic bench beside him. It's the first nice thing I've seen Rob do for the man. Gregory sits and folds his hands on the table. He looks different, even serene. He has a sunburn on the bridge of his nose. His new jacket is broken in.

"How was today for you?" I ask.

He shrugs. "Educational."

According to Rudy Bradley, the day began poorly. Gregory took big, careful steps over fallen trees and walked around mud and puddles, slowing down the line. None of the other volunteers said a word as they waited for him to catch up. But after a while, he got wise and stopped trying to keep clean. At some point, he grabbed a stick and used it to beat back the foliage. He wasted a lot of energy slashing away like this, but Rudy said it seemed to do him good emotionally, so no one said anything. Midday, they crossed Orbeton Stream. The river had a good pace to it, and the searchers had to leap across on stones. Halfway across, Gregory slipped off a stone and landed in knee-high water. He paused there, looking down, while everyone else continued to cross. Rudy wasn't sure what he would do. After a moment, Gregory sloshed across the river and walked up the opposite bank without a word. He made it to the end of the grid and back, at which point he vomited discreetly into the underbrush.

"I'm going home," he announces. "Back to Northampton."

"Right now?"

"Right now. Unless that's a problem."

"Well, of course you're free to go where you want," I say. "But we should stay in close contact. In case."

Gregory shrugs. "Valerie would not want me to sit here like this. We wanted peace and freedom for one another. She'd want me to go home, to our home."

"I can understand how you'd feel that way," I say.

"I need to do something to honor her. I want to gather with people who loved her. Maybe have a service. A ceremony. Something outdoors, so she can hear?"

Rob raises his eyebrows. "We're still searching the woods," he says. "We're gonna keep searching first thing tomorrow."

I nod. "People might say it's too soon, Gregory. I mean, to have a service."

"We never lived that way, worried about what people would

say." He raises his empty hands. "Her spirit doesn't want me here anymore. Her spirit wants me to be free."

Tanya sighs. "Personally? I think you've got the right idea."

Rob and I both look at her.

"I do," she says, blowing her bangs out of her eyes with a puff of air. "He's done everything he can. You don't honor someone like Valerie by sitting around driving yourself nuts. Is that what she would want?"

Gregory looks at her gratefully. "Thank you," he says.

Outside, in the night air, my throat tightens with emotion as I shake his hand.

"Everyone went rough on you," I say.

"I don't care," he says. "I just miss her."

Except for Gregory's taillights, the night is dark as pitch. We stand for a moment in the silence that comes after he drives away. I think about the little girl in Belgrade. She's someone else's Treasure.

Gregory is right. It's time to move on.

Lena

She is embarrassed at how searchable he is, how easy it is to see the other sides of Daniel Means. He was a wise soul on r/foraging, but when she searched up all his comments on the site, she'd read his embarrassing, puerile comments on subs like r/AmItheAsshole and r/AmericaBad and even, tragically, r/JusticeForJohnnyDepp. To the question on r/AskReddit "What organization or institution do you consider to be so thoroughly corrupt that it needs to be destroyed?" he responded, "US MILITARY." To the question "What do you think when you see a woman in public without a bra on?" he replied, "Wear what you want to wear. No one should be allowed to tell you how to dress." He was, at times, what he'd often accused others of being—a shitposter. On r/Maine, he responded to "What are some helpful tips for a newbie to the Maine winter?" by reposting an image of a castle made out of mashed potatoes. He was, like many people, tyrannized by his changing moods. By an absence of coherent personality. He was a mockingbird. She sighs and leans back in her chair. She puts her hand to her throat and feels an agitated fluttering.

There's a soft knock at the door.

It's Warren, holding a tuna fish sandwich on a plate.

Late-afternoon light is canting through his windows, the apartment already dim. He turns on a lamp by the door. She watches him drag the lamp over to her so she can see better. He lays the sandwich on the desk. His kindness leaves her speechless.

"Thank you," she whispers. She can't even look at him. Emotion wells in her throat.

He comes to her rescue. "Have you cracked the case, Fletcher?"

She shakes her head no, takes a bite of the sandwich, looks around. Despite their frequent forages, she's never been inside Warren's apartment before. She's surprised at the elegance of it. Two porcelain lamps with white linen shades frame a low chesterfield sofa in the small living room. The rug has the sheen of real silk, with sunburned patches from a life full of light. Everything nice but not too-too. She recognizes, on a shelf, the banded quail feathers the two of them found together. Atop a tiny bistro table by the windows, in a repurposed jar, a mangy bouquet. He sees her looking at it.

"I thought they were daisies," he said. "But then I looked it up. They're invasive mayweed. You don't have to tell me."

But she wasn't going to tell him.

She takes another bite of the sandwich, unable to eat it delicately.

"This is delicious," she says, mouth full.

It's not the afterglow of loyalty that keeps her from calling the Warden Service and telling them about her misgivings about Daniel Means of Bethel. She could just call the tip line. She doesn't need a justification. The head warden had said, on TV, "We want to hear from you." But the wardens haven't found the woman on their own, have they? Hundreds of searchers with radios and dogs and planes. And Valerie was still stranded in the woods.

She holds up a finger.

"Let's see if his mother blocked me on Telegram," she says.

"Whose mother?"

"My online friend."

She logs in. Security check leads her back to her Gmail. Warren's computer is a brand-new flat screen with a silent keyboard, far nicer than her own.

TerribleSilence liked Telegram because it was "for paranoids." Their chats were secret, using end-to-end encryption. No one could see the messages but the two of them. But despite his bluster, Daniel Means hadn't taken the basic precaution of blocking his password manager. He'd been easily hacked by his own mother. She scrolls through their messages. Oceans of messages. She had been, as they say, extremely online.

"Wow," Warren says, with a sniff. "You two were very good friends."

I know what happened to Sparrow.

She returns to the moment when he swerves toward his theory.

I can't wait to hear!

Did u know that there is a secret
military training facility along the trail
where she went missing???

??? Do tell.

I've known about the place for years.
I used to play out there as a kid.
Watched them w/ my own binoculars.
One time I was threatened. This big man,
with horns. He told me he'd kill me if he
ever caught me there again.

She scrolls further, deep into Operation Sparrow and what are now ringingly clear signs of his break with reality. Horns!

Psst.
I did something I shouldn't have.

                What?

I took a souvenir.

                What is it?

You want to see?

    Over her shoulder, Warren points at the photo of the stolen NO ENTRY sign. "Your online friend is into stealing signs?" he asks. "A criminal mischief charge can land a person in jail for six months."

    She stares at the photo in disgust, then scrolls away.

    Too bad you can't serve jailtime for being a pretender, an over-promiser, a false friend.

    "Let me show you Valerie," Lena says, brightening. As if she knows her. "Her trail name is Sparrow."

    The photograph from the last morning she was seen alive appears in various sizes and captions on the computer screen. Her thumbs hooked through her pack. Her gummy smile. Her expression one of merriment mixed with irony that belongs exclusively to the no-longer-young. The bright pink bandana loops her neck, tied on the side with a flourish, as on the bobby-soxers of Lena's own youth.

    Something sours her. She imagines this beatific smile out there alone in the woods.

    That bright flag around her neck.

These people. There is no
arguing w/ them.
They are sexually turned on
by fascism.

HEARTWOOD

Who?

EVERYBODY.
EVERYBODY IN THIS DOOMED AND
MALIGNANT COUNTRY.
I NEED TO LEAVE.
FOR GOOD.

    A Polish proverb rings in her mind.
    "Where an angel builds a church, the devil builds a chapel."
    Lena's heart begins to pound. She toggles back to Telegram, to the photograph of Daniel Means holding the stolen sign. *Yes, thank you*, she thinks. She pounds the desk.
    "Whoa," Warren says. "What now?"
    Wrapped around Daniel's wrist is a bandana.
    A bright pink bandana.
    Valerie's.

My dear mother,

You would think I'd be afraid, but I'm not any longer.
    Deep into my lostness, I came to this ridge, and I stopped.
    Sometimes you just have a sense of timing. You can't say why.
    I pitched my tent on a bed of moss.
    I zipped my tent closed against the darkness.
    The rain stopped. The mosses and I, we dried up.
    The forest is dry.
    The creek is distant.
    My arms and legs are fragile.
    At times, my heart pounds, for no reason.
    Some last tantruming. I ignore it.
    Meanwhile, days are traded for days.
    A chevron of geese crosses the sky.

When Santo left the trail, I almost went with him, you know.

I knew we could pick up where we left off the following season. I knew quitting would be the smartest choice. And no one would fault me. Everyone would be relieved. They would put up a banner in the hospital break room. I'd have a hundred stories to tell. I wasn't too proud to quit. I wasn't trying to prove anything.

But I was only halfway to answering the question I'd gone to the trail to answer.

My question was, When would my heart be whole again?

* * *

Have you ever hiked above the tree line? You should some day. It's holy up there. My first time was on Moosilauke, a four-thousand-footer in the Whites of New Hampshire. The steep slog up the mountain flattened toward the top. I walked through a lane of wind-sculpted krummholz until the gnarled trees, too, fell away and there were only the coppery grasses shushing in the roaring wind. The mountaintop was a kind of tundra, a beautiful boneyard in the mist, studded with cairns and broken rocks from the ruins of some old hotel. There were days on the trail when I felt like I could walk forever. On such days, my mind was quiet. A body does not need to be instructed how to move. It knows. On those days, climbing lost its drama, and even the tremendous goal of finishing seemed beside the point. I was plugged into a collective strength, the human story, the shared earth. I sat on Moosilauke a long time, strafed by the fresh wind. Ahead of me lay a row of farther peaks of the same grandeur, behemoths sided with green, cloud shadows big as lakes darkening their massive skirts.

That's when I understood the answer to my question, about my broken heart.

I was built to feel, so I felt. I was built to give, so I gave. All my life, I gave to my friends and to my family. When I became a nurse, I gave to my patients. We all did. In our medical training, we praised the person who stayed up the longest or who violated duty hours. We told stories about the times we ignored our own needs to care for other people. Every single nurse and doctor I knew had worked sick, through the flu or worse. It was something to admire.

Then along came this virus that demanded all of that giving and more. I hadn't known that I could give myself to death. And there was no language. No way to speak of it, even among ourselves. Exhaustion became our identity. The mindless way we put our scrubs in the wash and scrubbed our skin with soap to spare those we lived with.

We were called heroes.

But we were only given two options—being a hero or falling apart.

As for Gregory, I loved him still. I knew I'd helped him get sober. He deserved to be held when he trembled. Love's demands are beautiful and right. But standing on the top of Moosilauke, I realized that, at least for the time being, those demands were for other people. Some day my heart would be put back together, maybe missing a piece or two. But for now, love was another act I couldn't bear to perform without the proper tools.

I wake with the taste of bile on my tongue.

In the dark, I sit up and click on my headlamp.

My stomach convulses. I contract around the pain, not sure if I will vomit or defecate.

Vomit or defecate? Door three, please.

I pause, waiting. The nausea ebbs.

A starving body tries everything before quitting. It can shrink its organs, it can devour its own muscles. It shuts down its major systems—for example, digestion. I have fed my body so little that it is rejecting even the single rectangle of chocolate I held on my tongue all morning.

I can't throw up in my tent. But I don't want to leave my tent at this dark hour. In the children's book, when the lonely moose and his orange bird friend must travel through the forest at night, all is dark but for the flaming eyes and luminous incisors of various snakes, raptors, and antlered beasts.

A gag wrings my throat.

Swearing, I unzip my tent fly and poke my beam of light into the air. It is immediately swamped by darkness. I stand and stagger forward, crunching across the sticks and pine duff in my socks.

My fading headlight glows weak as candlelight. The narrow beam rests here upon a tree trunk, there on a log. I'm afraid of what I might see. I do not belong out here. I drop to my knees and am sick in the creeping dogwood. I retch and retch. I throw up the contents of my stomach, then I throw up my stomach itself; I throw up my goals, my loyalties, my past, my future, my attachments. I throw up my name. And still more contractions come.

I suppose I am meant to disgorge my life.

In the corner of my eye I see a flash of white.

I turn my head in time to see a pale bird veer in and out of my light.

I sit on my haunches and catch my breath. The headlamp turns the night into a solid wall. The beam of light searches the treetops. Nothing. I can see my tent in the moonlight just beyond, a humped shadow. As I stand and begin to shuffle toward it, the white bird sweeps past again, more aggressively. I pause. My beam of light follows the bird, but it's gone.

What was it? A nocturnal dove? A gull of the woods? A white bat?

Curiosity keeps me there for another moment. The knot of pain in my gut is gone.

Out of sheer dark, the winged creature rushes at me, beating my face and arms as if it is not one thing but many. It wants to enter me, to eat my light. I slice the air weakly. I do not have the strength to fight it off. "Please!" I beg. "Leave me alone please!" There is nothing to do but shield my head, to stand there swaying on uncertain legs. I am nearly weightless. The things of the woods know what a sickly creature looks like.

Finally, the harassment ends. I open my eyes.

There, in my beam of light, suspended about six feet in the air, looking down at me, is the hovering thing. Kitelike, not a bird, nor white bat, nor tiny owl. No—it's a *fairy*. Like a child, I believe totally.

We face one another as if the meeting were planned. I step forward. She flinches, ascends. Her outstretched wings waver. Streamers hang from her hind wings. She has an extraordinarily human face. Her gaze is impartial beneath her headdress, two red gems. She flits higher, then returns to her seat in the air.

I smile. My bird is a moth.

"You're a moth!" I say. "A really, really, really big moth. A *luna* moth."

She dips in response and continues to hover.

"You're beautiful," I tell her.

But she must think the same of me. We are mutually transfixed.

It has been days since I have been seen. It is tempting to believe I don't exist.

But that's not true—I *do* exist. My moth sees me.

Having drunk my light, she withdraws into darkness.

I stumble home, my stomach calm, my heart consoled.

Guess what, Mom? She brings the rain.

My moth! Brings rain!

In my wrung-out dreams I hear a persistent tapping on my tent, like a second hand. Tip, tip, tip. I figure it for a solo, but soon contrapuntal beats join in. Tiptap, tip, tip, tiptoptap. I inch my torso out of my tent, commando crawling onto my moss mat.

I blink up at the sky, which is dimly bright.

There they are. Storm clouds. Their misty bellies sweep the treetops.

I reach back in my tent for my Nalgene bottles. I can't get the tops off. My fingers don't work. I try to use my teeth. I bite the plastic cord that anchors the top to the neck of the bottle and tug. Tip, top, tip. How did I let myself get so weak? What was I doing when I stopped getting water? Necromancer! Self-killer! Drink! I breathe hard. I wrap one hand around the bottle and one hand around the top, and I twist. As I twist, I holler. The hollering does it. I get the bottle open. I dig a hole in the dirt and plant the bottle there. Somehow I accomplish the same with the second bottle, and then I drag my filthy hands back inside and I leave the tent flap open so that I can watch the rain.

The moss seems excited. Alert.

The air is charged with energy. I can *hear* the air.

The atmosphere thickens.

A flash of paparazzi lightning, then the rain comes sheeting down.

At first, no rain falls through the overstory. I can hear it banging on the canopy.

Gradually rain filters to the forest floor.

Water plonks into my bottles, so little, just a swallow.

I miss, with sudden passion, the sound of windshield wipers. Ub-dub, ub-dub. In my memory, cars speed past, spraying rain, while I sit in the back seat of your car lulled by their metronomic squeegee. Ub-dub, ub-dub. Rain turns daylight greenish, doesn't it? A faint pistachio. Traffic lights ponder at every intersection. Green, yellow, red, green, yellow.

I miss the smell of tobacco in the rain and I miss wet playing fields and rain-slicked streets pearly with engine oil and human footprints filled with rainwater and the fury of housebound children.

I miss all that.

Poetry. Life. One more hour on earth.

One more sacred day. One *shard* of a day.

Yes, please.

Sometimes, when I'm in the grocery store or somewhere, I'll see a toddler clinging to his mother's leg, giving me the stink eye, and I think, That's exactly how *I* felt. My mother was the Queen of Light and everyone else was a piece of crap. Of course, as a black-clad, nose-ringed, three-headed teenager, I couldn't stand you.

During those years, the very home I loved as a child appeared as a place made of cardboard, bad candles, laugh tracks, and clichés. Who buys signs with cheerful sayings to decorate the bathroom? You did. At the foot of the driveway outside our prefab beige colonial, Dad had constructed a mailbox that was a miniature beige replica of the house itself. Why didn't the two of you just kill me? I was going to die a slow death by humiliation. I was embarrassed by your small-time complaints, and your honky-tonk life. You didn't even own a passport. Why had I feared growing up? Suddenly, I couldn't wait to leave. *I'm, like, dying inside. Death by suburban Maryland.*

I screamed, I hate you! You drive me nuts!

For once, you said nothing.

* * *

Suddenly, I understand how pissed off you would be if I succumbed out here.

You'd be so mad! I have painted you as a sweetheart because I miss you but you can be very exacting. You'd be pissed off that your dead daughter is being pitied by everyone. You hate funerals, all that sad, defeated music. You'll read my journal and think, She sat around writing about *moss*?

No excuses! you always said. You hate excuses.

And maybe there's something to that.

Isn't it clear, at this point, that no one is coming to save me?

I reach my hand out and grope my moss. Well, I'll be jitterbugged! It's already soft. I squeeze it and rain juices out. The stalks have straightened up. The moss is *taller*. I apologize to it and then I rip a small clump of moss from the mat and bring it up to my face. Look, perfect pearls of rainwater are poised in the fronds.

I tip my head back and wring the rainwater into my mouth.

Maybe I need a bigger mother.

My earth, my Mother. Gaia.

Thank you, Mother!

I weep.

Been raining all day. Raining biblically.

I fall in and out of—

Whenever my bottles contain an inch or two of water I filter it and drink.

I can taste childhood puddles in it.

The water revives me. I mean it literally brings me back to life.

The creek has been rising without my knowing and now look, it's risen all the way up to my ridge. All sorts of things sweep past in the rush: tree limbs and bushes, a plastic lawn chair. That tiny grocery cart and the plastic food I used to play with soon follows, including my plastic hamburger, my cans of "peas" and ears of "corn."

A crushed and unmanned canoe sweeps past. An inner tube. Another inner tube.

The next inner tube has a teenager inside it. Joyriding on the flood.

The teenager sits in her inner tube kicking her legs, giving me a side smile.

She beckons me. She wants me to follow her.

Teenagers these days. They think everything's funny.

"I am too weak to pack up this tent," I tell her. "I'm too weak to carry it! I'm too weak to carry anything! I've waited too long!"

She twirls around on her tube. I don't think she can hear me.

"And where would I go anyway?" I shout to her. "There's nothing out here for miles! Should I just wander around until I die in the open air?"

Just before she rounds the bend and is out of sight, the girl cups her hands to her mouth.

"No excuses!" she hollers.

We both laugh.

I wake to wet silence.

It's late in the afternoon. My tent glows.

With a wrench of will, I open my tent fly.

The sun is bright. A clear halo around it.

A rabbit sits in the midde of the Green Sea, her ears illuminated.

I am not a moss. I'm a woman. A daughter. A nurse.

I know what I have to do.

I reach for my rain poncho. It takes a long time to fit my emaciated arms through the nylon sleeves. As I try to stick my left foot in my boot, it keeps glancing off the hole. Finally the foot fits. I don't even try to tie the bootlaces. It takes a lot of pecking to pull my driver's license out of a zipper pocket.

I leave my driver's license on top of my backpack.

I take one last look around this place.

I've heard it said that the sorrow of human life is that it ends. But I don't think that's the source of our sorrow. Everything ends, not just human lives. Days end. Species disappear. Planets die.

No, the real sorrow of human life is that we *feel*. That's our affliction.

That's why I wanted to walk for months on a trail through the woods.

The world and its people are too much for me.

I am crushed between empathy and impotence.

I don't think I'm important. Not at all!

In fact, I am embarrassingly insubstantial.

Then why was I given this heart?

It is so much more than I need.

Lt. Bev

SUNDAY, AUGUST 7. EIGHT A.M.
DAY 12 OF THE GILLIS SEARCH.

I call the colonel and tell him that I need to talk to him in person.

"Yes," he says. "I need to talk to you too."

I'll meet him in the main office in Bangor.

But first, I take a long, wasteful shower. I rub my scalp with shampoo. In my bathrobe, I brush my hair out like I used to as a teenager, over and over until the waves are smooth and almost pretty. I dress in civilian clothes. A salmon-colored button-down and tan fleece vest. All of my clothes are multipurpose, made of fast-drying material for the kind of person who might go out to dinner then stop and fish on the way home. I pack an overnight bag. I hang my reading glasses from my neckline. Until two years ago, the Warden Service didn't provide uniforms for a woman's body. For nearly three decades, I wore a shirt one size too big so that it didn't gap across my chest, and pants one size too tight so that they weren't comically loose in my crotch. The bulletproof vest, forget about it. You've got to zip that thing on any time you're in uniform and away from your desk. I'm a solid 40D, but in my vest, I'm flat as a board.

Money is never a factor in calling off a search. We don't put a price on a life. The problem with an extended search is that conditions degrade. Search areas are polluted with scent. Volunteers dwindle. So do leads. Folks run out of steam. Nobody wants to look for a corpse. The world keeps turning. I need to talk to the colonel. Couldn't we adjust protocol in this one case? Couldn't we keep the thing going for another week for her sake—Janet's? I'm not ready to give the speech: "Closing the search doesn't mean we stop searching. We never really stop searching. We'll look for her every day. I'm so sorry."

I can't even tell the woman I need one day off.

"Morning, Lieutenant." The colonel stands to greet me.

"Morning, Colonel." We shake hands and exchange a look of mutual condolence.

The Warden Service is taking hit after hit in the press. Not just fringe media, but stalwart papers like the *Portland Press Herald* and the *Boston Globe*. So much for our 97 percent success rate. The world now thinks we can't find a donut in a paper bag.

I don't sit. I sigh and put my thermos down. "This work has been my life," I begin. "For thirty years, the woods have been my world. As you know, I didn't get married or have kids. My fellow wardens have been my family. Some of them are like brothers to me. And now I even have a couple warden daughters. But eventually all good things come to an end. Maybe it's time for me to start thinking about the next phase."

"Wait, wait, wait," the colonel says. "What the hell are you talking about? The next phase?"

I blink back at him. I figured we'd been thinking the same thing.

"Jesus, Bev. What's going on? Are you blaming yourself about Valerie Gillis? Your teams searched more miles than if they'd walked back and forth to *China*. Something bizarre happened here, and maybe we'll never know what. But you are not to blame. You and I both know this is not your fault. Stop talking like this, damn it. Holy *crap*."

The colonel sighs, bows his head, and comes around and sits right in front of me, on the edge of his desk. He's a compact man, a head shorter than me. But he's undeniably good-looking, with his fitted shirts, honey-brown eyes, and dark lashes. I remember when he joined up in the aughts, in a class of young men who were like a breath of fresh air, ushering out the previous century, so different from the old gatekeepers who groaned whenever a woman spoke in a group. "Secure" is the right word. And sometimes my heart would start throbbing to see one of them dressed in a suit, a shiny thumbprint of aftershave on his neck. If they caught me looking, they'd smile. Now, having risen to a place he deserves, the colonel fastens his famous eyes on me.

"Listen," he says. "I need you. There is no other you. There is no other Beverly Miller, man or woman. You *are* our search program. I'd call you a legend, but you're too young for the word."

I pause. For a moment, I feel the presence of the naysayers in my life, many of them dead now, the ones who tried to chase me out of the service, or worse, the ones who did nothing to rise to my defense, even after I had proved myself a thousand times, and I think, *Hear that, ghosts?*

"Take the day off," pleads the colonel. "Take the *week*. Take time off. You've been working how many days in a row? Twelve? Sixteen-hour days? I bet you haven't even logged your overtime."

"My mother is really sick," I say.

"Jesus," he says. "Go see your mother. Is she down in Massachusetts?"

"Leominster. Hospice."

"Go see your mother." He rubs his face, looking stricken. "I kept thinking—I kept thinking we would find Valerie, each passing day. I should have stepped in and given you a break long ago."

"I wouldn't have taken it."

I grab my thermos. I regard the colonel.

"I'll go see my mom," I say.

"Good. Thank you."

"Can you please wait to close the search until I get back?"

He pauses. He nods. "Yes. Yes, I can do that."

"Just another day or two."

"Good. Yes."

"I'll see how I feel when I get back."

"That's fine," he says. "That's more than enough."

"Santo" Phone Call, 8/7/22, 11:15 a.m.

So, I already gave my pops's eulogy. I cried like a baby up there. Said shit I didn't mean. I was like, thank you, Pops, for protecting and teaching us and for putting food on the table—

Cody Ouellette: Everybody bullshits at a funeral, don't you think?

Abso-fucking-lutely. It's a holy tradition. But then a couple days later I was sitting around thinking of some of the real chestnuts of wisdom he offered during his lifetime, and I started laughing. So I wrote them down. Hold up, here's the first one.

"My mother taught me how to drive. My pops taught me how to drunk drive."

Cody Ouellette: That's good! It's punchy.

Right? How about this one.

"'Torture?' Pops used to say. 'What's wrong with torture? I'm tortured every day by the tears of pussies!'"

Cody Ouellette: Christ Almighty.

Here's a good one.

"When I started to hike, I was so excited. I went straight home and told Moms and Pops that I was going to hike the Appalachian Trail someday. Moms was like, 'That's great.' Pops was like, 'Wait. You trying to get mouth-raped by a redneck?'"

Cody Ouellette: Your dad sounds like a Bronx version of my dad. I got a call last winter. Some drunk ice fisherman disturbing the peace.

Turns out, I had to go ticket my own dad.

Damn! That's a good one! I wish I could put that one in my eulogy.
Where you at anyway, Warden?

Cody Ouellette: Sitting in my car. With a six-pack. Um, well, a two-pack.

Yo, cheers! I'm having *un chin* myself.
They're not gonna fire you, are they?

Cody Ouellette: Fire me? For what?

For not being able to find Sparrow.

Cody Ouellette: No. No. It's not like that.
It's worse than that. We get to lie awake at night going over and over the case in our heads for the rest of our lives.

Damn.
That's a lot. That sounds heavy.
It's not your fault either, man.
If it's not my fault, it's not your fault either.

Cody Ouellette: If you say so.

Hey, Cody. Are there really moose up there? I never got to see myself a Maine moose. I saw bobcats, deer, skunks. But I wanted to see a moose so bad. Seeing a moose was, like, the thing that kept me going. Me and Sparrow would meet southbounders and they'd be like, "We got swept down the Kennebec!" "We had to eat our friend during a blizzard in the Presidentials!" and I'd be like, "Yeah, but did you see any *moose*?"

Cody Ouellette: We got moose. We got moose galore. I saw about ten in a cut yesterday.

HEARTWOOD

No shit! Ten?

Well, maybe I'll finish my hike someday after all.

Just so I can walk through Maine.

Cody Ouellette: I don't doubt you will, man. I *know* you will.

When you get up here, call me.

Can we go on a high-speed chase?

Cody Ouellette: Yeah. Yeah. We'll chase down my dad.

Jevi *nais*! Let's do it.

Uh. How fast are you allowed to drive in a high-speed chase, exactly?

Cody Ouellette: A lot faster than your UPS truck.

Ha ha. Over fifty miles an hour? Watch out, Maine!

Cody Ouellette: It's a plan, city boy.

Tip Line Call from Lena Kucharski, Caller from Connecticut—8/6/22

Dispatch: Maine Warden Service tip line. Can I have your name?

Caller: My name is Lena Kucharski. I'm seventy-six years old. I'm calling from Connecticut.

Dispatch: You are on a recorded line. Go ahead.

Caller: I'm calling about the Valerie Gillis case.

Dispatch: Got it. You have information on the search for Valerie Gillis?

Caller: I do. I want you to go talk to someone up there. A young man.

Dispatch: You have a name, ma'am? Hello?

Caller: His name is Daniel Means. He lives with his mother in Bethel.

Dispatch: Why do you think he has information, ma'am?

Caller: I'm afraid—I'm afraid he might have knowledge about what happened to Valerie Gillis. He's in possession of an item of hers. Also, he was in the area when she disappeared.

Dispatch: What's the item, ma'am?

Caller: Her bandana. Her pink bandana. It's in the photograph.

Dispatch: Did he tell you the item is hers? Did he tell you he interacted with the subject? With Valerie?

Caller: No. No . . . He's unwell.
   He's an inpatient at Dorothea Dix Psychiatric Center.
   His mother took him there. He's there.

Dispatch: OK. Dorothea Dix.

Caller: He wanted to disappear. He had a campsite. He was going to live off the land and—and resist the expansionist military. At least, that's what I've construed.

Dispatch: Hold on. Do you know where this campsite is, ma'am?

Caller: I don't. I know *he* can tell you, though. I hope he didn't do anything terrible. I hope she's—I hope she's OK. I hope she's alive.
   (crying)
   He was a friend of mine.

Dispatch: It's OK, ma'am. It's going to be OK.

Caller: I'm sorry. I should have called much earlier.
   (crying)

Dispatch: It's OK, ma'am. I'm going to patch you through to a warden investigator right now. It may take a minute. Please stay on the phone.

Caller: Yes. OK. Yes. I'll wait as long as it takes.

Dispatch: Please hold.

Lt. Bev

Leominster is the birthplace of the pink flamingo lawn decoration, and that says a lot. The place seems to resist change. Deep into the franchise era, main street is still dominated by mom-and-pop stores. With time to kill before meeting my sisters at the care center, I pull up to the corner of Mechanic and Manning Avenue in a light rain, and there it is, Pilgrim Furniture & Mattress. A young man in a cheap suit stands next to an oversize sofa, staring out the window. Dad spent so much of his time at that store, it always feels more appropriate than visiting his grave. Then I keep driving down Mechanic, my chest growing tight with emotion. Leominster's downtown is festooned with flowerpots and banners, there's flags and signs and promises all over the place, and it remains, if you don't think too hard about it, pretty convincing. You are here. These are your parking lots, your baseball diamonds; those are your chain-link fences, your prisons; that way to Fitchburg, this way to Lunenburg.

Kate meets me in the lobby of Sunrise. She looks a little stiff in the joints as she stands up from the institutional sofa. She and Faith are both rail thin. I used to be jealous, but these days thinness looks a little breakable to me. I lean down to hug her.

"Big sister," she says. "I've missed you."

I hold her tight. "I've missed you too."

Ma has been living at Sunrise for over a decade. The people there take good care of her. When she arrived, they got her taking the right pills the right way, without her washing them down with sherry. They kept her fed and clean, and for a while, she herself seemed relieved. "See?" I'd say to her. "You don't have to deal with the mail or the stove or the neighbors." And she'd agree, those neighbors *were* loud, and the stove *didn't* work right. Faith sent me photos of her girls crowding onto their grandmother's bed, horsing around or putting sunglasses on her. The walls bear gifts from their schooldays—paper turkeys, valentines, a photo of Hailey in her ice hockey uniform. Before I made lieutenant, I'd go down nearly every weekend. Then Ma started to call me Claire, who was her older sister, long gone. Other days, she'd smile and call me "special angel." After the dementia took hold, she wasn't all that different than she'd been in health. She still complained about the noise. She was still totally incurious about the work that gave my life meaning. She still relished a glass of cold Coke.

Faith waves us into the room.

"You just missed the doctor," she says. "I can't believe it. She's stabilized."

We step to Ma's bed, my sisters on one side and me on the other. My mother's eyes are closed, her skin shiny with ointment. Her nightdress is bunched around her neck, as if she slid down into it.

"Is she asleep?" I whisper.

"A little more than asleep, but a little less than dead." Faith pulls a stray strand of hair off her face. "Great job, Ma. Bev came all this way from Maine and now you're not even going to *die*."

I stare at her body, which barely disturbs the top sheet. "When did she get so small?"

"You really haven't been home in a while," Faith laughs.

I shake my head. "She looks like a little girl."

"Well," Kate says. "She *was* like a little girl. A girl we all cared for. Even when *we* were girls."

I feel the urge to disagree, to untangle, but no words come. I stare down at the woman around whom so many of my memories coil, like bindweed up a column. She was going to die and to change, and I was going to be left unchanged and alive and somehow still waiting for her to show up. What I wanted from her seemed like very little, but there at the edge of her life, I wish I wanted even less.

"She had a good heart," I say.

"Sure," Kate says, tentatively.

"Come on, Bevie," Faith says. "When I was little, you were more of a mommy to me than anyone."

"You took up the slack," agrees Kate. "And there was a lot of slack."

"Well," I say. "She had a hard life. Losing Dad and everything."

Finally, I touch her. Her arm seems light and hollow as a tail feather. When I look across the bed at my sisters, their faces are full of pity.

"What?" I ask.

"You are so full of shit," Faith laughs.

"She's not," Kate objects. "She's not full of shit. That's what she really thinks."

"We're your *sisters*," cries Faith. "You can be *honest* with us."

"All right, all right," I say. "Listen, it's been a long day. A long drive. A long year."

"OK," Kate says. "What do you need? Are you hungry? Coffee, what? A drink?"

I think about it. I know exactly what I need.

I want to see my nieces.

Kate and I follow Faith to her house in my truck. Once we get to the old neighborhood, Kate starts reciting the names of the families who used to live there and telling me who lives there now. The woman has a photographic memory. She is the smartest of the three of us, by a lot.

We pull up to Faith's ramshackle ranch. Powder blue, Christmas lights all year. In the small yard, the pink flamingos flock with witches and pinwheels and faux stone bunnies on their hind legs. Grass grows in between patches of necrotic ring spots. Faith gets out of her Corolla in her driveway and balances a brown paper bag of groceries on her hip.

I sling my overnight pack onto one shoulder. On the sidewalk, I touch Kate on the arm. "So, listen," I say. "Before we go in, I wanted to tell you something. You know the lost hiker up in Maine? The one hiking through Maine on the Appalachian Trail?"

"Yeah, of course, it's in the papers even down here."

"We didn't find her. We're not going to find her in time to save her."

"No. Oh no."

"Yeah. We're about to close the search."

"That's really sad."

"It is sad."

"You feel responsible?" Kate asks.

"I *am* responsible."

"Did something bad happen to her, some kind of accident, you think?"

"It's anyone's guess. She's been out there for fourteen days." I stare down at my boots. "I'll have to tell—I will have to tell her family that—that we're too late. That we're going to have to leave her body out there. Their daughter's body."

"Jesus, Bevie. I'm so sorry. What a terrible, terrible thing."

Faith holds the screen door of her house open with her rear

and shouts, "What are you two bitches talking about? I can see you judging me! Picking on the youngest one, what a surprise!"

"Anyway," I say. "It hurts."

"I'm glad you told me," Kate says.

Faith's house, to be honest, is a mess. Tables are always strewn with craft projects, hairbrushes, and textbooks. Oversweet, unattended candles gutter in every corner. The TV is always on and blaring. But the place smells lived-in, meatballs and brownies and clean hair. When I walk in, my three nieces are sprawled like teenage satyrs on the couch.

"Aunt Bev!" they cry, piling on me. "Aunt Bev! We love you! Where've you been? What did you bring us?" They pull off my pack.

"Let the woman *enter*," Faith says, elbowing them aside. "Holy crap, girls. Pick *up* your *shoes*."

"You're so soft," Kelsey sighs into my bosom.

"Yeah, what *are* you wearing, exactly, Bevie," Faith says, "a pelt?"

"You shouldn't shoot animals," Hailey says.

"That's fleece, you dummies," Kate says, throwing her tote on a chair. "It's recycled plastic."

Faith puts her grocery bag on the floor and shoves the abundance of sneakers under an entryway table, causing a pile of unsorted mail to cascade to the floor.

"Oh God," she groans. "I can see Aunt Bev writing tickets in her mind. Health hazard. Fire hazard. Biohazard."

"Don't write us tickets!" the girls cry.

"This is out of my jurisdiction," I laugh.

Mackenzie, the oldest and the tallest one, just a couple of inches shy of my own height, puts an arm around my shoulder. "Did you bring your gun, Aunt Bev?"

"Do *not* give Mackenzie your gun, Bev," Faith says, walking to the kitchen.

"I didn't bring my gun," I say.

"Can I just see it? You don't have to let me hold it."

"She doesn't have it." Kate mockingly shakes Mackenzie by the shoulders.

Mackenzie winks at me sideways. "You can show it to me later, Aunt Bev."

My sisters are seven and eight years younger than me, and it seems like when I left home, a different historical period began, with a separate government and separate mores. They are bolder than I am. They say what they mean. As teens, they left Ma to her troubles and refused to stick around drying her tears. But I think their true power was one another.

Or maybe they were just more realistic. They learned to live with the mother they got.

That real mother, the mother that you get, you've got to love her, there's no choice. She is the mother you needed. She gave you strength, either because she loved you well or because she loved you poorly. She gave you your mission.

It's the dream mother that you have to let go of. The one you pined for, the one you thought your decency promised you. She's the one you've got to bury.

She's a mirage. She'll only break your heart.

"You shouldn't go to this trouble," I tell Faith as we peel potatoes.

"I don't cook enough," she says. "I just reheat shit. This is nice."

"You work all day. What are you supposed to do?"

"My girls are such lunkheads. I don't even think they realize that french fries come from *these*." Faith laughs her brawling laugh. "I've failed, Bevie. Those girls are a ton of fun, but they are slobs."

"We can *hear* you, Mom," one says from another room.

"I get dinner ready *all the time*," moans another.

"Besides," says the third, from the TV area, "maybe you should take a good hard look in the mirror."

Kate calls out, "All four of you are the same person anyway. You are exactly alike."

"Oh my God, girls," Faith shouts into the general area, "we should get Bev to look at the haunted toilet."

"Oh yeeaaah. I bet *she* could fix it!"

"We're not sure if it's haunted," Faith explains. "But it does seem to have these moods . . ."

"What the heck," somebody says. "Whose phone is that?"

"Aunt Bev," says another, "your pack is buzzing."

"Who cares? She's off duty!" shouts Faith, continuing, "*Four* females and we have *one* toilet. I think the toilet wants more *rights* or something. You know, better working conditions."

I shrug. "Call the plumber."

"We did," Faith says. "He's like, 'There is technically nothing wrong with this toilet.'"

Laughter rings from the other room. "So Mom was like, 'Do you think it's possessed?'"

"Yah, no. I did not actually say that."

"The plumber starts, like, backing out of the door."

"Aunt Bev. Honestly. Your backpack is *blowing up*."

I glance across the table at Faith, puzzled. I can hear the various ringtones. Work phone, personal cell. A silence follows. I mean a silence inside me. Kate comes to the doorway, her face serious.

"Maybe you should pick up," she says.

I put down the potato and walk to my pack in the hallway. Kate follows me, patting my back. She's murmuring something about maybe this is good news. I remember comforting her little body with the same kind of encouraging taps over hurt feelings, a lost blanket, mean kids at school. I unzip my pack and fumble for my work cell.

Rob: Pick up the phone
Tanya: Can you call me? Where are you???
Rob: PICK UP YOUR PHONE.
Mike: I AM SHITTING MY PANTS. I heard about it on the car-to-car.
Colonel Ben: Sorry, change of plans. Get here when you can.

As I am reading the texts, a call comes in. Tanya.

"Tanya," I say, my mouth dry. "Hey. What's going on?"

"Thank God." She's breathing hard, like she's been running. "Thank God."

"What's going on? I'm down in Mass. I'm a couple steps behind here—"

"I just came from Dorothea Dix."

"OK," I say. "You OK?"

"Yes. I'm just—a little lightheaded."

I want to shout "Is she dead?" but my mouth clamps shut. There wouldn't be all this urgency if she were dead. My sisters and nieces all gather in the open arch of the hallway, eyes wide. Kate gives me a thumbs-up in a questioning way.

"You won't freaking believe this," Tanya says. "It was a tip. We got the tip yesterday. This elderly woman had an online relationship with this kid, this local kid. The woman was starting to suspect he knew something about Valerie. We cross-checked and realized we had some priors on the guy. Daniel Means. A sovereign-citizen type. We've had brushes with him in the past. He's got a beef with the military survival school. Thinks the woods are his."

"OK," I say carefully.

"So I get in the car this morning and head over to Dorothea Dix, where he's involuntarily committed. They made me wait there three hours before authorizing a conversation. You need a doc there, various witnesses, et cetera. I thought, 'Here goes another wild goose chase. Yet another nothing.'"

"And?"

"And the kid walks in and nods at me. On his meds, he's sane as the day is long! I'm about to start asking him some questions and he just puts up a hand, like, 'I know who you are and I know what you want.'"

"And?"

"He told us where Valerie is."

"Where?"

"At his campsite, where he left her."

It's a kind of interior flash-bang. Disoriented, I stagger to the side. My nieces come over to support me by my free arm.

"Did he kill her?"

"No."

"Did he assault her? Did he hurt her?"

"Not according to him. He says she followed him out there. Says he left her there at the campsite. On the northern border of the military training grounds. Way up north by Black Nubble Mountain."

I regain my balance and step toward the front door, looking out at the empty street through the beveled window, the asphalt rain-dark. After a moment, they gather around me again, all five of them. *Way up north by Black Nubble Mountain.* Not within our search area. Not even close. Also, near a road.

"I never would have looked there," I murmur.

"Bev. He left her there *alive*. He drew us a map. We have a *map*."

"No way she just waited there," I say. "She must have made a run for it."

"Yes. But now we have a point last seen."

"Holy crap," Faith whispers, looking from face to face. "This is nuts!"

The girls run into the kitchen. Somebody starts packing me a sandwich.

"Tanya," I say. "You did it. You found the missing piece. You stuck with it. And you *did it*."

Tanya starts laughing. More like laugh-crying. "This hasn't worked out like it was supposed to at all!" Tanya has a lot going on under the surface, I realize, which softens me toward her, since the same could also be said about the people I admire most.

I pick up my pack and start hugging my family one by one, phone to my ear.

"You're a warrior, Tanya," I say. "Or as they say around here, a *warriah*."

Back on Mechanic. Past Dad's furniture store. Onto the Leominster Connector.

I-495. Lowell. Lawrence. Haverhill. Just before I-95, I get a glimpse of ocean glittering through the billboards and the feather grass. How many times I've driven this route, numbed by the miles. How frequently I've slipped between the state lines, never really feeling like a Mainer in good faith.

Meanwhile, I'm on the horn with everybody. It's approaching

evening and the team is in disarray. The chaos that had been politely waiting out the Gillis search has come to call. Five wardens plus the dive team are on a major water search down in the Narrows. Tanya is in Bangor, driving back from the psychiatric hospital. Half the state troopers are over in Skowhegan waiting out a barricaded felon. And me just north of Portland, feeling like the coastline has lengthened in my brief absence. Surprises? Yes. We searched as if she was lost. But Valerie and the local kid had moved in a straight line, north by northwest. Lost people never travel directionally like that. How could we have known?

I drive without stopping.

"DEEMI is putting together a team," Rob reports. "But they won't make it here until the early hours. Let's have them head west from Crocker Mountain. But you, you come in on Mountain Road and head north. It's shorter. The campsite is 7.2 miles north by northeast. I just texted you the coordinates. You've got a functioning DeLorme with you? And a PLB?"

"*I'm* going in? Just me? No one else is available? What about Cody? Anyone?"

"Cody is . . . Cody is . . . well, he's inebriated."

"Jesus." Cody. Cody. I should have recognized a fellow compensator. "OK. What about a K-9 team?"

"Glad you asked. Because that's the good news. Guess who's in Rangeley? Miles away from Mountain Road?"

"I don't know, Superman, hopefully."

"Regina. Regina and Badger."

The best K-9 team in Maine.

Super*woman*.

* * *

Regina and I are only about three miles into the woods when darkness falls.

We click on our lights. Regina's got a headlamp—she's holding the lead—but I've got a fully charged Maglite with a fifty-foot beam. My light has the effect of a photographic flash, making the woods seem stranger and more still than they really are. Back in the old days, I used to frequently stake out night hunters, but it's been years since I've walked the woods in darkness. My Maglite illuminates the trees, casting its stunning glare on the surrounding trunks and the weft of leaves overhead. Everything else is sheer blackness, which seals itself the moment I swing my light elsewhere.

Badger doesn't seem to mind the dark. He's not looking with his eyes anyway.

I catch up to Regina. "How's he doing?"

"He doesn't smell anything yet. But he gets it. He gets what we're doing." The woods are fairly open, and walking isn't hard yet. When Badger darts ahead, Regina pays out the lead. When he wheels around and darts back, she strips the lead back like fishing line. They do this over and over. The air is thick with a thousand messages he's reading. Bear, moose, bird, maggot, decomposition. There is nothing he cannot smell.

The woods are dripping from the day's rain. A raindrop hangs at the end of each fascicle, blade, and leaf. Whenever I brush my shoulder against a tree, I am doused by the throughfall. I'm as soaked as if I've gone swimming.

"Conditions are perfect," Regina says, which would make anyone but me laugh. "Just after a rain is perfect. It'll keep the smells in place."

Badger makes yet another pirouette. He's a beautiful dog, a pure black German shepherd with sky-high ears. It takes years to train a dog for searching. But you can't train just any dog. The dog has to be agile and intelligent, but most of all, he's got to have the drive. Unquenchable drive. Badger is that kind of dog. When I drove up to the roadside where Regina's truck was idling, he was slobbering on the window glass, his ears cocked, whining to get started.

"I'm glad to be back out here," Regina says. "It was tearing me up, you know. I *knew* she was out here. He *told* me." She gestures with her chin to the dog. "He's been a mess, to tell you the truth. I had him on another search out Corinna way once you guys postponed this one. He wouldn't do it. His heart wasn't in it. He only wants to find Valerie." The dog springs noiselessly over a fallen tree, while we follow, laboring over one leg at time. "Dragged off the trail by some nutjob," she says. "Christ on a cracker."

"It doesn't let me off the hook," I say. "We could have searched up here."

"For what reason?" Regina looks around at the unremarkable woods. "I don't know, Bev. I think you just like it there, on your hook."

We fall back into silence. The woods thicken. I'm walking just behind them, sweeping my beam, casting for—well, anything. An article of clothing. A naked arm. The Maglite is less useful in dense foliage. It projects one object onto another, so that all I see is moving shadows upon a screen of tree trunks. The shadows scroll, a parade of ghoulish forms. Sight grows tricky, full of fictions. Dried leaves look bloody in the light. The ground writhes. I feel watched, and when I sweep my beam up into the canopy, low and behold, a great horned owl glares back at me, her ear tufts flat. She takes flight, leaving me in the rain of down feathers, my heart racing.

I check my DeLorme. We're five miles in and two to go. It's getting harder to see Regina through the foliage, but I can hear Badger's little bell. We come across a patch of blowdown, too wide to skirt, and I take a snag in the side of the gut that would have impaled me if I didn't have my vest on.

Above our heads, the moon wrestles clear of the clouds. I glance up at that bright rock and mentally prepare myself for what I might find at that campsite.

"Please, dear God," I whisper. "Let her be alive."

I have seen my share of corpses. More than I expected to when I first signed up for this job, to be honest. I have grown, like a lot of first responders, unevenly used to it. I've seen bodies frozen in ice. Crushed under tires. When it's your job, when you are expecting it, the horror is overridden by relief, because thank God it's you who was first to the scene, not the deceased's spouse or kid. But I never got used to the suicides, the way they neatly arranged themselves, tidied the area, left a warning on the car window or the camp door.

I check the DeLorme again and see that we've veered slightly off course. I jog ahead.

"Hey, Regina?" Her headlamp flares in my direction. "The campsite is east of here."

"He wants to go this way," she says. "Should I get him to change direction?"

I swing my beam toward the given coordinates. The campsite is only a hundred yards away. My light lands on a ridge of sudden steepness. Rainwater trickles down the rock slabs. Meanwhile, I spot Badger's eyeshine in my beam. Two ethereal green orbs.

"No," I say. "Let's let him search."

I can hear the dog's rhythmic panting in the darkness. He has quickened his pace. We follow through the foliage for another brutal interval. I stop to take a sip of water, and by the time I fit my canteen back in my pack, they've disappeared from sight.

"Regina?"

Suddenly I'm hit with a rank smell. Putrid, like a cemetery.

"Hello?"

Faintly, far off, I hear his bell. I sweep my Mag. Ahead is a clearing, filled with moonlight. I can see the mercury-bright reflection of water. A bog.

Regina shouts, "Bev!"

"Yeah?"

"Bev!"

"What is it?"

My heart starts to gallop. I run as best as I can, my boots sinking.

Badger is sitting, as he's trained to do when he finds something. Beside him is a clump of something covered in muck.

I shine the Maglite. Regina stoops and rubs the muck off.

She looks back at me, eyes fierce. "It's a hiking boot."

I shine the light across the bog. I know its hers. I can see the puzzle now.

"She was trying to cross the bog," I say.

Regina stands. "She was in a rush."

"She was running away from him. Why else would she fall out of her boot? She was running away from the campsite." I turn west, where the moon hangs. The opposite direction from where Rob wants me to go. She had to go around the bog, but which way?

"She sat here," Regina says. "Then she went over here. There's a scent pool here."

I shine my light on the loamy forest floor. Her one-shoe footprint will be unique.

"Badger can't track her, track's too old," Regina says.

At the sound of his name, the dog pulls his long tongue back in his mouth.

Waiting for the go-ahead.

"But he can find things we can't," I say.

I grab my whistle from my shoulder strap.

I blow hard. The sound shrieks for miles.

At every single decision point—an obstacle, a fork, a river—the lost person makes a choice. Go around? Climb over? Wade across? To find her, we will have to make exactly the same choice she made at every point. It's crazy, if you look at it that way.

It's 2 a.m., and we haven't found anything since her boot. A cold track, washed away by days of rain. Maybe I guessed wrong, taking us up this no-name mountain. But if I were trying to put space between me and someone I was afraid of, if I were trying to find a spot with a view, I might head uphill. We keep laboring up, inching over boulders, crawling beneath blowdown. These ridges don't peak. They slope up until they start sloping down, pulling you backward both ways with their sticky-fingered witch hazel. I stop and blow my whistle again. Badger glances back at me, and for the first time, he seems unsure. The day catches up with us. I spent eight hours driving to Massachusetts and back, only to gear up and hike all night in the dark. My lower back is throbbing. We reach a flat moss-covered rock. I sit and peel open a PowerBar. Regina sits down next to me. I pass her half. It's our first break in five hours.

"Way leads on to way," I sigh, chewing. "So the poet says."

Badger sits, but immediately gets up again.

Regina strokes his flank. "Sit, buddy. Sheesh."

He refuses. Regina slackens the lead, and he disappears behind the rock we're sitting on.

Regina says, "I always thought they got that poem wrong. About the paths. It's not saying that you should take the less traveled path. It's saying that you'll never have to stop making decisions about *which* path to take."

"Exactly," I say. "That life's an endless series of decision points."

"Well, not endless."

"Ha, not endless. But the poem is much less encouraging than they make it seem."

"It's depressing, is what it is. Depressing and true."

I douse my neck with bug spray and nudge her in the side. "That's more words than I've ever heard you use in a row."

"Ah, go sail a kite."

That's when Badger starts to whine from behind our rock.

I shine my light and see that he's sitting again.

At his feet is a wrapper. Bright green. An energy bar.

I pick it up. The brand Valerie had with her.

We can barely keep up with the dog now. He's proud of himself for finding the wrapper. We're hiking at a pace, as fast as we can, when a soft rain begins to fall. Just then we hit a creek, maybe five feet across, rushing with the day's rain. Badger wades across.

With a twist in my gut, I remember her poor sense of direction. How easily she got turned around toward the end. More and more frequently, we were rescuing folks uselessly seeking higher ground to find a cell phone signal, when the route back to civilization was always downhill, following drainages, power lines.

I'm winded, hoarse, but still I holler her name.

"Valerie! We're here! We're here to take you home!"

I pause. The silence answers.

"We're friends! From the Warden Service! Valerie!"

The rain picks up.

"Can you let him off the lead now?" I shout as the rain hits the canopy.

"No," Regina shouts back. "She could still be miles away. He'll take off, and we'll lose him."

We're side by side, wading through a patch of creeping dogwood, when we almost stumble into it, pitched there under a small clearing, ground zero—

Her tent.

She's not inside it.

I crawl in. Her sleeping bag, her pack.

On top of the pile, her driver's license.

It makes me uneasy, like the neatened scenes of suicides.

I glimpse the photograph on the driver's license. A mistake. I feel socked in the gut.

She's smiling that trademark smile, full of all the hope in the world.

Outside the tent, Regina is pacing back and forth.

"Why did she leave everything?" I say.

Regina looks stricken. "Too weak to carry it, maybe?"

I try to slap some sense into my limbs. My legs and fingers are numb from the cold rain. I fix the bright orange tent with my light, the steam of my breath billowing in the beam. The human being I have been looking for for two weeks had been here, waiting for us. Whispering reassurances to herself. Praying for dawn.

"We could stay here and I could activate my PLB. Examine the scene. But—"

I look up. Regina is stepping downslope on the far side of the ridge.

"Bev!" she shouts. "He's got a track!"

Just when my legs can't run anymore, they do.

"Good job, Badger! Good boy!"

We take sliding, sloppy steps downhill. Maybe Valerie had finally done what she was supposed to do—follow a stream. Because stream leads on to stream as way leads on to way. The stream meets another and grows into a runnel that pours down the ancient rocks. The rocks grow larger as we descend, the steps more severe and more difficult for Badger to navigate, until they turn into a stepped wall. Just as I'm thinking no woman who has subsisted on such a calorie deficit for two weeks of life could climb these, I see her tread in the mud by the stream.

One sock, one boot.

"Valerie!" I shout. "We're here, sister! We made it! Where are you, Valerie? Sparrow?"

Sudden and torrential, it starts to rain.

"Damn it," Regina cries. I can barely hear her over the downpour. "No way he can track in this. We just needed one more goddamned hour!"

My beam is useless. All I can see are slashes of illuminated rain. I click off the Maglite and wait for my eyes to adjust to the dark. Water runs into my mouth and eyes. Through my bleary vision, I make out the faint hint of daybreak in the gap in the canopy.

"We're *this* close to Ridge Road," I shout. "Maybe she made it there."

"What?" Regina cries. "I can't hear you."

The rain batters my face as I feel my way forward.

I almost trip over her.

She's sitting upright, small as a child, her back against the rock.

Stick legs. One socked foot, one boot. At most, seventy pounds of a person.

Her eyes are open, but in an empty way.

I fall to my knees. "Valerie!" I clutch her small, weightless hands. "Valerie?"

I reach beneath her sodden windbreaker to feel for a pulse. As my fingers circle her fragile wrist, my gut sinks. I don't feel anything. I don't feel a pulse. I'm too late. Badger arrives, matted with rain. He squeezes himself next to the woman and lies down beside her, done at last. Blinking back tears, I blow furiously on my numb, inoperative fingers to warm them up. There's Regina's hand on my shoulder. I shove my hands into my armpits, staring into the unseeing eyes of the lost woman. Rain runs over her tranquil face. Drops gather in her eyelashes. I reach for her again.

That's when her eyes drift toward me and she smiles.

Like she knows me.

"Well, look at you," I say, laughing through my tears. "You're almost as wet as I am."

Lena

Lena takes a deep breath, then she dials. It's a landline—who knows if it's still in use.

An unfamiliar voice answers. "Hello?"

"Hello," Lena replies. A young voice—a boy.

"Hello," the boy says. "Who's this?"

"I'm—my name is Lena. I'm Christine's mother. Does she still live at this number?"

"What?" the respondent says. "Ummm . . . OK. You're Mom's *mom*?"

"Yes," she says, smiling. "I'm glad I have the right number. Can I ask with whom I am speaking?"

"My name is Austin."

"Hello, Austin. Nice to meet you."

"Umm. Okaaaay. Mom is at the *stoooore*. She'll be right back. We ran out of eggs."

She pauses. So. She has a very strange grandson.

"But I can tell her you called when she gets back."

"That would be helpful. Thank you."

"So . . . I should tell my mother that *her* mother called?"

"Yes, thank you."

"That sounds *so weird*. 'Hey, Mom, your mom called. Grandma called!'" The boy laughs, not unkindly.

Lena opens and closes her mouth. All she can manage to say is "What do you need eggs for?"

"Pancakes," the boy replies. "It's pancake night."

Now that they seem committed to the conversation, Lena asks something she idly wants to know. "Does she like to cook, your mother?"

"No. She *hates* it. We order takeout *a lot*," Austin says.

This makes Lena smile. Somehow it is wonderful, and right, and perfect, that Christine hates to cook. Who the hell likes to cook, day after day after day?

"Can I ask how old you are, Austin?"

"I'm twelve, Grandma."

This moves her. His voice is roughening. He's got one foot out of childhood already.

All these years pass, the theories sift away, and it seems, in fact, that Lena had never tried the simplest path, that of least resistance. Loggerhead turtles swim 7,500 miles from Mexico to reach Japan. Bar-headed geese migrate over the Himalayas, enduring changes in elevation that would kill a human. And yet she, a grown woman living in relative comfort and safety, could not say the words "I'm sorry" and mean it?

She is sorry, she is truly sorry. Most of all, she is sorry for how long it has taken her to say she is sorry. For a moment, the regret feels unendurable. But then the boy repeats, with some sass, "I said I'm twelve."

"Well," she says, her voice cracking. "Your mother probably doesn't want you talking on the phone with strangers."

"You're my grandmother," he points out. "So. Where do you live, Grandma?"

"I live in Connecticut."

"That's not far. We live in New Hampshire."

In a small voice, she says, "I know."

"We are in the Hiking Buddies NH 48 club. We are hiking

all the four-thousand-footers, me and her. My mom loves being outdoors. She can't stand being inside for long."

Lena's hand flies to her mouth. She cannot go on, she will break. Already, her body rocks with emotion, and it has only been two minutes.

"Grandma?"

"I'm here," she says, steadying her voice. "That's wonderful that you and your mother are hikers. I have an interest in the outdoors too."

"Facts?" he says. "Is there mountains in Connecticut?"

"Not very good ones. The truth is, I—"

And then Austin says: "Hey! It's Mom!"

Lena freezes. The sound of a door closing.

"Guess what, Mom? Your *mom* is on the phone! *Your mom*, I said."

Lena waits. The world hovers. She forces her gaze outside. *Now, now, Lena,* she hears a voice in her mind say. *Breathe.* Perhaps the most shocking thing out of everything—that her online life was an illusion, that she provided the clue that brought Valerie Gillis home alive, that she loves Warren Esterman, that she has a grandson—is this voice inside that speaks to her so softly, that says her own name without acid. *Now, now, Lena.* A self-mothering, a gentleness.

Shuffling. Cloth against receiver. Whispering.

Don't be alarmed, she tells her daughter in her head.

She will tell Christine, if she accepts the phone call, "I have been on the phone with your son for less than five minutes and I already know you are a much better mother than I ever was. You do not have to protect me from what you want to say anymore."

"Hello?" Christine says.

HEARTWOOD

Occasionally, the human mind becomes aware of the fact that it spins around the earth's axis at a speed of about one thousand miles an hour. Lena grips the edge of her desk.

"Hello, Christine," she says. "I was wondering if we could talk."

Lena

NOVEMBER

To the forager, winter always feels like an abandonment. The aboveground plants shrivel and break from their stems. Without this referent, the forager is lost. In winter, it is impossible to tell the difference between, say, an edible camas from a death camas. One stays inside. Lena still studies late into the night, and any residents who care to look up from the courtyard can see her peering into her screen, searching the cyberverse. Sometimes she sleeps in until lunchtime, arm flung over her eyes to block the sun.

She starts a life writing club. She appoints herself president.

"You may think your life story is not worth telling," she says. "Or that you are not important enough to write it. Back when we were kids, we were told that only certain men—*anointed* men—were worthy of being called writers. But that was a lie. Think of all the works of genius never seen, written in extremis. Books have been written on banana leaves, birch bark, cardboard boxes. Works of genius have been scratched on the walls of cliffs and prison cells..."

All three attendees look on, wide-eyed. Bobbi and Warren nod vigorously.

"In any case," Lena says with a shrug, "we're all on death's door. Who gives a crap what anyone thinks? All righty..." She checks her notes. "We have one new member today: Dick."

"That's me," Dick says.

She smiles. "Welcome."

She doesn't get Christine, but she does get Austin.

Christine is unyielding in her position, but she is willing to transport Austin to Cedarfield from Keene for several long visits. Each time, Lena waits in the lobby as the blue compact car pulls up in the porte cochere. Lena smiles in case Christine can see her. The passenger door opens, shadows move, and soon the huge boy comes pushing through the glass doors. Behind him, the car he arrived in pulls away.

Austin is not a hugger, but he *is* a sharer. He shares every thought in his head. He tells her how he woke up early, with a boner. He is full of things he wants to tell her, and he loves the flower arrangement in the lobby and he loves the wallpaper.

Wouldn't you know, her grandson is right at home staring for hours at Lena's reference books and Audubon sketches. He barely speaks to her sometimes, so absorbed is he in minute comparisons. They go to the Bistro-To-Go for lunch and he eats half his body weight in hamburgers and awes anybody who dares to sit with them. He is gentlemanly. He has an almost princely way of fluttering his eyes and bowing his head when introduced to an elder. He wants to be tested on his new knowledge before he leaves, and Lena is absolutely shocked by his ability to retain what he has read.

The similarities between Lena and Austin are embarrassingly clear. The difference between, say, a house sparrow and a Eurasian tree sparrow. This realization makes her feel an intimacy with Christine, who has lived with this irony for years. Should the boy want to go to college some day—and she hopes he does—he'll have the untouched sum of the reward money waiting for him in a 529 account. $25,000 plus interest.

On this visit, Austin's third, Cedarfield is decorated for the Thanksgiving holiday. Gourds spill out of cornucopias, pumpkins line the security desk, and a centerpiece of assorted grasses is poised on the welcome table. Lena sits in the lobby waiting for Christine to drive up. They're late. Maybe this is the day they do not come. A young man from a food delivery service opens the doors and plunks the package of white plastic on the security desk. As he passes Lena, he smells deliciously of peanut oil.

Fifteen minutes later, a van pulls up. A dozen women emerge. The women keep coming out, as from a clown car. From tidbits of conversation, Lena understands that they have just come back from a matinee at the Bushnell theater in Hartford.

Lena tries not to check the time.

Years of birding have taught her patience.

Just wait. Be.

At last, the familiar blue car arrives. The two shadowed figures in the front seat converse. Lena's heart flutters as the driver seems to hesitate. Austin opens the passenger door. As he moves his shambling legs to the ground, Lena tries to see inside the car. Each time the car has come, Christine's face has been partially obscured in the glare of the windshield. In the shadow of the porte cochere, Lena would catch only the silhouette of her face or the toss of her hair. Today, she sees the sleeve of Christine's white sweater as her daughter hands Austin his backpack.

The bird-watcher is used to identifying the bird by a single detail. The birder might glimpse only a flash of color—a barred eye or an orange wing band. Sometimes the birder only hears the song and never sees the bird at all. But with this one detail, this field mark, the birder *has* seen the bird.

A fellow resident passes by, on her way inside with a shopping bag. Lena points out the window.

She gestures to the car, eye moist with pride. "That's my daughter."

Lt. Bev

There's a sign taped to the cash register at Melby's:

> IF YOU ARE AFRAID OF
> CHANGE, LEAVE IT HERE.

November's frost rimes the window. Winter has arrived. In the lot, several cars carry a half inch of snow on their roofs. Mike is telling me about a complaint filed against a warden over in District 11 who ran over someone's dog during a pursuit. Mike still spends his days eavesdropping on the public safety two-way radio system. Part of me thinks I should pry his receiver out of his arthritic hands, but the truth is, keeping tabs makes him happy.

"Well, a heartfelt apology would help," I say. "Don't you think? That dog was somebody's pet."

"Ah," Mike says. "You think he should join the cult of the apologizers. Mea culpa! Mea culpa!" He puts his hands on his ill-shaven cheeks. "Not everybody wants to be a guilty little liberal church mouse like *you*, Bev. Taking blame for everything. Wetting your sissy pants."

My mouth drops open facetiously. "Did you just call me *little*?"

Mike slaps the table and laughs.

I loudly chew some ice. "It feels funny to get a lecture from the only warden in the history of the service to suspend his own license."

Mike pauses to remember the story, then laughs uproariously.

Years ago, while filling out the paperwork for an Operating Under the Influence charge on some fisherman he'd arrested for using an ice drill while drunk, Mike had mistakenly written his own name in the box of "the offender." Later, when trying to renew his driver's license, he was unable to do so due to an apparent OUI on his record—the one he'd given himself. It quickly became a favorite collective joke among the wardens.

"Ouch, ouch!" Mike clutches his chest. "You are hurting my feelings!"

Gretchen brings our food, and Mike quickly drops the schtick. I can tell he doesn't want me to know how hungry he is.

"Enjoy," says Gretchen.

It's my last breakfast with Mike, but neither of us knows it yet. I retired two weeks before. Soon, in December, I will pack up a suitcase and head down to Leominster. I'll give Kate some plane tickets to Puerto Rico for her fiftieth, reminding her that it's my turn to sit at Ma's bedside for a while. Ma, who's still hanging on. I will sit with Ma for many hours, and I will speak at length even though she cannot hear me, but it's OK, because the mother I'm talking to can hear me. I'll spend most nights over at Faith's, fixing the CO_2 detectors and mediating their four-way fights and mixing up pitchers of Crystal Light and placing bets on *The Bachelorette*. Kelsey teaches me how to play *Mario Kart*. Mackenzie cuts my hair short. When Ma passes, it will be me who is there at her bedside, holding her hand.

When I return to Maine in the dead of winter, nothing will feel right without them. The following summer, I'll find a job running the Nature Shack at a camp in the Wachusett Mountain State Reservation just outside Leominster in exchange for free tuition for Hailey and Kelsey. Returning to Maine at the end of the summer, I miss them all too much. Even the loons and the late-summer asters won't gladden my heart. Finally, I put my camp up for sale. On a magnificent day in September, before I get a chance to tell him I'm leaving Maine, Mike dies of a heart attack in his bear stand.

Neither of us knows any of that on this November morning at Melby's. And yet, for some reason, the visit is touched with lastness. I pause a minute to really take Mike in. I watch him eating his corned beef hash with gusto. He's got a handsome head of hair despite his age. His eyes flick up whenever the door opens, as if he's still on duty. I was only twenty-seven and brand-new to the force when he clapped me on the back in front of all our peers, and I stepped under an invisible dome of his protection that lasted for years, until I didn't need it anymore. He believed in me. I've been shoved and punched and wrestled with aplenty since then, but the first time an armed man lunged at me, and I was dumbstruck by his grimacing face inches from my own, Mike was there to throw the man back, shouting *You're an idiot! You're not half the man she is!*

"When I grow up, I want to be like you, Mike," I say.

He crumples up his napkin and throws it on the table. "Aww, now."

"No, I mean it." I take the bill off the table and say, "Allow me."

"Well, gee," he says. "OK. Look how enlightened I am!"

I gather my stuff and pull on my coat while Mike asks Gretchen for one more refill on the coffee. I stand up and give Mike a nod. I'm about to turn and go when I stop. He's pecking at his oversize cell phone.

"I love you, Mike. Ugly as you are. You've always been a friend."

A heartsick look flashes across his face, and then he says, "Bev. How many UMass freshmen does it take to change a light bulb?"

"Bye, Mike!" I wave over my shoulder as the door to Melby's closes behind me.

AMITY GAIGE

* * *

When I get home that day, a package is waiting for me. A brown padded mailer forwarded to me from the Bangor office. I sigh, throw it on my reading chair, and change into my work clothes. Winter is already here, and I have much left to do to prepare for it. Since my retirement, I've worked six or seven hours a day on my long-neglected home and land. I've repointed the chimney, graveled the walkway, sealed the cellar, caulked the shower, limbed trees, oiled hinges, evicted critters. I spend unthinking hours clearing brush, burning brush, feeding brush through the wood chipper, until the sky turns from blue to black. I stand dog-tired by the lakeside, listening to the dialogue of loons or the sounds of the lake as it sips at the shore. Something about the physical labor moves me. It's as if I'm saying, "All right, Maine, all right, winter, all right, time—you win."

I don't get to the package for several days. One cold evening, when the world is dark early, and I've eaten dinner and built a fire, I open it up. It's a composition notebook, the same black-and-white kind I used to write my tests in in school. I turn to the first page.

"Dear Mother, you used to call me Sparrow," it reads. "Why Sparrow? Well, because the woods are full of sparrows, and you loved everything outdoors. Songbirds, wildflowers, wind. You could read the weather like a poem."

It's Valerie Gillis's journal, crammed full of entries in blue pen. I dig back through the mailer and find a note.

Dear Lieutenant Miller,
   How's it going up there in Vacationland? Good, I hope.
   Mom and Dad and Ruben Serrano just came for Thanks-

giving. Ruben and I reminisced about our AT sufferfest. Mom and Dad held me close. I have more thanks to give than there are hours on earth. We all spoke of you so fondly.

I'm settled in my new apartment a block away from the Smith College botanical gardens. Gregory and I still see each other all the time. He comes over to my place every Monday and we cook dinner together. Because who doesn't hate Mondays? In the New Year, I start training to become an APRN.

Otherwise, I'm trying to keep life simple. I want to be a good person. A caring nurse.

Sometimes, the sound of the wind in the trees takes me back to the woods.

My experience has given me a strange kind of wealth.
I just wanted you to know that.
Yours,
Valerie

P.S. Oh! The whole point of this is I'm sending you my journal. Writing saved my life in the woods. But the journal is a little too much for me to handle emotionally, so my therapist said maybe I could send it to someone else for safekeeping. I thought you might like to read it. You can read it on the toilet.

Chuckling, I go make a cup of tea. I try to do other housework, bill paying. But I keep eyeing the journal across the room. Then I go outside with no coat and walk down to the lake. I think of that line about the stars again, from the poem: "Looking up at the stars, I know quite well / That, for all they care, I can go to hell." But that's not the whole poem.

> *How should we like it were stars to burn*
> *With a passion for us we could not return?*

AMITY GAIGE

If equal affection cannot be,
Let the more loving one be me.

Poetry? Maybe there's hope for me yet.

Then I climb my four back steps, walk over to the fireplace, sit back down, and read the whole damned thing, start to finish. The fire crackles as I read.

When I'm done reading, my eyes wet, I put the pages down, and I stare into the fire for a long time.

Wood gives structure to backcountry life. So much time is taken choosing a tree, felling it, limbing it, chopping it into stove-size logs, hauling the logs to the yard, stacking the logs, bringing them inside in armfuls. What do I get for all my work? I get something wonderful—the crisp conversation of fire at night as it pops and creaks, like a storm in a jar. A fire is a bedtime story. It starts fierce, in high flame, but it's in the dying down that the fire is most itself, when the heat from the embers enters you and hushes all your intentions, both your goodness and your graft.

Here's an idea: All emotions start out as love. Later, that love is worked on by the forces of luck and suffering.

Hate is just soured love.

Fear is wounded love.

Longing is homeless love.

Love, not pain, is the mother. Love is the taproot.

I have no regrets. I do not regret anything.

Author's Note

While the spark for *Heartwood* came from a real event, this is a novel. In 2013, sixty-six-year-old Gerry Largay was hiking the Appalachian Trail when she got lost. A massive search was unsuccessful and Gerry lost her life. My novel borrows some details from Gerry's story, such as the location where she got lost, the range of conspiracy theories that grew in her absence, and the fact that she was a nurse. I thought of Gerry's bravery often when I was writing this novel. Everything and everyone else in *Heartwood* is completely invented by me. The characters, action, and dialogue are wholly fictional and not intended to portray any real person or represent real events.

Acknowledgments

I would like to thank my editor, Olivia Taylor Smith, for her faith in this novel, and for bringing warmth and creative spirit to everything she does. I'm grateful to have agent Kim Witherspoon in my corner, as she has been for many years now. She wisely told me to stop caring so much about the leaves and to concentrate on the tree. The following people made a marked impact on this novel with their expertise in copyediting, fact-checking, and designing: Nicole Brugger-Dethmers, Morgan Hart, Linda Sawicki, Andrea Monagle, Paul Dippolito, Matt Roeser, and Jackie Seow. My deep thanks to stellar publicist Anne Tate Pearce and marketing pro Danielle Prielipp. Thanks to Brittany Adames and Maria Whelan for the crucial support, and to Lyndsey Blessing for bringing my books to international audiences. I'm grateful to the team at Fleet/Little, Brown UK, especially Rhiannon Smith, Lucy Martin, and Katy Bridgen.

I would like to thank the following members of the Maine Warden Service: Josh Bubier, Aaron Cross, Maddie Killian, and retired wardens Deborah Palman and Dave Georgia. Warden Josh Bubier has been an exceptionally generous advisor on this project. He allowed me to observe his work life firsthand, and also made the time to correspond with me for years until I was slightly less ignorant. My admiration for conservation officers and first responders grew with every interaction with Josh and his colleagues, who proved that even amid danger and tragedy, sensitivity and kindness can prevail.

ACKNOWLEDGMENTS

I'd like to thank the author of *When You Find My Body*, D. Dauphinee, whose wise book taught me about the moving parts of a search as well as lost person behavior. Dee took me out to these woods so that I could see and feel them. I'd also like to thank Doug Comstock for the joke about the dog biting the out-of-stater. Other books that were essential for my understanding and inspiration were Robin Wall Kimmerer's *Gathering Moss*, Helen Macdonald's *Vesper Flights*, Carolyn Finney's *Black Faces, White Spaces*, and Kyle Rohrig's *Lost on the Appalachian Trail*. I read Annie Dillard's masterwork, *Pilgrim at Tinker Creek*, most mornings before writing. I learned much from the courageous podcast communities for *She Explores* and *The Nocturnists*, as well as the entire Appalachian Trail family.

Thank you to the extraordinary women in my writing group: Janice P. Nimura, Megha Majumdar, Sarah Shun-lien Bynum, and Marisa Silver. Thank you to Jennifer Egan, whose example and whose belief in this book has been life-changing.

Thanks to Yaddo for the precious time and space.

Thanks to the readers of my previous books. I wrote this with you in mind.

The following people have sustained me in all weather, by helping me finish this book or just by showing up: Sarah Moore, Susan Pourfar, Kelly Proulx, Paul Witiniski, Shou-jie Eng, Rosie Emlein, Moriah Gillis, Emily and Natalie Wagner, Artie Hill, Brian Wilson, Tony Hale, Jane and Mike Shauck, Gail Canzano, Adam Haslett, Richard Demming, Jeff Holmes, and my two faithful Tiny Book Club mates, Catherine Blinder and Michael Robinson. The only thanks that felt sufficient to the decades of refuge and friendship that Mira Kautsky and Keith Flaherty have given me is this book's dedication. I'm grateful to my sister, Karina Gaige, and my extended family of Watts, Thompsons, and Groffs.

ACKNOWLEDGMENTS

I would like to thank my mother, Austra Gaige, for being an early reader of this work, for the countless hours in which she stepped in to help in my absence, and for a lifetime of love and attention. I would not be a writer without the unqualified support of my mother and my late father, Fred Gaige. Special thanks to my children, Freya and Atis, for their remarkable compassion, humor, and engagement with life. As for Tim Watt—there isn't enough space on this page to enumerate the reasons your family and your community treasure you, nor to count the moments you put my head back on straight.

Freya, Atis, and Tim, you are my heartwood. I've remained standing for this long, with this much faith in storytelling, because I am strengthened by your love for me and mine for you.

Amity Gaige is the author of four previous novels: *O My Darling*, *The Folded World*, *Schroder*, and *Sea Wife*. *Sea Wife* was a 2020 *New York Times* Notable Book and a finalist for the Mark Twain American Voice in Literature Award. *Schroder* was also a *New York Times* Notable Book, and a best book of 2013 according to *The Washington Post* and the *Wall Street Journal*, among others, and was shortlisted for the UK's Folio Prize in 2014. Her work has been translated into eighteen languages. In 2016, Amity was awarded a Guggenheim Fellowship in Fiction. She lives in West Hartford, Connecticut, with her family and teaches creative writing at Yale.